Start Here

Start Here

TRISH DOLLER

Simon Pulse

New York London Toronto Sydney New Delhi

To the girls who know where they're going.

And to the girls who are still finding their way.

This book is a work of fiction. Any references to historical events, real people, or real places are used fictitiously. Other names, characters, places, and events are products of the author's imagination, and any resemblance to actual events or places or persons, living or dead, is entirely coincidental.

SIMON PULSE

An imprint of Simon & Schuster Children's Publishing Division
1230 Avenue of the Americas, New York, New York 10020
First Simon Pulse hardcover edition August 2019
Text copyright © 2019 by Trish Doller
Jacket photograph close-up of rope copyright © 2019 by iStock.com/AlKane
Jacket photograph of girl on rope copyright © 2019 by iStock.com/Hakase
Jacket photograph of sailboat copyright © 2019 by iStock.com/Meghan McGrath
Jacket photograph of girls in sunglasses copyright © 2019 by Daniel Grill/Getty Images
For information about special discounts for bulk purchases, please contact
Simon & Schuster Special Sales at 1-866-506-1949 or business@simonandschuster.com.
The Simon & Schuster Speakers Bureau can bring authors to your live event.
For more information or to book an event contact the Simon & Schuster Speakers Bureau
at 1-866-248-3049 or visit our website at www.simonspeakers.com.
Jacket designed by Tiara Iandiorio
Interior designed by Mike Rosamilia
The text of this book was set in Adobe Caslon Pro
Manufactured in the United States of America
2 4 6 8 10 9 7 5 3 1
Library of Congress Cataloging-in-Publication Data
Names: Doller, Trish, author.
Title: Start here / by Trish Doller.
Description: New York : Simon Pulse, 2019. |
Summary: Willa and Taylor fulfill the dying wish of Finley, who had held their friendship
together, by sailing from Ohio to Key West after high school graduation.
Identifiers: LCCN 2019005401 | ISBN 9781481479912 (hardcover)
Subjects: | CYAC: Sailing—Fiction. | Adventure and adventurers—Fiction. |
Death—Fiction. | Grief—Fiction. | Friendship—Fiction.
Classification: LCC PZ7.D7055 St 2019 | DDC [Fic]—dc23
LC record available at https://lccn.loc.gov/2019005401
ISBN 9781481479936 (eBook)

"Let yourself be gutted.
Let it open you.
Start here."

—Cheryl Strayed,
Tiny Beautiful Things

Finley

FINLEY SITS CROSS-LEGGED ON HER BED, WEARING the glossy blue Coraline wig she bought last Halloween. Her parents had put the kibosh on trick-or-treating when she became a teenager, but she and her friends still dressed up to hand out candy to the neighborhood littles. Last year Finley wore the yellow raincoat and matching boots of her favorite literary character. Today, along with the blue wig, she's wearing a T-shirt that says THE FUTURE IS FEMALE. She has great expectations for the rest of the world, but for Finley Donoghue, the future is now.

She checks out her mirror image on the laptop screen in front of her and crinkles her freckled nose. She doesn't look much like herself anymore. There are dark circles under her eyes that no amount of concealer can hide. And under the wig, her actual light-brown hair—which used to hang almost to her waist—now resembles baby duck fuzz. Which is fine for baby ducks, but not so much for a girl who loved the way her ponytail would swing as she bounced on the sidelines at football games. All her clothes have gotten baggy, but not in an intentional, sexy way. She dusts a little bronzer across her cheeks to tone down the paleness of her skin and shines her lips with some rose-colored gloss. Satisfied—at least as satisfied as she's going to get—Finley presses the record button on her computer and smiles until her cheeks dimple.

"Two years ago, we bought an old boat and made a plan to sail to Key West. We circled a date on the calendar, and by my calculations, that day is tomorrow." Sadness sinks like a stone in her heart, stealing her breath, and her smile slips. "I always believed the three of us would be going together. I never expected my body to have plans of its own. But here we are. Or rather, here *you* are."

Coach Kaman was big on posture. At the beginning of each season, she'd tell the cheerleaders to pretend they were marionettes with strings running through their spines and out the tops of their heads to keep them up straight. "Strings, girls!" she'd shout, whenever they were slouching. Finley pulls her imaginary string and sits taller to keep from slumping back against the pillows. Once upon a time, she could make a running roundoff into a back tuck look effortless. Now the simple act of living is exhausting.

"Since I can't be there, I've created a list of clues to points of interest along the route. I'm sure most of them will be super easy, but others . . . okay, so . . . I'm never gonna know if you don't follow the clues. Or even what you might discover if you do," she says. "But if you decide to play along, the list and some other stuff you'll need for the trip will be waiting for you on the boat."

Tacked to the wall beside her bed is a photo that Taylor snapped with her instant camera just a few days ago, the day Finley's friends promised they'd take the trip without her. Finley had been wearing her Coraline wig that night too. In a show of solidarity, Willa wore a gray plastic Viking helmet with horns and yellow yarn braids, while Taylor's hair was stuffed up into a giant rainbow-colored puff like you see sports fans wearing in crowds at football games on TV. The colors have the same washed-out quality as the pictures in her grandma's old photo albums, as though their friendship has already stood the test of time. Finley smiles at the photo and turns back to the laptop to continue the video. By the time Taylor and Willa see it, she will be past tense.

"You know . . . the dying part doesn't scare me anymore." The first time Finley faced death, she was four years old and the oncologist told her parents she had six months to live. She's not unaware of how fortunate it is that she's had thirteen years instead, and she's tried to live them as fully and fearlessly as possible. "But I don't want to leave everyone I love behind. I just . . . I don't want you to forget about me."

She presses pause with one hand as she scrubs away a tear with the other. She can edit the video later, but now she needs a break. She curls into a fetal position and sobs, wishing she could start her life over again, this time without leukemia.

Finley already misses the weekly meet-ups she used to have with her dad at the coffeehouse across the street from his condo downtown. Living full-time with her mom, Finley didn't always see him every day, so they would order the featured coffee of the week before settling down on the comfy couch to catch up. The last time, her dad confessed to joining an online dating service. They browsed profiles together, and Finley talked him through his first contact with a pretty woman (his own age, thankfully) who looked nothing like her mom (also, thankfully). Now he visits Finley daily, just in case it's the last day. Maybe, she thinks, she should ask her dad to break her out of home hospice for one last latte.

Finley will miss Decembers. She and her mom would pick a date, cue up a holiday playlist, and spend an entire day baking Christmas cookies. Finley's favorites were the frosted cutouts. She loved rolling out the dough on the floured kitchen island and trying to cut as many cookies as she could with each pass. She loved smashing candy canes to make peppermint bark. She loved browning the butter for chocolate chip cookies. She loved the smell of the spices they used to make German *lebkuchen* for Grandma, since she was the only one who ever actually ate them. Finley and her mom would sing along with the Christmas songs and sample so many of their creations that they'd be sick of cookies before the holiday season had even really begun.

Finley will miss her sister starting high school. She worries about how Regan is going manage without someone to guide her. Finley considers leaving a list of things her sister should know, but Regan has spent the better part of a year in the shadow of cancer. Maybe she wants to forge her own path and make her own mistakes. Still, Finley makes a mental note to give Regan all her old World History exams. Mr. Rupp uses the same questions every year.

Finley will miss sailing. Pep rallies. Yellow roses. School dances. Blue raspberry slushies from the Dairy Frost. Her little green Fiat. And her unrequited crush on her best friend's brother.

But most of all, Finley will miss Taylor and Willa.

Taylor, her very first friend. They bonded over the sand table on the first day kindergarten, and when Finley's mother came to pick her up from school, the two girls were sitting together in the big claw-foot bathtub that their teacher had converted into a reading nook, sounding out the words in

Don't Let the Pigeon Drive the Bus! Over the years Finley has made so many friends, but she loves Taylor, who laughs with her whole body. Taylor, who won't admit she cries when she watches Nicholas Sparks movies. Taylor, who makes her feel the most like home.

It was different with Willa. First, because Finley wasn't always kind to her. Finley suffers private shame whenever she remembers how all the girls in their grade—including her—used to shun Willa because her school uniform was too big and she only ate peanut butter sandwiches for lunch. They'd squeeze together at the opposite end of the lunch table as though poverty were contagious. Now Finley knows that Willa is resourceful and brave and funny and so fucking smart—and Finley considers it a privilege to be her friend.

It's physically painful to know that their lives will go on without her. That Finley's best friends will make new best friends and *these* people will be the ones to celebrate the good news and commiserate the bad. They'll be college roommates, wedding attendants, godparents. They'll know things about Willa and Taylor that Finley will never know.

Her tears take a long time to subside and a bit longer after that before her eyes aren't quite so puffy. She unfolds and sits back upright to repair her makeup and finish the video. Her nose is a little pink, but maybe they won't notice.

"Even though I won't be with you, I hope you have an epic adventure. But more than that, I hope it will be the kind of trip that changes your lives. So, if you're ready to begin . . ." Finley leans close and gives her friends one last dimpled smile. *"Start here."*

41.4489° N, 82.7080° W
Start here.

Willa

SUNRISE IS LITTLE MORE THAN A SUGGESTION, A pale golden smudge on the horizon, when Willa pushes her keycard into the slot outside the sailing club. The gate rolls back slowly and the car muffler splutters as her mom steps on the gas. Tires. Brakes. Muffler. The list keeps getting longer and longer. Willa supposes she should be grateful they even own a car, but soon the costs will outweigh the value and she doesn't know what they'll do then.

The clubhouse is dark and the parking lot deserted, except for Cam's chalky green pickup parked out on Springer's Wharf, and at the sight of it she feels a flutter of ... something she has no business feeling.

"You know you can come home whenever you want," her mom says as she shifts the car into park at the head of B-dock. "Finley wouldn't hold you to this."

Willa was eleven years old when Finley decided the two of them should sail to Kelleys in Optimist dinghies. They provisioned themselves with sunscreen, bottled water, PB&J sandwiches, and a pair of walkie-talkies, then set out across Sandusky Bay. Everything was fine until they reached the mouth of the bay. The weather was clear—and Finley's dad was on standby in case they needed to be rescued—but the distance and the choppiness of the waves were scary, especially in an eight-foot boat.

Finley's voice crackled through the walkie-talkie. "Willa! We have to keep going or else we won't know how it feels to do this!"

Willa wanted to suggest they wait until they were twelve or seventeen or twenty-five, but she also wanted Finley to see her as brave enough, as *worthy* enough to be her best friend. Willa kept going, and now she knows how fun it is to sail to Kelleys in an Optimist dinghy. She also knows her mom is wrong. Finley would *absolutely* hold her to this.

Once the trunk is empty, Mom folds a one-hundred-dollar bill into Willa's palm and says, "I've been saving this for a special occasion."

From here, Willa's mom will drive up to the FriendShip gas station, where she'll spend the next eight hours selling gas, snacks, and coffee to tourists on their way to Cedar Point. She's already wearing her blue smock, which is both endearing and dorky. Before this job, Willa's mom served drinks at the strip club out by the tracks. Groomed dogs. Detailed boats. Waited tables. Developed film in an hour. Delivered pizzas. But she has trouble making jobs stick, which leaves their budget endlessly stretched. One hundred dollars could buy groceries, a few tanks of gas, or extra minutes for their pay-as-you-go phones.

"You should keep this." Willa tries to give the money back, but her mom jams her hands into her smock pockets, reminding Willa of a stubborn child. "The muffler is about to fall off the car."

"It'll be fine."

She wishes she had her mother's knack of letting responsibility float away like a helium balloon. Instead, it sits like a weight in her chest. "What if it's not?"

Willa knows—especially now that Finley is gone—that she shouldn't be so hard on her mother. Colleen Ryan was barely older than Willa when the love of her life was killed by a bomb in Iraq. She got pregnant with Willa a short time later and has been a single mom for eighteen years. She's a *survivor*. But Willa is wired differently. She wants to understand how someone can flake out on their own life, but her brain just can't make that connection.

"With you gone all summer, the bills will go down," her mom insists, the honeysuckle scent of her body spray tickling

Willa's nose as they embrace. "A hundred bucks to get rid of you seems fair."

She doesn't want to smile because she still fears the rent will go unpaid and her mom will wind up homeless, but Willa can't help herself. She shakes her head. "So cold."

Her mom's laugh splits the stillness. "I'm going to miss you, honey girl."

Family has always just meant Mom. Willa's grandpa died of lung cancer before she was born, and her grandmother suffered a fatal stroke when Willa was too young to remember her. Willa's father is a blank line on her birth certificate, and her mom swears she has no idea who he might be. The only clues to his identity are Willa's brown eyes, deep brown curls, and skin that is darker than her mother's. Sometimes she wonders about the other half of her chromosomes, but most of the time having her mom's smile and the Ryan-family freckles is all she needs.

Until now, the longest Willa has been away from home is junior race week at Put-in-Bay every August, and even then her mom could hop on the ferry at Catawba and be there in twenty minutes. Her throat constricts when she thinks about being gone for nearly three months. "I'll miss you too."

Her mom tucks a stray curl behind Willa's ear. "Maybe send me a postcard or two?"

"Obviously."

"And I'm too young to be a grandma, so if you have sex, use protection."

"Oh my God, Mom. Gross." Willa's skin warms, and she's thankful the air is cool. Hooking up with strange boys is not part of the plan. Even so, it's not something she wants to discuss with her mother.

"Listen, as someone who used to be a veritable United Nations of sex—"

"Those are words I could have lived my whole life without hearing," Willa says, slinging her faded red duffel over her shoulder. "So I'm going to go stab my eardrums now."

When her mom smiles, it erases all the bad, and Willa is flooded with love.

"I guess this is it," she says.

Her mom gestures at the pile built from Willa's floral sleeping bag, pillow, backpack, and Aldi shopping bags filled with food. "Want a hand with this stuff?"

"Don't be late on my account."

Willa's mom touches a kiss to her forehead, then wipes her lip gloss away with her thumb. "I love you, do you love me?"

Willa's cheeks dimple into a smile. "Yes, I love you, do you love me?"

When she was a little girl, they'd go back and forth with this until Willa broke into a fit of giggles. Now her mom offers another, softer smile as she climbs back into the car.

"More than anything in this world, so be safe. Be *smart*."

Smart is the thing Willa does best, but the lump in her throat is too big to say so. Instead, she waves until the car reaches the gate. The right taillight fails to illuminate when her mom steps on the brakes—one more repair for the list—and tension tightens around Willa's spine. She sends up a silent prayer that her mom won't get ticketed by the police on her way to work. And that she'll hold down this job until Willa returns.

The car is out of sight when she gathers up her bedding and heads down the dock. The wood creaks beneath her tennis shoes, calling back memories—the crackle of sails, the scent of sunscreen, and the wet footprints their bare feet would make on the sun-warmed dock boards. Willa glances back, half expecting Finley to come running, her hair streaming behind her like a brown ribbon.

"Let's go!" she would shout if she were here. "The world is waiting for us!"

Willa would give anything, *everything*, to hear her best friend's voice again. Just a couple of days ago, she was riding her bike down Meigs Street when she passed a teenage guy with a monster Afro pulling a little red wagon down the sidewalk. In the wagon was a birdcage with a brown-and-white rabbit inside. The whole scene was so sweet and absurd that she automatically hit Finley's speed dial to tell her about it. The recorded voice—*this number is no longer in service*—reminded her again that Finley was gone. The pain is lodged like a pebble in her shoe, and no matter how much she tries to shake it out, it won't go away.

She reaches the boat and stops in her tracks when she sees the name stretched out across the transom in a half-cursive handwriting font.

Whiskey Tango Foxtrot.

It took them forever to settle on a name. Taylor argued that it was bad luck to change a boat's name, but she was overruled by Finley and Willa, who agreed the original name—*Honeybee*—didn't suit them at all. It was Finley who came up with the idea of using the nautical alphabet code words that correspond with their first initials. Whiskey Tango Foxtrot. Willa Taylor Finley. WTF? Every interpretation just worked.

Willa researched renaming ceremonies online, and after they'd removed every trace of the old name, wearing dresses and heels—well, except Taylor, who mistakenly believed she was too tall for heels—they christened the boat. Taylor found a mini bottle of champagne from her cousin's wedding, which they splashed on the bow of *Whiskey Tango Foxtrot*, saving just enough for each of them to have a celebratory sip.

Finley had ordered the lettering, but that was before her leukemia came back. The last Willa knew, the name was still rolled up in a box somewhere. Seeing it here now is another painful jolt to her already battered heart.

A dark head appears in the companionway, and Cam steps up into the cockpit from the cabin. He's shirtless, and bathed in the rays of a brand-new sun, he looks golden. His sleepy brown eyes wander a lazy path up from Willa's ruby toenails, and a warm shiver raises goose bumps on the backs of her thighs. His grin holds the smugness of someone who knows the effect he has on girls—even girls who have no intention of falling at his feet. "Hey, little Willa."

Campbell Nicholson is a literal genius who dropped out of Cornell after his freshman year with no real explanation. Now he spends his days holding a SLOW sign at highway construction zones and his nights getting stoned with his friends, just like he did in high school. Willa can only dream of having the kind of privilege Campbell tosses so casually aside. She doesn't understand making that choice. Just like she can't understand why her mother takes one low-paying job after another instead of wanting something more. If Willa learned anything from Finley it's that you get only so many trips around the sun. Why would you waste them?

Willa cocks her head, trying to play it cool. "What are you doing on my boat?"

His grin widens. "Come aboard and I'll show you."

Willa ignores the hand Cam offers as she steps off the dock, but in the cockpit he stands so close she can feel the warmth radiating from his skin. She fists her fingers to keep from touching him.

"So, you saw the name, right?" Campbell asks.

Willa nods.

"Finley asked me to do it," he says. "Also, the outboard had a little stutter I wanted to check before you left. I think it's fixed."

These tiny moments of sweetness are the ones that make Willa want him, even when she knows he is not for her. "Thank you."

Cam ducks through the companionway and beckons her to follow. "There's more."

Down in the cabin, he's looped strings of tiny white lights around the handrails above the bunks. And on the low half walls that separate the main cabin from the v-berth at the front of the boat, Campbell taped little doodles of Taylor and Willa with Shakespeare quotes written beneath.

For Taylor: *What is past is prologue.*

For Willa: *Though she be but little, she is fierce.*

She touches her fingertips to the doodle, tracing the black Sharpie bun on the top of her black Sharpie head. He's even drawn the baby curls that won't stay in.

The quote is from *A Midsummer Night's Dream*. Her

favorite. Willa has always loved words, but this was the play that made her fall in love with language, with story. When she received her acceptance e-mail from Kenyon College, she entertained a brief fantasy of being the next Emily Gould and walking the same halls that John Green and Ransom Riggs had walked. Then she tucked it away—in the same place she kept her inexplicable attraction to Cam—and enrolled at Case Western as a business major. Studying business was smarter. Better. Even though Campbell has no way of knowing any of this, it feels as though he's been rummaging around in Willa's brain, and she doesn't like it.

"How did you know I'd come?" she asks.

He cocks his head, his brows furrowing as if the question is absurd. "Because you're Willa."

"What does that even mean?"

"You always do the right thing."

She's not sure if she should consider that an insult or a compliment, so she doesn't reply. Especially when she's not sure if this is the right thing.

Willa's original plan for the summer was to work as many hours as possible at Plato's Closet. Her college scholarships would cover the major expenses, but she needs her own laptop. She wanted to hit up garage sales to find a dorm fridge, get started on her fall reading, and try to figure out how life works without Finley. Despite Willa's deathbed promise, spending the entire summer on a boat with Taylor Nicholson was never really part of the plan.

Then two things happened that changed her mind.

First, Willa delivered her valedictory address to the tops of people's heads while they thumbed through their commencement programs and played games on their phones, and the feeling she'd wasted the past thirteen years snaked through her like a strangler vine. There were no trophy cases for valedictorians. She would not leave a lasting impression. The only reward for all of her hard work would be four more years of hard work, and the thought of that made her want to cry.

Afterward, Willa went home and slept fifteen hours—right through Taylor's graduation party and straight on into the following day. When she woke, Willa found an instant photo lying on the edge of her bed. It was the one Taylor took a couple of months before Finley died. She'd been almost bald from chemo, so they all wore silly wigs—and Taylor snapped three shots, one for each of them. It was their last sleepover, but also the night Willa and Taylor swore to take the trip without Finley. The tape on the back of the picture must have come unstuck in the night, but it felt as though Finley had left it on Willa's bed to say, "Suck it up, buttercup. You promised."

Now Willa crosses her arms and levels a serious look at Campbell. "I'm not here for your sister."

"Doesn't matter why you're here." He shifts closer, and the

tiny hairs on her arms stand on end. Sparks dance under her skin. She wishes she could control her body's response to him, but she can't. "Only that you are . . . honey girl."

Her mom's favorite term of endearment lands like a bucket of cold water. "Are you making fun of me?"

"No. I swear, Willa. I'm not."

"I'm not your honey girl." She moves away, ignoring him as she drops her duffel on the bunk below the Willa doodle. She's slightly annoyed he gave Taylor the bunk that slides out into a double, but Taylor is almost a foot taller than Willa. To be fair, she needs the bigger space.

"You could be," Campbell says.

"No," she says. "I could not."

For most of her friendship with Taylor, Cam was just part of the landscape. An unofficial big brother. A solid pair of shoulders to sit on during chicken fights in the Nicholsons' pond.

Until one night last summer.

Willa and Finley were doing a marathon watch of an old sci-fi TV series called *Firefly* when Finley suddenly burst into tears. Her voice cracked as she said, "I can't do this anymore, Willa. I just want to die."

Willa wrapped her arms around Finley and held her tight, blinking back her own tears. "Please don't say that. You can't give up when you're almost done."

Finley's chemo and radiation left her exhausted, and with a host of other side effects that made her feel even worse. But she had only a couple of weeks before the treatment would be over.

"I've pooped so much today I might as well start wearing adult diapers," Finley said. "And right this minute I feel like I'm going to puke."

Willa poked her side. "If you vomit on me, our friendship is over."

Finley sniffled a laugh as she wiped her eyes with the cuffs of her pajama top. "I'm sorry for bringing down the room. I just—sometimes I can't be strong."

"No one expects that from you, Finley. Some days are going to be shitty." Willa crossed her eyes and stuck out her tongue. "Literally and figuratively."

Finley laughed. "I hate you."

"No, you don't. Especially when I have an idea that will make you feel better. Hand over your phone."

Willa had never actually needed his services, but everyone knew Campbell Nicholson was the go-to guy for any illicit thing a person could want. Drugs. Alcohol. When it came to fake IDs, Cam was the juvenile delinquent version of Jason Bourne. Willa had read about cancer patients smoking pot to keep pain and nausea at bay—and if anyone could get his hands on some weed, it would be Cam.

She scrolled through Finley's contacts until she found his number, then sent him a text. **It's Willa. Finley's having a rough night. She needs . . . something.**

It was a Friday night and Campbell was sure to be at Ben Mantey's party, but fifteen minutes later he strolled into Finley's bedroom with a bag of weed in his pocket. Cam rolled a joint, and they propped themselves against the wall beneath Finley's open bedroom window, getting high and playing Would You Rather . . . ? until Finley fell asleep with her head on his shoulder.

"Thanks for coming to help," Willa said after they tucked Finley back into her bed. "That was really . . . sweet."

"You seem surprised."

"Maybe a little," Willa admitted. "I figured you were busy."

"I'm never too busy for Fin." He leaned in so close that Willa almost thought he would kiss her, and her heart stopped beating. Instead, he grinned. "Need a ride home?"

She'd planned to spend the night, but Finley was finally comfortable and deeply asleep. "If it's not out of your way."

"Grab your stuff."

Willa left a note and followed him out to the truck. The bench seat was covered with a striped Mexican serape, and mounted in the dashboard was an old-fashioned radio with tuning knobs instead of preset buttons. She focused on those things—things she loved about his truck—instead of the jittery feeling of being alone with Campbell. Willa had no reason to be nervous—he was Taylor's brother—but she was not completely oblivious to his good looks. Or that Finley had been crushing on him since the beginning of time. As he swung up into the truck, the space suddenly felt too small.

"Relax, little Willa," Cam said as he started the engine. "I don't bite."

He clicked on the radio, and they listened to the Indians game on WLEC as they headed down the Chaussee and across the Causeway. Instead of turning onto First Street, Cam drove to the Dairy Queen and pulled up to the drive-through menu.

"Blizzard?" he asked.

"Um . . . sure. Butterfinger. Small."

Campbell ordered for both of them, and when they had their ice cream, he drove Willa the rest of the way home. He pulled into a parking space in the lot outside her apartment and cut the engine. "I have to tell you . . . I had you pegged as a cookie dough girl."

She laughed. "I think you're confusing me with Finley."

"I'm definitely not confused."

She glanced in his direction and her smile slipped. He wasn't looking at her like she was one of his sister's friends. He was staring. Willa's gaze bounced away—to the radio, to her backpack on the floor, and finally, out the window.

Anywhere but at Campbell. Her face burned with pleasure and shame, and she had no idea where to put all this brand-new, not-wholly-unwelcome attraction.

"So, um . . . ," she began, changing the subject. "Big plans for tomorrow?"

"Farm stand in the morning, beach in the afternoon. Want to come?"

"I have to work."

"Maybe another time."

"Yeah. Maybe." The lie killed her appetite for ice cream, and for a split second she hated Finley Donoghue. Then she hated herself. She opened the truck door. "Thanks again for helping with Finley. I really—"

Campbell cut her off with a kiss. His mouth was soft and tasted like vanilla ice cream, and she really wanted to kiss him back. Instead, she pulled away.

"This . . . can't happen."

"Willa."

"I won't hurt Finley like that. Not when she's sick. Not ever."

She ran up the stairs to her apartment and went straight to her room, but the memory of kissing Cam kept her awake all night. In the morning, her phone chimed with a text from Finley. **Tell me last night wasn't a dream. Campbell was in my bedroom, right?**

Yep, Willa responded, her face burning with betrayal. **It was real.**

"Willa." Cam reaches for her now, his fingertips on her hip as he takes a step closer. She has tried so hard to stay away from him. Out of respect for Finley's feelings. And because there's no room in Willa's future for a guy like him. But even now she still wants him. Fire rushes through her veins, and when he licks his lower lip, she leans in. Then the boat sways and Campbell steps back.

"Cam?" Taylor comes into the cabin carrying her cat, Pumpkin, and her eyes narrow when she sees Willa. "What are *you* doing here?"

"Same thing as you, I guess."

This day has been circled on their calendars for two years, ever since Finley suggested they pool their money to buy a cheap sailboat and spend their post-graduation summer sailing from Sandusky to Key West.

"There's no such thing as a cheap sailboat," Willa pointed out at the time, but Finley waved her hand like Obi-Wan Kenobi and said the right boat would appear when they needed it.

Like magic, Taylor's dad was taking a shortcut on a back road in Lorain County when he spotted an old Mirage 25 sitting in someone's barn. The paint had faded to a chalky yellow and the name was almost completely worn away, but the hull was sound. And the price was cheap, relatively speaking. Willa's share took a considerable bite out of her college savings, but she paid it because she knew it would be worth it. Like sailing to Kelleys in an eight-foot dinghy.

It was also pretty magical that their parents agreed to the trip. Willa wanted to believe it was because the Force was strong in Finley, but the truth was that they were the kind of girls who didn't give their parents reasons not to trust them. And because they'd never be so far out of cell phone range that they couldn't call home in an emergency.

"Why did you change your mind?" Taylor demands now.

"I thought you might need my help," Willa says, earning a sharp glare. Sometimes talking to Taylor is like stepping on gum. They're not even two minutes into summer and Taylor's hackles are already up. Two *months* is going to feel like an eternity if Willa has to measure the weight of every single word. "I just mean—you were right. We have to do what Finley wanted. So I'm all in."

Taylor's stance softens, and she nods her approval.

"I, um—" Willa moves toward the steps to go fetch the rest of her gear, but the boat sways again and Taylor's mom crowds into the small cabin. She beams at Willa, and the exclamation marks are practically visible in the air as she says, "Willa! Thank goodness you're here! You girls are going to have such a wonderful summer!"

Mrs. Nicholson is one of those unflaggingly cheerful sorts, who always sees the glass half full. She still believes Taylor and Willa are the best of friends, even though that hasn't been technically true since the summer before high school, when Finley chose Willa—instead of Taylor—to be her crew on the junior race team. Taylor was convinced Willa had poisoned Finley against her. Rather than talking it out, Taylor quit the sailing team and stopped hanging out with Willa unless Finley was there as a buffer between them.

"It's going to be great." Willa puts more conviction into her words than she actually feels. She steals a glance at Taylor, and what passes between them is an unspoken *if we don't kill each other first*.

Taylor

TAYLOR HAS BEEN AROUND SAILBOATS HER ENTIRE life. Her granddad was the commodore of the sailing club back in the 1970s, and her parents have always owned a boat. According to family legend, her mom and dad went out for a sail on the day her oldest brother, Carter, was born, and her mom almost had to give birth in the middle of Sandusky Bay. The tale has gotten taller with time and telling—her mom didn't *actually* almost give birth on a boat—but sailing is definitely in Carter's blood. H_2O-positive. His dream is to sail with Oracle Team USA in the America's Cup, and it constantly gets under his skin that Cam's trophies and awards—Campbell won so, so many of them as a junior sailor—are collecting dust in the attic.

The sailing gene must have skipped Taylor because she doesn't understand the physics of wind and water. She forgets everything during the winter, so when summer rolls around, she feels ignorant and left out. Even worse, sometimes she gets seasick. Taylor prefers land-based sports, especially volleyball. She played on the varsity team all four years of high school, and the volleyball court was the one place she didn't feel like a freak. Objectively, she knows she's not actually a freak—the US Olympic volleyball team is loaded with women over six feet tall—but Taylor is glad she finally topped out at six one.

Her growth spurt in fifth grade had been particularly rough. Almost overnight she went from tall to tallest, towering over her mother, her teacher, and all the boys in her class. Jared Fantozzi started calling her Hagrid—until Finley threatened to punch him in the face. Finley was sent home from school for bullying another student, but that kind of loyalty was what drove Taylor to save her farm stand earnings to help pay for a boat even when she didn't really enjoy sailing. She sanded, varnished, and painted because Finley was worth it. And even after she died, Taylor was bound by a promise she had no intention of breaking. Not like Willa, who bailed almost immediately.

Everyone was returning to their cars after the inurnment ceremony at the cemetery when Willa and Taylor met up in front of Finley's little vault. Taylor couldn't even look at it without welling up. She hated the idea of Finley being all by herself in a cold, dark marble box. She wished the Donoghues had added some of Finley's favorite things, like the one-eyed teddy bear she swore she didn't sleep with anymore. Or her pink cardigan with the rhinestone buttons. Or the pictures from the bulletin board in her bedroom. That day, it made sense that ancient Egyptians buried their pharaohs with all their possessions. Forever is such a long time to be alone.

"This sucks." Willa tugged her black jacket a little tighter around her body and shivered. Even though it was April, there were still small mounds of unmelted snow on the grass. As if spring didn't want to bloom in a world without Finley Donoghue.

Finley had kept a list of things she wanted at her funeral, like a bonfire on the beach with music and fireworks. She'd wanted her ashes planted in a living urn that grew into a tree or launched into space to become a shooting star. The one thing Finley had not wanted was for her family and friends to stand around the beige common room at church, eating dry ham sandwiches with plain yellow mustard and talking about how she was in a better place. Taylor knew funerals were meant for the living, but Finley deserved fireworks. "We have to go to Key West."

"Taylor, listen—" Willa took a deep breath, and Taylor was absolutely certain she didn't want to hear what would come next. "This trip is going to take the entire summer, and I really need to save money for Case."

Anger boiled up inside Taylor. "God, you're just as bad as everyone else. You *promised*."

"What was I supposed to say? She was dying."

"You promised," Taylor repeated. "Doesn't that mean anything to you?"

Willa's voice was flat as she said, "I wanted to take this trip with *her*." She didn't say *not with you*, but Taylor heard it anyway.

"You're such a bitch."

Willa tried to shrug it off, but not before Taylor saw the flash of hurt in her eyes. "If you want to go," Willa said, walking away, "don't let me stop you."

That was where they'd left it.

Until Taylor decided maybe this was something she *could* do on her own. To her way of thinking, the biggest challenge would be the actual sailing part of the trip. Motoring through canals and down the Intracoastal Waterway would be kind of like driving a car, and she was an okay driver. Just one tiny fender bender when she backed her mom's SUV into a telephone pole. Taylor would just have to keep the boat between the channel markers, and those were like roads, right? Her dad could teach her how to set an anchor. And if she needed to dock the boat, she would go slowly and use lots of fenders.

Taylor wanted to believe she was brave enough to go it alone. She fantasized about keeping a blog of her adventures, and maybe the newspaper would do an article about how she was solo sailing as a tribute to her dead best friend. Finley would be super proud of her.

But the closer Taylor got to the leaving date, the more her nerves twisted into knots. What if she fell overboard? What if the boat sank? What if a freighter plowed over her in the middle of the night? There were so many ways the trip could go wrong. More than once she considered apologizing to Willa, but pride pulled her back every single time.

Today, when her mom drove through the sailing club gate and Taylor saw Willa's sleeping bag and pile of grocery bags, her insides went soft with relief. But now she's relieved and irritated at the same time. She hates the way her own mother makes it seem like Willa's last-minute change of heart is heroic. Like she never believed Taylor could do this on her own.

"Oh, goodness!" her mom exclaims. "We forgot Pumpkin's food. I'll run home and get it."

"And, uh—I need to get something from my truck," Cam says, making Taylor wonder if he's just trying to keep from getting caught in the crossfire. Especially when the next thing Willa says is, "You're bringing your cat?"

Taylor's teeth clench as she says, "Looks that way."

Her family has a mess of outdoor cats that live in the barn and prowl the fields for mice, but Pumpkin is their only indoor cat, a calico that Taylor chose from the shelter when she was eleven. They've grown up together, and Pumpkin sleeps wherever Taylor sleeps, usually curled in a ball against the back of her calves. Taylor couldn't bear the idea of leaving her cat behind. She's taken by surprise when Willa tickles Pumpkin behind the ears and smiles.

"She'll be good company."

Taylor wonders if Willa means the cat will be better company than her, but she decides not to overthink it. She doesn't want to fight before they've even left the dock. "I thought so too."

"You have to deal with anything that comes out of her butt, though."

Taylor laughs, and a twinge of guilt pings her heart. It seems too soon for laughing, even though Finley probably would have found it funny too. "I, um—I shouldn't have called you a bitch. She wanted us to do this together, and I need your help."

"I shouldn't have left you hanging until the last minute." Willa looks around. "So . . . what's the plan?"

It's not lost on Taylor that neither of them actually apologized, but it was close enough. "Maybe get everything arranged first? So I—so *we* know where to find things when we need them."

Willa nods. "Good idea. That gives us time to remember what we forgot. There's always something."

Taylor's dad built some shelves inside the empty engine compartment under the stairs, creating a makeshift pantry for their nonperishables—ramen noodles, cans of soup, granola bars, instant mac and cheese, and a giant Tupperware of her mom's homemade snickerdoodles. They have no oven or refrigerator, only a built-in cooler and a small propane camp stove, and the toilet is little more than a glorified Porta Potti that will need to be emptied regularly. It will be like living in a floating camper for the next two and a half months.

"God, this boat is tiny." Willa stashes a couple of textbooks in the hatch beside her bunk. "Three of us would have been stepping all over each other."

Taylor bristles, until she realizes Willa is just making conversation, not pressing a bruise. They haven't spoken to each other since the funeral. Taylor's mom sent Willa an invitation to Taylor's graduation party, but Willa never showed up.

"Finley would have figured it out," Taylor says. "Remember that time she crammed six people in her Fiat to go looking for Gore Orphanage?"

One of the most popular local urban legends was one in which an orphanage near Vermilion had reputedly burned down with all the children inside. The ruins of the house were said to be haunted and that if you went there at midnight—especially on Halloween—you could hear the children screaming. Finley was a sucker for weird attractions and urban myths, so they'd all piled into her car to go looking for the remains of Gore Orphanage.

Willa laughs. "How can I forget? I was smashed in the back seat between Owen and Brady, and all the while she was driving in the wrong direction."

"At least you didn't get poison ivy." Taylor had gone home that night with an itchy red rash circling both her ankles and, in places, climbing up her shins. She still has a faint scar from where she'd scratched herself raw.

"Ouch." Willa's nose crinkles as she winces. "True."

They fall silent, and in that long moment Taylor misses Finley with a longing so fierce it steals her breath. She doesn't want to cry anymore, but she doesn't know how to keep the tears from coming. "I wish we had to figure out how to fit three of us on this boat."

"Yeah." There's a note of wistfulness in Willa's sigh. "Me too."

Finley would have offered Taylor a hug, but Willa has always been the opposite of touchy-feely. Prickly-resisty. So Taylor ends up wiping her eyes on the sleeve of her T-shirt. By the time her brother returns with a large kraft paper box, it almost looks as though she hasn't been crying at all.

"We need to do this before Mom gets back." Campbell pulls out his phone and cues up a video of Finley wearing her blue Coraline wig. Taylor and Willa lean in as he clicks play.

"Two years ago, we bought an old boat and made a plan to sail to Key West," Finley begins, and Taylor covers her mouth to hold back a sob. She remembers this Finley from their last sleepover, before the Donoghues brought in a hospital bed and a round-the-clock hospice nurse. That night they'd watched a *Doctor Who* marathon and made Belgian waffles at two in the morning. By the time the short video is over, tears are streaming down Taylor's face and Willa's fingers are threaded tightly through hers.

"Where is the list?" Taylor demands. "Why did Finley give it to you?"

"Because I'm Switzerland ... and she wanted you to work together." Cam points a look at their linked hands before working open the lid of the box. Willa lets go.

"Just give us the list," Taylor says.

"Relax. There's an order to this."

The first thing Campbell pulls from the box is a plastic baggie of marijuana. Even though smoking pot is one of her brother's favorite pastimes, Taylor has never touched the stuff. Just seeing it makes her nervous, and she imagines the drug dogs at the nearby police station suddenly sniffing the air. She has no frame of reference to know how much is in the baggie, but any amount feels like too much.

"Thanks." Willa takes the baggie, and Taylor's jaw drops. This is a side of Willa she has never seen, and now she can't help but wonder if Finley smoked pot too. Did the two of them blaze up whenever she wasn't around?

Cam senses her outrage. "It helped Finley feel better during chemo," he explains. "And getting high is way more fun with friends."

"I was her friend." Taylor has always been privately paranoid that Willa and Finley had more fun without her. In Taylor's imagination, they had smarter conversations and did more interesting things. She hates that her brother may have been part of their secret world. "You could have invited me."

Willa rolls her eyes. "Not everything is about you."

Taylor opens her mouth to retort, but Cam cuts her off.

"We have no time for arguing," he says, rummaging around in the box like some sort of degenerate Santa Claus. This time he comes up with a pair of fake IDs. Even though the Ohio DMV has tried to make it impossible to counterfeit driver's licenses, Campbell is a wizard with passport photos and an X-Acto knife.

"Seriously?" Taylor is aware she's quickly becoming a buzzkill, but she can't help herself. She's not a fake-ID kind of girl. She's a listen-to-records-in-her-bedroom kind of girl. "I'd like to make it to Key West without ending up in jail."

Cam laughs. "Finley wanted you to have them."

"Why would we even need fake IDs?"

"Why wouldn't you?" He looks perplexed for a moment,

then skeptical, as though he's wondering if they even share the same DNA. Taylor often wonders that herself.

"Please don't let the next thing in that box be a gun," she says.

Again her brother laughs. "It's not, but there is a speargun in one of the cockpit lockers. Just in case."

In case of what? Taylor can't imagine a scenario in which she would need a fishing speargun or a bag of weed, but she supposes she should have faith in Finley's plan, even if it doesn't make much sense yet.

The next thing Campbell takes from the box is a spiral-bound book called *Getting Loopy with Captain Norm*, a self-published guidebook to America's Great Loop. The Great Loop is a series of connected waterways that form a circle around the eastern half of the United States. Some "loopers" spend months, or even years, traveling the full circle, but Finley narrowed their trip to just one section. She bought the book because of the silly title, but it's actually filled with marina recommendations, anchorage locations, and boating tips.

Finally, something useful.

"Is there a list in there?" Taylor asks impatiently.

"I'm getting to it," Cam says, pulling out a Jolly Roger. Above the skull, in pink lettering, it says NO QUARTER, and below the crossed cutlasses, it says NO SURRENDER. "This flag was in the box with the boat name lettering. So she probably meant it as a surprise."

"So cool." Willa breaks into a huge smile, and even Taylor has to admit the flag will look badass fluttering up in the rigging. Willa wraps it around her shoulders. "What's next?"

Campbell reaches into the box and brings out a sheet of paper.

This is it.

Before Willa has a chance to react, Taylor snatches the list from her brother's hand, greedy for this last bit of Finley. Taylor has a shoebox stashed on a high shelf in her closet filled with all the notes they ever wrote to each other, dating all the way back to kindergarten, when they drew pictures of their favorite animals, giraffes (Taylor) and elephants (Finley). Taylor takes comfort in Finley's familiar sloppy scrawl.

1. Start here.
2. Music is good for the soul.
3. Make time for wonder.
4. Time travel whenever possible.
5. Don't lose your head.
6. Take a bite out of life.
7. Make your own luck.
8. Give a "ship."
9. Get a little wild.
10. Believe the unbelievable.
11. Stay young.
12. Reach for the stars.
13. It's not the destination . . .
    (You know the rest.)

Willa

THE FORGOTTEN THINGS HAVE BEEN REMEMBERED— including the cat food, Taylor's retainer, and Willa's bike—and the boat is ready to sail, when Mrs. Donoghue shows up unexpectedly. Seeing her is like looking at Finley through a time machine. She is Finley in middle age, her light-brown hair highlighted to cover the gray and crinkles at the corners of her eyes. Willa feels a squeezing sensation in her chest—as though a fist just tightened around her heart—at the loss of a Finley she'll never know. It takes everything not to excuse herself for some air. She stays because Finley's mom has done more for her than she can ever repay.

Willa and Finley were in the same grade at school—but not friends yet—when the Boys and Girls Clubs partnered with the sailing club to offer lessons to underprivileged kids. That summer Willa showed Finley that the tiny girl who was always picked last in gym class was the first to learn how to sail. Finley saw Willa in a new light. She saw her as a *sailor*.

When school started in the fall, Finley invited Willa to sit with her friends in the cafeteria, and Finley always found spare lunch tickets in her backpack for Willa so she could join them eating terrible tuna casserole and Friday pizza. Mrs. Donoghue altered Willa's uniforms to fit her properly. Once Finley's mom gave Willa a pair of shoes, claiming she'd accidentally bought the wrong size for Finley. Even after Willa was old enough to realize the depths of their generosity—that Mrs. Donoghue had been buying extra lunch tickets all along—Finley and her mother never made Willa feel like a charity case.

"It looks like you're all set." Mrs. Donoghue smiles, but sadness lingers in her eyes. Willa has no idea how she'll ever get over losing her best friend, but she can't begin to imagine how Finley's mother must feel. Mothers aren't supposed to lose their daughters. "But before you go, I have a couple of things for you."

She hands Willa a prepaid debit card. "It's Finley's savings for the trip."

"I really—I can't accept this."

"Please don't be stubborn, Willa. Finley wanted you to have it, and I don't want you girls to be caught short."

Being given a substantial amount of money is a much

bigger deal than a pair of school shoes or lunch tickets, but Willa's biggest fear is that her meager savings won't carry her through the entire trip. Taylor frowns at the debit card, and Willa worries this will become another wall between them, but she needs the money. "I'll, um—I'll pay you back."

"Don't be silly." Mrs. Donoghue wraps her arm around Willa's shoulder and kisses her temple. "If I learned anything from my daughter, it's that you only get one life. Make the most of it."

Willa nods. "I will. Thank you."

Finley's mom turns to Taylor and offers her a small glass bottle filled with what looks like gray sand. "We didn't honor any of Finley's funeral requests because . . . well, can you imagine my eighty-eight-year-old mother at a bonfire party on Cedar Point Beach? But Finley's dad and I thought you girls might like to scatter some of her ashes when you reach Key West. She'd approve, don't you think?"

Taylor nods, her eyes shining with tears as she takes the bottle, leaving Willa to speak for both of them. "Definitely."

"Well." Mrs. Donoghue smiles again. "I should go." She embraces Taylor first, then Willa. "Finley would be so proud of you. Have a wonderful summer."

"Okay, so the first clue is 'start here,' which is obviously Sandusky." Willa pull a notebook and a pen from her backpack and unfolds a small map of the United States to compare against the list. "And 'music is good for the soul. . . .'"

Taylor finishes the thought. "That sounds like the Rock and Roll Hall of Fame. Do you think she wanted to go there?"

"Possibly," Willa says. "But I was thinking that she might have written these clues after she realized she wouldn't be coming with us. These might be places she thought *we* would like to go."

Taylor is quiet for a moment, then sniffles as her tears begin again. Willa's conscience prods her to be kind, but she refuses to offer any comfort. Every time Willa starts to feel sorry for Taylor, awful memories bubble to the surface. She can still hear Taylor screaming at her in front of the entire sailing team, calling Willa a backstabber and a friend-stealing bitch. Willa weathered those insults without flinching because they weren't true, but she still gets mad when she remembers how Taylor called her trailer trash.

Willa and her mom had been living in Greenfield Village at the time, which sounds like a tidy little mobile home park with tiny squares of green grass and smiling neighbors. There *were* a few friendly senior citizens who lived in the park, as well as some kids that Willa played with after school, but mostly living in Greenfield Village was like living in an episode of *Cops*. More than once Willa had been awakened by red and blue lights flashing on her bedroom wall.

The thing is, Willa can shake off being called poor. It's as much a fact as having brown eyes or being right-handed. But *poor* carries the implication that someday your status can change; *trash* suggests that if the bottom of the barrel is right beneath you, that's exactly where you belong.

Taylor never apologized. She pretended she never said it and—for Finley's sake—Willa pretended she never heard it. Now, as Taylor wipes her tears with the sleeve of her T-shirt again, Willa knows Finley would expect her to be the mature one, but instead of offering sympathy, she says, "The third clue is 'make time for wonder.'"

"That has to be Niagara Falls," Taylor says. "You know how weird she was about that place."

Finley's obsession with the falls began after her family vacationed there when she was ten, when her parents were still married. Afterward, she read every book she could get her hands on about Niagara Falls. She did a fifth-grade science fair project about hydroelectricity so she could build a model. And in middle school Finley wrote a persuasive paper arguing that Niagara Falls should replace Victoria Falls as one of the seven natural wonders of the world.

Even in high school, when her obsession had finally waned, Finley kept a framed photo on her bookshelf of her family wearing the translucent yellow tour ponchos, their hair flattened by the mist coming off the falls. Finley and Regan were happy little girls in the picture, but their parents wore the forced smiles of a couple who would be divorced a year later. Maybe Finley never noticed—or maybe she chose to ignore it—but Willa wonders if Finley loved Niagara Falls because it was the last vacation her family took together.

"I've never been there," Willa says.

"I'm not going through the Welland Canal or sailing on Lake Ontario," Taylor says. "So if you want to go to Niagara Falls, we'll have to take a bus from Buffalo."

"What if I want to sail Lake Ontario?"

"Then maybe you should have shown up sooner."

Willa's eyebrows arch. "It doesn't matter when I showed up. I'm here now and it's *our* trip. You don't get to make all the decisions."

Taylor moves to her side of the cabin, drops onto her bunk, opens a tattered copy of *Outlander*, and pointedly ignores Willa, who moves on to the next clue. 'Time travel whenever possible.' This one is so vague that it could refer to anything in any town along the way. She slips the list inside the Captain Norm book, as irritated with Finley as she is with Taylor, and feeling sad about both.

Willa steps into her flip-flops and walks down to the junior barn, where she and Finley spent hours hanging out on the battered old couch, drinking Gatorade and playing Uno with the other kids on the sailing team. Her chest aches as she thinks about how her life came full circle two summers ago, when she and Finley taught sailing to the kids from the Boys and Girls Clubs.

"I was one of you guys," Willa told them at their first lesson. "The closest I'd ever been to a boat was seeing one out there sailing in the bay, but right here at this club, I discovered that anyone can learn how to sail."

There was a little girl in the class named Aaliyah, who idolized her. If Willa wore her hair in a bun, Aaliyah would show up the next day with her hair in a bun. She was delighted that her light-brown skin was the same shade as Willa's skin. She listened with a fierce intensity when Willa talked, and when the class finally hit the water, Aaliyah was determined to be first in all things. At the end of the week, she sobbed as she gifted Willa with a red and purple friendship bracelet that she'd made herself.

"I'm going to miss you so much," Aaliyah said, her face buried in Willa's neck. "But I'll come back next year and all the years after that until I can be a teacher like you."

Willa touches the woven bracelets circling her wrist, Aaliyah's among them—the colors faded from water and sun—and wonders what happened to that little girl. She didn't return the following summer, and the director of the Boys and Girls Club said only that Aaliyah had gone to live with her grandma in Cleveland.

"She might not remember your name forever," Finley said. "But you left an impression on her that will never go away."

Willa didn't believe it at that time, but now she knows that someone can leave you with an indelible mark that will change you forever. Finley's mark burns hot enough to make her want to scream sometimes, to rage at a God who would take one of the sweetest human beings on the earth, while leaving murderers and rapists to do business as usual.

All the lights are turned off when Willa returns to the boat, and Taylor is asleep with Pumpkin curled in the hollow behind her knees. Willa bunks down on her side of the boat, and through the open hatch she can see a handful of stars. She doesn't know if she believes in heaven anymore, but all the same she whispers to Finley, "I hope you know what you're doing."

Taylor

THE NEXT MORNING THE SUN IS MISSING IN ACTION and the clouds are swollen with imminent rain. It seems like a bad omen to Taylor, who is reminded of the day her family was returning from a long weekend on Kelleys Island when a storm whipped up on Lake Erie. The sky was nearly as black as night and the wind howled as her mom hustled the kids belowdecks, leaving Taylor's dad to battle the weather alone. In the stuffy confines of the cabin, with the boat pitching on every wave, Taylor felt her insides churn. She made it to the galley sink in time, but she threw up and threw up and threw up. Her mom dosed her with Dramamine and a can of ginger ale, and eventually Taylor fell asleep. Now, as she stands in the cockpit of *Whiskey Tango Foxtrot* with the first sprinkles peppering her cheeks, her stomach coils.

Taylor checks the weather radar app on her phone, the

forecast calling for all-day showers. No big winds. No thunderstorms. But she knows how quickly conditions can change.

"Do you think we should wait out this weather?" she asks, stepping back inside the cabin, where Willa is making up her bunk. It hasn't even been twenty-four hours and already Taylor's side of the boat is a wreck. "It's supposed to rain all day."

"It's just water."

"It should clear up by tomorrow."

"If we're going to make it to Key West before school starts, we can't waste time," Willa says. "We need to leave today."

"It's just *one* day."

"Look, Taylor, this whole trip was meant to be an adventure, and that includes the weather. Suck it up. We're leaving."

"Just last night you said it was *our* trip, so if I don't get to make the decisions, neither do you."

"Fine." Willa snatches a coin from the plastic bin filled with quarters for doing laundry. The quarters were a gift from Taylor's grandparents. "Heads, we leave. Tails, we stay."

Taylor nods. Willa flips the coin in the air, and Taylor holds her breath as it spins and falls. Willa catches the quarter, then opens her fist.

Heads.

"Shit." Taylor's shoulders sag. "Fine."

She jams her arms into her foul-weather jacket and stomps off the boat. Taylor knows she's being petty, but she doesn't want Willa to know she's afraid. When her dad brought them safely home from Kelleys, he'd had a lifetime of experience and Taylor had no reason to be frightened. Seasickness was the worst thing that could happen to her. Willa might be a good sailor, but Taylor doesn't trust that Willa will know what to do in gale-force winds or ten-foot seas.

Taylor stands under the awning of the clubhouse porch and phones her dad. "It's raining."

He laughs a little, but not in an unkind way. "That happens sometimes."

"I keep thinking about that time at Kelleys."

"I saw the forecast that day, Taylor, and thought I could outrun the storm," he said. "I made a mistake. But today the weather is not like that. It's just rain."

"But what if—"

"Trust me," her dad says gently. "Go."

They exchange *I love you*s and *goodbye*s, and Taylor is tucking her phone into her pocket when Brady rolls through the front gate in his big putty-colored Buick Riviera. Ever since he bought it, his friends call him Grandpa Guerra, but Taylor loves the car because it has velour seats, fake wood trim, and a cassette player. One Saturday they went to a bunch of garage sales, looking for cassette tapes.

"What are you doing here?" she asks, sliding into the passenger seat.

"Were you just going to leave without saying goodbye?"

"No. I mean, I was going to call you."

"Really?" he says. "Because you've been kind of hard to reach lately."

Ever since Finley died, Taylor has felt like a big empty hole. She doesn't know how to explain to Brady—or anyone, really—that there was no one in the world she loved more than Finley. Or that she is lost without her.

Twelve years ago, Taylor didn't understand what she felt the first time she saw Finley, with her swingy brown ponytail and pink backpack with her name embroidered across the pocket. Taylor remembers being overcome with an intense yearning to be Finley's best friend, and when Finley asked her to read *Don't Let the Pigeon Drive the Bus!* in the bathtub reading nook, it was like a wish come true. It wasn't until she was at a birthday sleepover a few years later—when the girls started giggling about the boys they liked—that Taylor's kindergarten yearnings suddenly made sense. But when Finley confessed that she liked Dominic Vaccaro *and* DeAndre Grant, Taylor understood that her feelings for Finley went one way and she kept them to herself.

A few more years later, in freshman biology, Taylor and Brady were looking at plant cells through a microscope when he asked if she wanted to get ice cream with him sometime. It wasn't the most romantic invitation ever, but Taylor didn't mind. Brady has been an easygoing boyfriend. Funny. Sweet. Uncomplicated. He's bigger and taller than Taylor, so she felt small wearing his football jersey on pep rally days and she felt special wearing his face on a badge on her jacket at games.

"I think we should break up," she blurts out, looking at the fake burl-wood glove compartment so she doesn't have to look at Brady's adorable, earnest face.

"Do you want to date other people or something?" he asks.

"No."

"Did I do something wrong?"

"No."

"Then I guess I don't understand," Brady says. "What's going on?"

"I just need—"

"Please do *not* say you need space, because that's a bullshit excuse."

"I miss Finley so much I can't breathe," she says.

"And breaking up with me is gonna fix that?"

"Probably not."

He sits there for the longest time, softly drumming his thumb against the steering wheel. Finally, he sighs and says, "Okay."

That one little word rips Taylor open as though Brady is the one doing the breaking up. Tears trickle down her cheeks as she opens the car door and rain batters her face. "I'm sorry."

Brady doesn't look at her, but he nods. "Me too."

As Taylor walks down the dock, she isn't sure she made the right decision. There's so much she'll miss about Brady, like picnics on the rocks at the Marblehead lighthouse. Sharing an armrest at the movies as they held hands. Kissing him in the driveway until her dad flickered the porch light to signal that it was time to come inside. But Brady deserves someone who loves him as much as Taylor loved Finley.

Willa notices her tears as she comes into the cabin. "Are you okay?"

"I just broke up with Brady."

"Wow." Willa blinks with surprise. "Do you, um—do you want to talk about it?" The sympathy in her voice touches a raw nerve. Taylor is not used to sharing such personal things with anyone other than Finley.

"Let's just go."

"Sure. Okay." Willa is already wearing her foul-weather overalls, but she pulls on her jacket and twists her curls up into a bun. "For what it's worth, I'm really sorry."

There are no other boats on the bay as they motor through rain and sloppy waves past Cedar Point and beyond the breakwall into Lake Erie. Willa turns the boat toward the east, keeping a healthy distance between them and the shoreline. Sometimes, on a clear day, you can see hints of the islands to the north, but today the lake disappears into a gray haze. At the dock, the boat seemed sturdy and safe, but now it feels vulnerable, and all of Taylor's fears slam into her at once. The bagel she ate for breakfast comes back as a puddle on the cockpit floor, but Willa doesn't even spare a glance in her direction. As the rain slowly washes the vomit down the scupper holes in the floor, Taylor tucks herself into the smallest shape she can manage and tries not to cry.

She grows accustomed to the relentless rhythm of the waves after a couple of hours and some ginger ale to calm her stomach. Taylor is able to go into the cabin long enough to make sandwiches for lunch, but Willa does all of the driving. Willa is the one who stands on the wet deck to adjust the sails, the one who keeps the compass pointing in the right direction.

By car it would have taken them a little more than an hour to drive to Cleveland.

It takes them the entire day to sail there.

"Can you get some dock lines ready?" Willa asks as the lights of Edgewater Marina come into view. Aside from a terse *thank you* when Taylor brought her food, these are the first words she's strung into a full sentence all day. "Or you can drive and I'll do it."

Maybe on a sunny day, Taylor wouldn't be afraid of falling overboard, but the deck is wet. "I'll drive."

Willa tells her to aim for the Terminal Tower, an easily recognizable landmark on the Cleveland skyline. As Willa moves steadily across the cabin top, tears blur Taylor's vision. It was unrealistic to think she could have done this by herself. She doesn't love sailing the way Finley did. The way Willa does. Taylor struggles to keep the boat pointed toward the lights of the skyscraper.

Willa, she thinks, *must really hate me right now.*

Once they pass the breakwall into the protected marina, the waves subside. Taylor's mother and Mrs. Donoghue are waiting on the dock, huddled under giant golf umbrellas. Taylor rushes to tie the dock lines, wanting to get off the boat as soon as possible. She tumbles into her mother's waiting arms, leaving Willa to double-check the knots.

41.4993° N, 81.6944° W

Music is good for the soul.

Willa

"WILLA, HONEY, COME GET OUT OF THE RAIN!" Mrs. Donoghue beckons from under her umbrella. "We've got dry towels and a table reservation."

"I'll be right there," she calls back, retying a knot that Taylor got wrong. The fingers on Willa's right hand are cramped from nine hours of holding the tiller, and her bladder is about to burst. All she really wants is to collapse on her bunk and sleep, but it would be rude to refuse. And the cherry on top of this shit sundae is the fact that Willa was the one who wanted to leave Sandusky in the rain. Would it have killed her to wait one more day? Would it have killed her to be nice? She wipes her face with a wet hand, jumps off the boat, and runs to catch up with the others.

The dining room inside the yacht club is warm, and Willa feels practically naked after wearing her weather gear all day.

Her curls have become a wild mass, and she envies Taylor for having the kind of hair that dries straight without any styling products. It's not that Willa doesn't like her curls, but she's never been able to walk into school with wet hair and have it look great by second period.

"So, what are you girls doing tomorrow?" Mrs. Donoghue asks. "Will you keep moving, or spend the day in Cleveland?"

Willa waits for Taylor to tell them about the list of clues—she's never had the feeling that Finley meant for the list to be a secret—but Taylor seems preoccupied with the steaming bowl of clam chowder in front of her.

"We, um—we've thought about going to the Rock Hall," Willa offers, hoping Taylor will jump into the conversation. She has always been better at talking to Finley's mom.

Near the end, whenever Willa and Taylor would stop by to visit Finley, Mrs. Donoghue would give them their privacy. She'd ask the hospice nurse to take a break so they could be normal teenage girls. At the end of every visit, Finley's mom would hug them too long. Tears would glisten in her eyes as she said, "Thank you for being such good friends to Finley."

Taylor let Mrs. Donoghue's hugs go on as long as necessary, but Willa never knew how to buoy up Finley's mom when Willa felt like she was the one who was drowning.

"That sounds like fun," Taylor's mom says, and the

table falls into an awkward silence, punctuated only by the clinking of spoons against bowls. Finally, Taylor looks up at her mom.

"I can't do this," she says. "I want to go home."

"You have *got* to be kidding me." Willa keeps her voice level, not wanting to cause a scene in public, but she's one deep breath away from going off. "You're bailing after ten hours?"

"I just—it's too hard."

"Hard is having to do all the work by yourself." Willa removes the paper napkin from her lap and places it on the table beside what's left of her soup. "How nice it must be to just give up, knowing everything will be fine for you. I wasted my college savings and quit my job."

"You could come work at the stand," Taylor says, throwing a glance at her mom, who offers an encouraging nod.

The Nicholsons own a huge farm in Perkins Township that's been in their family for generations. Every summer people flock to their farm stand—which has grown over the years into a full-blown shop—for homegrown fruits and vegetables. Their tomatoes and sweet corn are legendary, and you're not doing autumn properly if you don't go to Nicholsons' Farm for pumpkins, hayrides, and fresh-pressed cider.

"That's not the point," Willa says.

"Today was terrible and I hated it."

Willa ignores Taylor and turns to Mrs. Donoghue. "Thank

you for coming all this way to buy us dinner. If you'll excuse me, I need to go call my mom."

If Willa were to look up, she would see slivers of clear sky and a few stars peeking out from between the clouds that plagued her all day. But she keeps her head down, her footsteps in concert with her head—*I hate her, I hate her, I hate her*—as she walks back to the boat. She climbs aboard and sits on the cabin top as she punches the speed-dial button for home.

Her mom is working tonight and usually silences her cell phone while she's on the clock, but Willa wants to leave a voice mail to warn her that she's coming home. Except someone who is not her mom answers on the second ring. Steve. The guy who sleeps over at their apartment whenever he and his on-again/off-again girlfriend are off. Sometimes he stays a night, sometimes several, but he always leaves.

Willa doesn't dislike him. In fact, she can tell he was kind of cute in high school because the outline of his eighteen-year-old self is still there. She understands why her mom likes him, but what Willa can't understand is why her mom is content to be someone's backup plan when she deserves to be someone's first choice.

"Willa? You there?" His voice is gravelly, and in the background her mom sings along to an old Foo Fighters song.

Not at work.

Something inside her cracks open and Willa is just . . . done. Done worrying about the car repairs. Done making sure the bills are paid on time. Done being afraid her mom will lose her job (again). Willa pivots her arm and flings the phone as hard as she can. It arcs high before it drops into the water and disappears. She feels a surge of panic as she realizes she will have to pay for a replacement, but Willa is done worrying about that, too. It's her mom's turn to worry.

"Did you just—" Taylor stops in front of Willa, her mouth falling open as she looks at the spot where the phone splashed down.

"I have nothing to say to you."

"I came to offer you a ride home," Taylor says defensively. "Campbell can bring the boat back to Sandusky tomorrow."

"You *completely* ruined my summer."

"You can come work at the farm stand."

Willa gives a strangled cry. "You stood in front of Finley's ashes, called me a bitch, and I still showed up! Now you get to just walk away? Fuck you, Taylor. I'm going to Key West."

"For real?"

Willa has no idea if her money will hold out the whole way or how she's going to sail by herself for two months, but she is not going to give Taylor the satisfaction of seeing her

65

uncertainty. Her voice is cold as she says, "It's what Finley wanted."

Taylor looks away first.

The boat sways as Taylor moves around the cabin, packing her clothes and gathering up her bedding. Willa sits on the deck as the breeze stirs the rigging of the sailboats in the basin, creating a soothing metallic symphony at odds with the boiling rage inside her. Finally, Taylor emerges as her mom comes down the dock with an empty cart. "You can have all my food and, um—I left Finley's ashes."

Willa nods, but she doesn't speak.

"So," Taylor says, scooping up her cat. "Be careful. Have fun."

Again she doesn't respond, and as she watches her former friend walk away, Willa hopes she'll never have to see Taylor Nicholson again.

At nightfall Willa curls up in the cockpit with her flashlight and an actual chart book, plotting a route to Niagara Falls. Tomorrow she'll sail as far as Ashtabula. The following day she'll cross into Pennsylvania and spend the night in Erie. And on the day after that, she'll make the crossing to Port Colborne in Canada. The days will be long, but Willa is already planning ahead. She'll keep a bucket in the cockpit to use as a toilet. She can prepare all her meals in the morning to eat throughout the day. Same with water. If she rigs up a beach umbrella over the cockpit, she'll have a little bit of shade. As long as the weather cooperates, she should be okay.

When she finishes, Willa turns her face skyward. The clouds are gone and the night sky is sprinkled with stars, and her memories roll back to the time she, Taylor, and Finley spent the night on the beach to watch a meteor shower. They treated it like an indoor slumber party, spreading a patchwork of blankets on the sand. Taylor made a playlist filled with songs about stars. They danced, toasted marshmallows over a little fire that Willa built, and watch the lights of freighters twinkle in the night like distant cities.

Around midnight, they lay back on the blankets to look up at the sky.

"Let's play Constellation," Finley suggested. When they were little, they'd try to identify as many constellations as they could and would race to locate the Big Dipper since that one was the easiest to find. Over time, the game morphed into making up constellations and an accompanying lore. "Willa, you start."

"Okay, so that one there"—she pointed to a cluster of stars not far from Polaris—"is Louise. It was named in honor of a 1950s housewife who clubbed her husband to death with a croquet mallet after he left his socks on the floor and criticized her tuna casserole."

Taylor laughed and Finley clapped with delight. "Now you, Taylor."

"The one over there, beside Louise, is Stan the Magic Fish," Taylor said. "Legend has it that Stan would grant three wishes to the fisherman who caught him. For centuries, men from all over the world attempted to catch him. Then, one day in the 1950s, a woman named Louise accomplished the impossible."

Finley snorted, then covered her face with her hands as the three of them literally rolled around laughing. When Taylor caught her breath, she continued.

"No woman had ever tried to catch Stan, so naturally he was curious about her wishes. Louise's first wish was for a million dollars. Her second wish was for a brand-new Cadillac. And her third wish was that she would get away with killing her husband. Once Stan granted the wishes, Louise filleted him and cooked him into a casserole."

They laughed until their stomachs ached, and even afterward, one of them would think about Louise and start giggling, making them crack up all over again. Eventually, they fell into an easy silence, just watching the sky until the first meteor streaked past.

Now Willa scans the stars, searching for Louise and Stan the Magic Fish with a whirlwind of anger and sadness spinning inside her. She never imagined losing Taylor would actually feel like a loss, but now both Finley *and* Taylor are gone. Willa catches the trail of a shooting star, but it's too late to make a wish. And she knows her wish will never come true.

Willa falls asleep in the cockpit and the morning brings a sky that's nothing but blue. She's slathering on a coat of sunscreen when Taylor comes walking down the dock with her duffel bag and her cat.

Taylor

ON THE DRIVE TO SANDUSKY, BOTH HER MOM AND Mrs. Donoghue assured Taylor that there was no shame in not wanting to continue the trip. Back at home, as her family sat around their backyard firepit, her dad said, "Not everyone enjoys sailing, Taylor." But she saw the mix of pity and confusion etched on her brothers' faces, like she'd been switched at birth and their real sister was out there somewhere, longing for water.

Taylor tried to convince herself that her parents were right, but it didn't stop her from feeling like she'd failed Finley. Or feeling guilty that she'd held Willa to a different standard. Now Willa would be the one to experience everything on Finley's list and Taylor would be the one missing out.

Her parents went to bed at ten, and Carter left to meet some friends at a bar downtown, leaving Taylor and Campbell alone. She poked at the fire, sending up sparks. "Did I do the right thing?"

Cam's attention was focused on rolling a joint, his narrow fingers deftly shaping the paper and filling it from a plastic bag just like the one Willa had hidden in a tampon box in the bathroom cupboard on the boat. His shoulder lifted in a half shrug. "Did you?"

"It was a pretty horrible day and I think Willa will be okay without me." But the excuse seemed anemic, even to Taylor. "She's probably glad I'm gone."

"Well, there's your answer," Cam said.

"So why do I still feel like shit?"

He slid his tongue along the rolling paper before speaking, then, "Because it's the wrong answer."

Taylor slumped in her chair. In the distance, their golden retriever rustled around in the peony bushes, bothering a feral cat that was trying to sleep. If Buddy didn't end up with a slash on his muzzle, he'd be lucky. Now that she was home, Taylor wanted to stay there, safe and dry. "I have to go back, don't I?"

Campbell nodded. "Yep."

"Will you take me?"

This morning, as he drove her back to Cleveland, Taylor practiced apologies in her head. But Willa doesn't look overjoyed to see her, and the words stick in Taylor's throat. She forces them out. "I shouldn't have left. I'm sorry."

"I'm done doing all the work," Willa says.

"No. I know. I promise I'll do more."

"Fine."

"I made a playlist," Taylor says as she steps aboard *Whiskey Tango Foxtrot*, and Willa actually smiles at the olive branch.

"Cool."

The air between them feels cleaner, but Taylor knows their relationship is like a house of cards. One strong gust and it will collapse again.

For the next few hours, they settle into a routine, taking turns steering the boat and making meals. Taylor reads the sex scenes from *Outlander* aloud, and Willa laughs at her terrible attempt at a Scottish accent. Taylor discovered the first book of the series in her mom's nightstand drawer when they were in middle school, and a good portion of their sex education came from the sex scenes between Jamie and Claire—which, Taylor thinks now, might not have been the worst way to learn about sex. None of them had put the lessons into practice—at least as far as Taylor knows—but Finley was the one who talked most about having sex.

"The real tragedy," she lamented, during one after-school visit, "is that I'm going to die a virgin."

Willa laughed and bopped her with a pillow. "The bright

side is that your chances of being canonized are that much better. Someday they'll be saying prayers to Saint Finley, patron saint of virgins."

Finley giggled. "Yeah, but if I had to choose between sainthood and having sex with Campbell . . ."

The two of them cracked up laughing, but Taylor always felt a little uneasy when Finley talked about Cam. Taylor understood that her brother was attractive, but the door to Campbell was revolving. Finley deserved someone who loved her more than anyone else in the world.

A tear beads in the corner of her eye, and Taylor puts down the book. Finley is woven so tightly into the fabric of her life, and now it feels as if she's coming unraveled. "I can drive for a while."

"Are you sure?" Willa asks. "It's still my turn for another hour."

"I'm sure."

From her seat beside the tiller, Taylor watches through the companionway as Willa stretches out on her bunk for a nap. She doesn't seem very emotional about Finley's death. Taylor has never seen her cry—not even at the funeral—but Willa has rarely ever given her feelings away. Maybe she mourns when no one is watching.

Sailing is infinitely easier without the rain. Willa gave her a compass heading, and Taylor does her best to keep the needle pointing in that direction. She tenses a little when she sees a freighter in the distance, but relaxes when she realizes it's heading away from them. She adjusts the beach umbrella for a bit more shade, and it doesn't take long before her eyes grow heavy—and then slide shut.

Taylor startles awake when she hears a hollow knocking sound on the hull of the boat and a male voice saying, "Hello! Is everyone aboard safe and well?"

Her eyes open on a small Coast Guard boat bobbing beside *Whiskey Tango Foxtrot* and two guardsmen wearing navy-blue uniforms with orange life vests and military boots. The older man has graying temples and a spot of pink sunburn on the top of his pale nose, while the dark-skinned younger man wears a navy ball cap and aviator-style sunglasses.

Her first panicked thought is that they're about to be arrested for possession of marijuana, but above her head, the mainsail flaps softly in the breeze and the boat is going slowly nowhere.

Taylor's next thought is that Willa is going to kill her.

Willa shoots a murderous glare at Taylor as she scrambles through the companionway, but her face transforms as she smiles at the coastguardsmen. Willa's floral bikini catches the attention of the younger guardsman, who removes his sunglasses for a better look. His dark eyes are fixed on her as she says, "We're okay. Everything's fine. Taylor must have fallen asleep while I was off watch."

"So, uh—where ya headed?" The threat of imminent danger past, his tone becomes less official, more flirty.

"We're on our way to Key West," Willa says. "But just as far as Ashtabula tonight."

"Well, you'll want to turn yourself that way"—the older guardsman points 180 degrees from the direction the boat is currently facing, and Taylor feels the heat of embarrassment creep into her cheeks—"and maybe get some rest tonight. It's a long way to Key West."

"We will," she says.

"So, are you just passing through Lake Erie?" the young guardsman asks Willa.

"We started out in Sandusky."

"We're stationed out of Ashtabula." He burrows his hand beneath his life vest and comes out with a business card and a pen. He writes something on the back of the card. "This is my personal number. If you want to hang out, hit me up."

Willa looks legitimately surprised that a cute boy is flirting with her in the middle of Lake Erie, but Taylor kind of respects that he saw his shot and took it. He could do a lot worse than Willa Ryan. She sneaks a peek at the card. "Maybe I will . . . Edison."

"And you are?"

"Willa. Oh . . . and Taylor."

"Okay, Romeo," the older guardsman says. "We need to get moving."

"Wait!" Taylor realizes she and Willa haven't done anything to document the trip yet. If Finley were with them, they'd have snapped dozens of pictures by now, but so far neither of Taylor's cameras have left their cases. She swings down into the cabin, grabs the instant, and returns to the cockpit. "Can I get a picture?"

The Coast Guard boat bumps softly against the sailboat as the guardsmen pose with Willa, who makes an okay sign with her fingers. Taylor's camera whirs as the photo slides out.

"Ladies." Edison tips his cap at both of them. The dent around his close-cropped hair is weirdly endearing, and Taylor wonders if Willa will call him.

"It was a pleasure. Be safe. And stay alert." As he follows the older guardsman back onto the Coast Guard boat, Edison grins at Willa and mouths, *Call me.*

The boat speeds off, and Willa takes over at the helm, putting the *Whiskey Tango Foxtrot* back on its proper course. She traps the tiller between her knees while she reapplies sunscreen to her exposed skin. Her lips are a tight line, as though she's holding back everything she wants to say, and Taylor wishes she would just yell. Fighting would be a lot easier than trying to penetrate Willa's frosty shield.

"I'm sorry I fell asleep," Taylor says.

Willa holds out the bottle of sunscreen. "Your nose is a little pink."

Taylor had hoped taking a picture would lighten the mood, but the fun they had this morning seems to have evaporated and Willa has gone back into bitch mode.

At her next turn at the helm, Taylor cues up the playlist she made together for the trip. Or, more accurately, threw together in the middle of the night because right now there is no music that feels good to Taylor's soul. It hurts to remember the adventures that went along with her best friend's favorite songs. She wants to believe that one day she will be okay, but that day seems so far away. Taylor touches the face of her phone and the music stops.

"Why'd you turn it off?" Willa comes out of the cabin with a bowl of white rice drizzled with Tiger sauce. Taylor never quite understood the appeal of plain rice, even with a splash of peppery sauce, until Finley quietly explained that rice is super cheap and stretches a long way on a budget. Taylor has never known an empty pantry—they even have a second refrigerator in the garage for beer and soda—so she wonders now if Willa actually likes rice.

"This playlist sucks," Taylor says.

"Sounds fine to me."

"It's just a bunch of recycled stuff from other playlists," she says. "It doesn't have any meaning."

Willa pokes at the rice with her fork. "Kind of like this trip."

Taylor wants to be pissed, but Willa is not wrong. So far, this trip sucks too. "Kind of."

"Without Finley, we're adrift . . . some of us more than others obviously."

At the note of humor in Willa's voice, Taylor scratches her nose with her middle finger and they both laugh.

"I thought for sure you were pissed about that," Taylor says.

"I was," Willa admits. "But, I mean—the Coast Guard showing up is exactly the kind of thing Finley would have loved."

"Totally."

They fall silent, and Taylor thinks maybe this trip isn't the kind that comes preloaded with a soundtrack. Maybe they have to find the music as they go.

Willa

ONE OF THE BIGGEST MYTHS ABOUT SAILING IS THAT it's romantic. The ads in fashion magazines feature impossibly beautiful people draped across the glossy teak decks of old wooden sailboats, clad in jaunty nautical stripes or glamorous ball gowns. Holding ropes that lead to nowhere. But Ralph Lauren never mentions the bugs, the inescapable heat of the midday sun, or the long stretches of boredom—the kind Willa and Taylor experience as they huddle beneath the beach umbrella, trying not to get fried as they make the crossing to Port Colborne.

They stopped in Ashtabula and Erie only long enough to eat, sleep, and shower. Willa didn't call Edison, but she kept his card—just in case. So far, the trip hasn't been much fun, but the next destination on Finley's list is Niagara Falls, and Willa is excited to cross into another country. She traveled with the junior sailing team to various regattas around Ohio, but the closest she's ever come to a real vacation is the long Memorial Day weekend she and her mom spent in Amish Country. They ate dinner at an all-you-can-eat buffet and slept just outside Millersburg in a no-star motel, where the icy air conditioner rattled at full blast all night. Even the narrow bunk of a thirty-year-old sailboat is an improvement over that bumpy bed.

Willa keeps her eye on the handheld GPS they borrowed from Taylor's dad as they approach the invisible boundary line between the United States and Canada.

"We're coming up on the border," she calls to Taylor, who is sprawled out on her bunk, reading. "We should do something."

"Like what?"

"I don't know," Willa says. She researched the shellback ceremony that navy sailors perform when they cross the equator, but this boundary isn't as significant—and they don't have anyone to play King Neptune anyway. "I've just never been outside of the United States, and I want to commemorate it."

No sound comes from the cabin as Taylor considers. Then, "I have an idea."

Willa can hear her rustling around, but she doesn't know what's happening until Taylor comes up from below with two handmade signs, one that says I'M IN CANADA and another that says I'M IN THE UNITED STATES. She colored the letters to look like flags. "You can stop the boat halfway across the line and we'll take a picture holding the signs."

"There's not an actual line. You know that, right?"

Taylor rolls her eyes. "Just get us in the ballpark."

Willa's anticipation ratchets up as she watches their progress on the GPS. About fifteen minutes later, she shifts the tiller, nosing the boat into the wind to bring their forward momentum to a stop. The sails flap as she and Taylor situate themselves—and Taylor's camera—on the front of the boat. Willa holds the Canada sign while Taylor holds the US sign, her thumb resting on the remote button for her camera. Pumpkin sits in the hollow between them.

"Ready?" Taylor asks.

Willa tucks a flyway curl behind her ear, feeling like Samwise Gamgee in *The Lord of the Rings*, preparing to take the step that will put her the farthest away from home she's ever been. She takes a deep breath and nods. "I'm ready."

"Finley on three," Taylor says. "One ... two ... three ..."

Her name shapes their mouths into smiles as Taylor snaps the picture.

A six hundred-foot freighter overtakes *Whiskey Tango Foxtrot* as Willa motors toward the entrance to the Port Colborne harbor, the black steel hull rising up beside their small boat like a wall. Willa's breath catches in her chest as the sailboat dips and bobs on the wake that ripples out from the colossal ship. Gulls cry and swoop in the wake, snatching at fish churned to the surface by the powerful engines. From the rear deck, a crew member waves down at Willa and Taylor.

"That was amazing," Willa says, at the same time Taylor says, "That was terrifying."

Willa would be lying if she said she wasn't afraid of being run over by a freighter, but she feels better when the next ship sounds its horn to indicate it has seen them. Ahead, docked inside the mouth of the canal, is yet another cargo ship, already waiting its turn to go through the locks that bypass Niagara Falls. Their boat looks like a toy in comparison.

"I don't want to go into a lock with one of those things," Taylor says.

"We won't," Willa says. "Freighters have priority, so we have to wait until they're through the first lock. We'll probably go with some other recreational boats."

"None of this sounds fun."

"I have a feeling it's going to be hard and tiring, because we have to keep the boat from hitting the wall of the lock . . . and there are eight locks," Willa says. "But no one we know has ever done anything like this."

Taylor laughs. "Yeah, because no one *wants* to do this."

"Finley did."

Taylor sighs. "Couldn't we just dock here and take a bus to Niagara Falls? I mean, the Welland Canal isn't one of her clues, and the one about time travel could mean the Erie Canal, couldn't it? It's really old."

"Do you honestly think that's what she meant?"

"I don't know! I hate that she's not here to tell us! I hate these stupid clues! I hate that she's dead!" The second ship overtakes them and the boat rocks, throwing off Taylor's equilibrium. She sits down hard on the cockpit bench, tears trickling down her cheeks. "And I really fucking hate freighters!"

A giggle escapes Willa. She clamps a hand over her mouth, but it's too late to hold back. Gales of laughter roll out of her until tears are leaking from the corner of her eyes. Until Taylor starts laughing. Until Willa's sides ache. Until the freighter is past and Willa raises both her middle fingers at the back of the ship, yelling, "And I really fucking hate freighters!"

She weighs the idea of sailing back across the lake and entering the Erie Canal at Buffalo. Like she said in her video, Finley will never know what they choose to do or not do— and it would make Taylor more comfortable—but Willa wants the challenge of the Welland and she wants to be able to say she sailed on two Great Lakes.

"Finley wouldn't take shortcuts," she says as they pass

between the breakwalls into the harbor. "She wouldn't want this to be too easy."

Taylor sighs again. "I know."

"It's been a long day," Willa says. "Let's crash here for the night and see if things feel different in the morning."

"She still won't be here," Taylor says. "She's never going to see any of this."

"Then we'll have to see it for her."

Willa radios the marina office on the handheld VHF, and she's given the okay to dock in one of the empty transient slips. Once the boat is tied up, Taylor calls home, while Willa uses a special videophone at the marina to notify the customs office of their arrival. Mr. Nicholson had warned them that Canadian officials might want to inspect the boat, but the man on the screen just verifies that Willa and Taylor are properly documented before welcoming them to Canada.

"Your mom called mine, wondering why you haven't called home," Taylor says as they meet back on the boat. "I told my mom you accidentally dropped your phone in the lake."

"Not completely a lie."

"You can borrow my phone, if you want."

Willa shrugs as she gathers her toiletry kit and towel. She's not ready to talk to her mom yet. "I might."

"She's probably worried," Taylor says.

"I said I might."

"I just think—"

"God, Taylor, leave it alone," Willa snaps as she steps off the boat onto the dock. "This is none of your business."

In the shower, Willa thinks about how whiplash fast she and Taylor can go from friendly to fighting. It was never that way with Finley. They debated pizza toppings or which movie to watch on Netflix, but they only ever had one big blowout. It came after a regatta at Indian Lake, during which everything that could go wrong, did. They were on the wrong side of the racecourse. The spinnaker halyard got tangled up. Finley blamed Willa, Willa blamed Finley, and they spent the two-hour ride home not speaking. Except that fight had ended with remorseful tears and sniffly apologies, not the giant, festering mess of a "friendship" Willa has with Taylor. The bad blood between them should have been laid to rest with Finley—and Willa wonders if it will ever die.

She returns to the boat, where a saucepan of water steams on the stove and Taylor is sitting in front of her laptop. "I'm making spaghetti," she says without looking up from the screen. "Do you want some?"

"Yeah, um—thanks," Willa says.

Taylor nods. "I'm also creating an Instagram account. We've been gone four days and I've only taken two pictures."

"That's criminal."

"Right?" Taylor says. "If we're going to be doing stuff no one we know has ever done, there should be proof we did it."

"So, wait . . . Does this mean you're okay with going through the canal?"

"Only if we can take a break and chill here for a day."

"That's fair," Willa says as the water in the saucepan rolls to a boil. She empties a box of spaghetti into the pan. "We could ride our bikes to the beach tomorrow."

"Yeah. Okay."

Growing up, they practically lived at the beach across the road from Finley's house. Their little-girl selves had sculpted elaborate sandcastles with margarine tubs, decorating them with bits of clamshell and seagull feathers. In middle school, they'd spent an inordinate amount of time doing their hair, then screaming when the neighborhood boys—the ones they were trying to impress with their cute hair—tried to splash them. By the time the girls reached high school, they were completely over those boys. Instead, they'd read books and listened to Taylor's playlists. They'd slept under the stars. If she were here now, Finley would say riding their bikes to the beach is an outstanding idea. But she's not here, so Willa has to accept that Taylor's "okay" is better than nothing.

Taylor

THE SUN HASN'T EVEN BROKEN THE HORIZON YET when the VHF radio crackles with an incoming call, informing Taylor and Willa that their transit window through the Welland Canal will open in thirty minutes. Willa scrambles out of bed to acknowledge the call, then quickly changes out of her pajamas and into her bikini with a pair of cutoff shorts. She seems perfectly at ease getting naked in front of Taylor, but Taylor still hasn't gotten used to the lack of privacy. She waits until Willa is out of the cabin before she changes into a tank top and shorts.

"I'm going to empty Pumpkin's litter box and get some coffee," Taylor says.

"Don't take too long." Willa pulls a misshapen fender from the cockpit storage locker. "We don't want to miss our window."

"We're not going to miss our window."

"I'm just saying . . ."

"Just because I fell asleep one time doesn't mean you can treat me like I'm going to fuck up everything else," Taylor snaps.

"What the—" Willa's eyebrows form a deep crease of confusion. "Are you seriously picking a fight with me right now? Over *this*?"

"I just—"

"The only thing I care about today is getting this boat through that canal without sinking," Willa says. "So if you want a fight, it's going to have to wait until we get to the other end."

"I'm going to get coffee." Taylor steps off the boat.

"Don't take too long."

She flings her arm back and flips her middle finger at Willa, but this time no one laughs.

Taylor wishes they could stay longer in Port Colborne. Yesterday, they rode their bikes along the canal—past art galleries, clothing boutiques, and antique stores—and stopped at a British bakery to buy warm, fresh cinnamon scones with real butter for breakfast before pedaling over the Welland Street lift bridge to the beach. Taylor took pictures of everything, from the charming buildings to the tumbledown sandcastle on the beach that reminded her of the castles she used to make with Finley.

The one thing that bothers Taylor about yesterday is how

little she and Willa had to say to each other. Finley was the talkative one. She'd have insisted on going into all the clothing shops to browse. She'd have struck up a conversation with the lady at the bakery. And she would have lost her mind over the fluffy little service-dog-in-training they met while waiting for a cargo ship to pass under the lift bridge. Finley provided the narration for their friendship, and Taylor misses her near-constant stream of chatter, along with Finley's endless sense of wonder. If she were here, she'd be excited about going through the locks, and maybe Taylor would feel excited too. Instead, she's stuck with serious, intense, bossy Willa.

Now, in the marina store, Taylor fills a couple of to-go cups with coffee, adding cream and sugar to her own. Willa prefers black.

"Like her soul," Taylor mutters on her way to the cash register.

She passes a display of boat fenders that are fat and shiny. Their old fenders came from her dad's collection of cast-off boat supplies, and Taylor isn't sure they'll survive the canal. A red sale tag above the display advertises a four-pack for ninety dollars. They're smaller than their current fenders and ninety bucks is not cheap, but it's one less thing to worry about. Balancing the coffee carrier with one hand, Taylor grabs the mesh bag and carries it to the register.

Willa is eating a bagel with cream cheese when Taylor gets back to the boat. Her eyebrows lift when she notices the bag of fenders. Taylor shrugs, handing her the cup of black-like-her-soul coffee. "I don't want anything bad to happen to the boat."

The first lock is eleven miles beyond Port Colborne. By the time they arrive, Taylor is nearly sick with anticipation. With no frame of reference, her imagination has spun up images of their boat being smashed to pieces against the lock wall. Pleasure boats travel through the Welland Canal all the time, so Taylor knows she's worrying too much. She just doesn't know how to turn off her brain.

Willa eases *Whiskey Tango Foxtrot* toward the wall of the lock, and a shoreman hands Taylor a long coil of rope.

"Most people run it around the cleat and pay it out slowly as the boat goes down," he instructs. "Do you have gloves? Might come in handy."

The Captain Norm book recommended boaters protect their hands while traveling through locks, so one of their last purchases before Taylor and Willa left Sandusky was a four-pack of heavy-duty gardening gloves. Taylor pulls a pair from the back pocket of her shorts and slides her hands inside.

"All set," she says, but she's not ready. Not really.

Ahead of them in the lock is a large white trawler called *Nauti-Gal* and an unnamed sleek red go-fast powerboat with a bank of outboard motors stretched across the back. Both boats are loaded with fenders to protect their shiny hulls, and Taylor is glad she bought a few more. *Whiskey Tango Foxtrot* is a small boat and they still have so far to go.

The steel doors close slowly and then the water begins its descent. From her place on the bow, Taylor eases out the rope, keeping pace with the water level, while Willa does the same at the back of the boat. It's less scary than Taylor imagined, but as the lock wall rises up beside them, the boat feels smaller than ever.

It takes about fifteen minutes for the water to drain to the correct level. The doors open at the opposite end of the lock, and *Nauti-Gal* peels away from the wall first and motors away, followed by the go-fast boat. Taylor releases the rope as Willa steers toward the middle of the channel.

"That wasn't so bad," Taylor says.

"I hate to be the bearer of bad news," Willa says. "But this was just the beginning. Next are the flight locks, and that's not going to be fun."

"Is there any good news?"

"Not unless you want me to make something up."

"Remind me again why we're doing this?"

It takes Willa and Taylor two hours to reach the first of the flight locks. The sun is higher in the sky and the other two boats have been waiting for their arrival. The owner of the trawler—a man who reminds Taylor of a grumpy version of her granddad—glares at her from his back deck as though she could have made their little outboard motor chug along any faster than it did.

Once Willa has the sailboat in position, the lock doors close and the water begins to drop. With each foot, the boat sinks, until the walls rise high above their heads, until only the top of the mast extends above ground level. Taylor is paying out the rope when a surge of water pushes the boat toward the lock wall. The fenders squish and Taylor's muscles strain as she and Willa push the boat away from the wall.

The water stops at forty-nine feet, and the doors at the other end are totally exposed. Water cascades down their massive surface, and they remind Taylor of something out of a fantasy movie, the kind of doors from behind which a horde of orcs would swarm. Instead, the doors open into the next lock. This one lowers them another forty-nine feet, and a third lock drops them yet another forty-nine feet.

It takes nine hours to go through the whole canal, and after they pass three giant cargo ships, Taylor's fear of freighters has worn away. She and Willa swap places periodically to catch a break from the sun under the beach umbrella, but Taylor can feel the heat on the end of her nose and the tops of her feet. The palms of her gloves are blackened with oily dirt and her arms are sore as the boat clears the final lock. Taylor takes over the tiller. "I swear to God, if I have to go through one more lock ..."

"You do know there are locks in the New York canal system, right?" Willa says, handing her a bottle of water. "And in the Chesapeake and Delaware Canal."

Taylor pops the cap and squirts Willa's forehead. "You shut your filthy mouth."

Willa retaliates, hitting Taylor in the cheek. "Then I guess you don't want the good news."

"What's the good news?"

"We conquered the Welland Canal."

Taylor grabs her camera to snap a picture of Willa flexing her biceps, then grins. "We did, didn't we?"

"Hell yeah, we did," Willa says. "Because we are Whiskey . . ." Her smile slips. When they first bought the boat, Finley came up with their own version of a pre-game huddle cheer, in which they'd slap a three-way high five while shouting "Whiskey! Tango! Foxtrot!"

Taylor's throat is too thick with tears to say her part, and there is only silence where Finley would shout "Foxtrot!" But after a beat, Taylor taps her water bottle against Willa's. "Foxtrot would be proud."

"Yeah." Willa nods. "She really would."

43.0962° N, 79.0377° W

Make time for wonder.

Willa

WILLA TURNS A SLOW CIRCLE ON THE WET DECK, her arms outstretched and her face tilted toward the swirling mist. The force of Niagara Falls crashes over the Hurricane Deck railing, splashing hard against her back and crashing over her head. She shrieks and links forearms with Taylor to keep them both steady, and when they look at each other, they crack up laughing. Water streams into the neckline of Willa's thin yellow poncho, soaking her T-shirt and her bikini underneath. Her makeup has washed away, but she doesn't care.

"This is the coolest thing I've ever done!" she shouts over the roar as the falls batter the rocks beside the deck. Another wave smashes into her and she shrieks again.

Taylor rolls her eyes, but she's smiling as she yells back. "You need to get a life."

"Don't pretend like you're not having fun!"

This morning, they boarded a bus in St. Catharines that took them to downtown Niagara Falls, where they rode another bus to the Rainbow Bridge. They crossed on foot, stopping to take pictures of each other with one foot in Canada and the other in the United States, kind of like they'd done on the boat.

The US border guard seems unimpressed that they'd come through the Welland Canal by sailboat. Maybe to him it meant nothing. Maybe to him, Willa and Taylor were just two ordinary tourists. But the guard didn't know they were doing something important, that they are on a quest.

At the lower levels of the Cave of the Winds tour, the Bridal Veil Falls tumbles over moss-covered rocks, and the photos Taylor took were scenic and beautiful. Now she attempts a selfie with her phone in its waterproof case as they stand with the falls, thundering and white, splashing them from behind. Willa bares fierce teeth, but laughs at the last minute, so she doesn't know how her face will turn out.

They return to a lower, less-intense deck to have a look at the results. The image is hazy around the edges from the mist and speckled with water droplets. Their hair is dripping, their ponchos are molded to their bodies, and Willa is actually doing the fierce thing with her teeth. But what stands out most is that behind them, shimmering softly in the spray, is a rainbow.

Taylor's eyes squeeze closed and she draws in a shuddering breath. She is so wet that no one would be able to distinguish tears from water, except Willa. There on the deck, surrounded by the constant rush of the falls and people yelling above it, she slips an arm around Taylor's shoulder. "It's okay."

"I miss her so much," Taylor sobs. "She should be here."

Willa has no faith left in the God who took away her best friend, but she touches her finger to the rainbow on the screen. "She's right here, Taylor. See?"

"It's not the same."

"Yeah." Willa sighs. "I know."

Taylor turns to Willa and wraps her arms around her. She's still crying and Willa gently pats her back. It has been years since they've shown each other any kind of real emotion, any true affection, and she doesn't know how to make Taylor—or herself—feel better. Finley *should* be here. It's not fair that she's gone.

"Do you want to skip the rest of the tours?" Willa says. "We could go back to St. Catharines or maybe take a walk."

"No." Taylor scrubs her eyes with the heels of her hands, sniffling. "We should stay and see all the things Finley would want us to see."

They ride the *Maid of the Mist* boat to get up close to the falls, watch a film about the history of Niagara, eat lunch at the top of Horseshoe Falls, and stand in a tunnel behind the

99

falls, watching the water rush past in a solid wall of white. None of it compares to the Hurricane Deck, but Willa can imagine Finley geeking out over everything. She'd want to keep the ineffectual ponchos and buy something in one of the gift shops.

Taylor has withdrawn since her breakdown on the Cave of the Winds tour, more focused on taking pictures than talking, and Willa gives her wide latitude. When they reach the Journey Behind the Falls gift shop, Taylor excuses herself to the ladies' room. Willa is revolving the rack of key chains, looking for her name, when she notices the snow globe display.

The big glass domes come with fancy white snow and high prices, but Willa finds a plastic novelty shaker that has the Niagara Falls inside, along with a tour boat and a rainbow that stretches from one side to the other. Willa pays for the globe and thrusts the shopping bag at Taylor when she comes out of the bathroom.

"Here. I bought you a present."

The bag rustles as Taylor reaches in and pulls out the snow globe. She laughs and gives it a shake, setting off a snowstorm of silver glitter. "This is so cheesy."

"I know, right?"

"Thanks," Taylor says. "For, um—you know."

Willa nods. "Sure."

They just look at each other for a couple of beats, and

Willa is unable to pinpoint why it's so hard to talk to Taylor, why it's so hard for them to be friends. Finley picked them both. Why can't they pick each other?

"Do you want to stay to see the fireworks?" Taylor asks.

"Um . . . *yeah*. Except the last bus leaves right after the fireworks start."

"We could spend the night." Taylor pulls her phone from her pocket. "I'll pay for it."

Spending the night in a hotel in Niagara Falls can't be cheap, but Taylor seems really determined. "Are you sure?" Willa asks.

Taylor nods. "Definitely."

Taylor books a room at a hotel overlooking the American side of the falls. Willa doesn't ask how much it costs, but the sheets have a just-laundered scent and the air-conditioning hums quietly in the background. The shower stall is bigger than Willa's entire bathroom at home, and she steams up the mirrors as she washes away several days' worth of sink baths. She hasn't felt this clean since they left home. After Taylor takes a shower, they head to the taproom of a local brewery just down the street.

"Can I get you some drinks?" the bartender asks as they claim a couple of barstools. "And our guacamole is amazing."

"Guacamole sounds great," Taylor says.

"Definitely," Willa says. "And I'll have a Niagara Lager."

Taylor nods. "Same."

"I'll just need to see your IDs."

They hand over their fake driver's licenses, and Willa holds her breath. The drinking age on the Canadian side of the falls is nineteen, but Willa wouldn't be surprised if the bartender threw them out on the street. Instead, she hands back the cards without question. "Thanks. I'll get that guacamole order in right away and be back shortly with your beers."

As she walks away, Willa leans over and whispers, "Oh my God! I can't believe that worked. My first beer in a foreign country."

Taylor laughs. "Calm down, Marco Polo, it's only Canada."

Willa watches the bartender fill two pint glasses from the tap near the middle of the bar. She brings them down, along with a pair of menus. "The guac should be up shortly."

Willa takes a sip of her illegally acquired beer. It's yeasty and a little tart, just like every other beer she's ever had.

"Well? Does it taste foreign?" Taylor teases.

Willa laughs. "Shut up."

Taylor takes a drink and crinkles her nose as she swallows. She's never really liked beer all that much. "I was hoping it might taste like maple syrup."

"Way to stereotype Canada."

"I could have said hockey."

"Hockey-flavored beer?" Willa says. "What would that even taste like?"

Taylor shrugs. "I don't know, but it would be served on ice."

Willa laughs. "Did you steal that joke from your dad?"

They plan their next move as they munch on chips and guacamole. Willa wants to go a little more slowly on Lake Ontario, but Taylor is still skeptical about sailing. Willa hates to compromise, but she agrees that they'll get to Oswego as fast as they can, then take a slower pace through the New York canal system. Before they leave the taproom, she buys a growler of beer to take back to the hotel, where they sit on the balcony, drinking from plastic cups and watching the falls. At night, the water is illuminated, and tonight the colors alternate from blue to purple to red.

"This was definitely worth staying for," Taylor says.

Willa only smiles and bites the rim of her cup to keep from saying *I told you so.*

At ten, a rocket whizzes up into the night sky, and the first of the fireworks bursts, huge and sparkly red, before shimmering into smoke. Willa's memories dip back to all the Fourth of Julys she spent at Finley's house.

Every year the people who live along Cedar Point Road throw beach parties and build bonfires. As little girls, Taylor, Finley, and Willa would swim in the lake until dusk. Then, while the adults drank and shot off bottle rockets,

Mrs. Donoghue would light sparklers for the kids. Willa loved writing her name in the air or pretending her sparkler was a magic wand. As they got older, the girls would walk the long stretch of beach, sneaking beers from other people's coolers until the Cedar Point fireworks began. But Willa's favorite part was how you could see the other fireworks displays in the distance—Put-in-Bay, Kelleys Island, Lakeside, Huron, even as far east as Lorain and sometimes Avon Point. From now until forever, Willa could go to the beach for the fireworks, but without Finley it just won't be the same.

Willa glances at Taylor. A tear tracks down Taylor's cheek, lit up by the glow from the city lights, and Willa knows she's caught up in her own memories. Willa opens her mouth to speak but changes her mind. Sometimes you need to be alone with your grief. Sometimes the only way around is through. Willa takes a sip of beer, turns back to the Niagara Falls fireworks, and pushes away everything else.

Taylor

THE SKY IS SO BLUE IT ALMOST HURTS TO LOOK AT, and Lake Ontario is calm as they sail away from Niagara Falls. Willa takes first watch at the tiller, so Taylor goes below to upload their photos from her cameras to their Instagram account. Since she created it, their followers have increased a little every day. Most are family and friends from back home—even Brady is following—but many are strangers, which is kind of exciting.

"There's a comment from your mom on the Coast Guard picture," Taylor calls up to Willa. "She wants you to call home."

"Sure. I'll get right on that."

Willa's mom is younger than Taylor's parents, so they've always seemed more like sisters than mother and daughter. More like friends. Taylor doesn't understand why Willa refuses to call home—and she still hasn't explained why she threw her phone in the lake.

"You can borrow my phone, if you want," Taylor offers again.

"I sent her a postcard from the hotel this morning," Willa says. "And she can see from your pictures that I'm perfectly fine. Better than fine. I'm picking up cute boys in the middle of lakes."

Taylor would laugh if Willa didn't sound like she wanted to bite someone. Taylor can't imagine cutting herself off from her mom that way, but she can't force Willa to call home. Instead, Taylor turns her attention back to the Internet. One of the comments is a question: "What made you decide to do take this trip?"

There isn't enough room to answer the question in the profile, so Taylor creates a free blog. She makes a page for *Whiskey Tango Foxtrot*, uploading the before and after pictures of the boat. On the next page Taylor adds some bio information about herself and Willa—but nothing too personal—along with links to their individual Instagram accounts and e-mail addresses. And, finally, Taylor makes a page for Finley's video. When she's finished tweaking the design and colors, Taylor adds the link to their Instagram. Now she has an answer for the question.

"Hey," Willa calls down. "It's your turn to drive."

"Be right there." Taylor closes her laptop and stows away her photo equipment, except for the cameras. As she steps up into the cockpit, she uses her phone to take a shot of Willa, sitting under the beach umbrella with Pumpkin on her lap. Thirty seconds later, the photo is winging its way through cyberspace.

Taylor sits and takes over the tiller. "Can I ask you something?"

"Um . . ." Willa's expression is guarded. "Okay."

"Why did you throw your phone in the lake?"

Willa sighs. "I really don't want to talk about it."

"Does your mom even know why you're mad at her?"

Willa goes down into the cabin, and Taylor thinks the conversation is over until Willa comes back with a bottle of water and a cookie. She trims in the jib a little bit, then says, "So my mom's been sort of seeing this guy—"

"Uncle Rico, right?"

"Wait. What?"

"That Steve guy," Taylor says. "Finley called him Uncle Rico like in *Napoleon Dynamite*."

"That's what I called him when I was confiding in her. At least I thought I was confiding in her." Willa shakes her head. "I can't believe she told you."

"What's the big deal?"

"I asked her not to tell anyone."

"You could have told me," Taylor says.

"Could I, though?"

Sometimes when she can't sleep, Taylor's mind will play a highlight reel of all the crappy things she's done in her life. Invariably, it snags on the memory of embarrassing Willa in front of the entire junior race team. Taylor will lie in the dark, her cheeks burning with shame, and try to justify the rage she felt that day. Except the rift between them is entirely Taylor's own making. She supposes she could apologize, but words don't seem adequate. Maybe that's why she used her mom's emergency credit card to book an expensive hotel room overlooking Niagara Falls, even if Willa doesn't know it was an apology. Taylor's face is warm as she says, "Maybe not."

She waits for Willa to continue the story of her mom's boyfriend, but after a few minutes of silence, it feels pretty clear that this time the conversation truly is over.

After three days of bouncing along the New York shoreline, they arrive in Oswego, where Campbell's old green pickup truck is a sight for Taylor's sore eyes. He is standing at the dock as Willa steers the boat into the slip and Taylor tosses him a dock line.

"You're both alive," he says. "That's a good sign."

Taylor and Willa filled their time reading and binge-watching bad movies on Netflix. They didn't talk about anything serious—they barely talked at all—but they didn't argue, either. Taylor considers it a small victory. "It's been . . . fun."

Cam's eyebrows hitch up. "Really?"

"Even the sailing part hasn't been too bad. The weather was good."

"Okay, where's my real sister?" Cam steps aboard, and Taylor playfully punches his shoulder, making him laugh. "Hit me again and I'll keep the care package from Mom."

"Did I mention you're my favorite brother?"

"Like I didn't already know that." He winks at Willa. "How's it going, little Willa? I like your outfit."

Taylor and Willa have worn their swimsuits almost non-stop since leaving Niagara Falls. The days have been too hot to wear much more. But Taylor hates the way Campbell looks at Willa like it's Christmas and she's a present he'd like to unwrap. Thankfully, Willa just rolls her eyes at him.

"Are you hungry?" he asks. "I was thinking we could get some food, then maybe hit up a party I heard about."

"You've been in Oswego for what . . . a couple of hours?" Taylor says. "How did you already hear about a party?"

She shouldn't be surprised. Campbell has always been like a bloodhound when it comes to sniffing out parties. He shrugged. "I stopped at Starbucks."

"And?"

"Girls go to Starbucks," he says. "And where there are

girls, there is information. Can I help it if they want to tell me all their intimate secrets?"

Taylor grimaces. "Ew."

"A party sounds good," Willa says, going down into the cabin. "I'm ready to get off this boat for a while."

Willa

WILLA GLANCES UP FROM THE CAPTAIN NORM BOOK as Campbell comes walking up the dock from the showers. He's wearing black jeans—the ones he wears almost constantly—but he's traded a baggy skateboarder T-shirt for a black button-down. His hair is slicked back from his face, and he is so beautiful that Willa has to force herself to look away so she can catch her breath.

"You even shaved," she teases as he steps aboard the boat. "The girls at the party don't stand a chance now."

The corner of his mouth hitches up. "Does that include you?"

"I'm not your type."

He drops onto the cockpit bench beside her. He smells good, like Castile soap and waxy pomade and just . . . *him*. "I think you're exactly my type. Just not sure why you're afraid to admit it."

"I am not afraid."

His breath is warm against her ear as he whispers, "Then say it, Willa. Admit you want me as much as I want you."

"That's not true," she says, though he is right about everything. She aches with wanting him, but Campbell Nicholson is the human equivalent of a bug zapper. Girls are lured in by his beautiful face, then burned when he gets bored with them. Willa doesn't want to be that kind of girl, but whenever he is near—when all she can hear is the rush of blood in her ears—it would be so easy to let him incinerate her.

He laughs as he stands. "Whatever you say."

Taylor returns from the showers wearing a navy-and-white-striped T-shirt dress with her flip-flops. Her toenails and fingernails are all painted turquoise.

"You look super cute," Willa says as three of them walk through the marina parking lot to the main road.

"Same."

Willa's multicolored off-the-shoulder top is one that Finley had bought for herself but never got around to wearing. The tags were still attached when Finley gifted it to Willa. This is the first time she's worn the top, pairing it with a dusty pink corduroy overall skirt she found at Goodwill. "Thanks."

Oswego reminds Willa of Sandusky, the streets lined with the same kinds of houses, the same kinds of trees. Nothing special, but at the same time, a good place to live. They turn onto a smaller side street where cars are parked bumper to bumper all the way down the block.

"This party is definitely going to get busted," Cam says. "If we get separated, meet at the big park we passed on our way."

The party house is a two-story affair with vinyl siding and an enclosed front porch. It looks like a normal house, but the Greek letters over the front door scream *fraternity party*. Campbell doesn't look like a frat boy, but he strides up to the house as though he belongs. He's a chameleon like that, fitting wherever he needs to fit. Willa wishes she had that ability, but she's not white enough to blend in comfortably at a frat party in Upstate New York.

The crowd inside is a mix of college students and high school kids, and no one seems to notice they don't belong. A couple of guys make eye contact with Willa over the tops of their Solo cups, but it's Campbell who gets the lion's share of attention from the girls, who stare as he leads Willa and Taylor to the keg.

As Cam fills their red cups with beer, two girls approach him. They both have long shiny hair—one brunette, one blonde—and pretty smiles, and Willa wants to punch their adorable noses.

"Go. Have a good time." The way he says it feels dismissive, like he's trying to get rid of Willa. Like the whole you-want-me-as-much-as-I-want-you conversation never happened. "Don't do anything I wouldn't do."

Willa and Taylor find a corner of the dining room, where they sip their beers and watch a beer pong match between two guys wearing Greek letters on their T-shirts. The living room couch is filled with guys playing—or watching—a video game. One couple is making out on a chair, while another couple is fighting just inside the front door. It's just like every other party Willa has ever been to, but at home she knew everyone. Including the police officers who'd break up the party if there were noise complaints from the neighbors. Across the room, Campbell is talking to a different girl.

"You know what? I'm playing beer pong." Willa pushes away from the wall, blocking the human bug zapper from of her line of sight.

"Do you even know how?" Taylor asks.

"No, but I didn't sail across two Great Lakes to stand in the corner of the room, waiting for something to happen." Willa walks up to the nearest frat boy. He towers over her by at least a foot, and his shaggy brown hair hangs in his eyes, but she's not looking for a date; she's looking for a beer pong partner. "I want to play."

His eyes widen in surprise and he's slightly flustered as he says, "Sure. Yeah. Hi."

"Hi."

"I'm Josh."

"Willa." She takes the Ping-Pong ball from his hand and

looks across the table at his opponent. "It's doubles now. Find a partner."

"Are you good at this?" Josh asks.

She shrugs. "I've never played before."

He gives her a rundown of the rules, but within a couple of rounds—after she's chugged two cups of cheap beer and her toes have gone tingly—it's clear that Willa is not good at beer pong. She wanders away from the table, oblivious to the groans of frustration as she abandons the game, and when she looks toward the corner, Taylor is gone.

Willa searches out Campbell and finds him leaning against a doorway with his red cup dangling from his fingers. The pomade has failed and he pushes his hair back as a tanned girl wearing frayed cutoffs and dangly gold earrings walks up to him. She leans in to say something over the music and party chatter, something that makes him grin. She cocks her head toward the kitchen, then says something else.

"Please don't go off with her," Willa says quietly to herself.

Cam couldn't possibly have heard, but he shakes his head a little and the girl's smile fades. He watches her walk away, then brings the cup to his mouth. Even though she—and all the girls that came before her—should serve as a warning, seeing him standing alone cracks open something inside Willa. Courage crawls out, filling up her chest. She is done playing it safe.

"Hey," he says as she steps into his space. Closer than

she's ever intentionally been. A smile takes over his face, but before he has a chance to speak, Willa rises onto tiptoes and touches her lips to his. Beer splashes her feet and his arms go around her, one hand cupping the back of her neck as the other pulls her against him. Only then does it register that he dropped his beer to touch her.

Campbell's lips are as soft as she imagined, but kissing him eclipses any kiss she's ever had. His fingers tangle in her curls, and she slips her arms up around his neck. The soft sweep of his tongue makes her dizzy, and the party falls away. At least until someone yells, "Get a room!"

They smile against each other's mouths, and Cam raises his middle finger to the room in general. "Let's get out of here."

Willa nods. "Yes."

"Boat?"

"Yes."

Taking her hand, he leads her through the crowd, out the door, and into the cool, quiet night. Taylor is far from her thoughts as Cam pins her gently against a tree and kisses her again and again. The five-minute walk to the boat stretches out longer and slower as they stop every few feet to kiss. The buzz is better than beer. Better than anything. Willa could so easily get addicted to him. He could so easily ruin her. But she follows him toward the lake, dark and glittering in the moonlight. Through the marina. Into the cabin. Onto her bunk.

Taylor

TAYLOR SLIPS INTO THE BATHROOM TO HIDE FROM A drunken frat boy named Skip. He seemed nice at first, someone to chat with while Willa was playing beer pong. And the cherry Jell-O shots were kind of fun, too. Except after the second shot, Skip's mouth came way too close to Taylor's mouth and his breath smelled like beer. "Come up to my room?"

Taylor was not interested in kissing a random boy, especially one named Skip. She pushed him gently away and pretended she saw Willa across the room. "Hey, I need to talk to my friend for a second. I'll be right back."

Now she sits on the closed toilet lid, wondering how long she'll have to wait before Skip forgets about her and moves on to another girl. He was pretty drunk, so maybe not too long. Taylor hasn't seen Campbell since they arrived, and she lost track of Willa when she followed Skip to the kitchen for Jell-O shots.

Someone knocks, and Taylor hopes it's not him. "You've been in there awhile," a muted female voice says through the door. "Are you okay?"

"Yeah, um—just a minute."

Taylor washes her hands even though she didn't use the toilet and wipes them on her dress instead of the grubby towels. Just outside the door is a girl, waiting for her turn. Her shiny black hair is swept into a messy topknot, and she's wearing a Sister Kismet T-shirt, which surprises Taylor. Sister Kismet is one of her favorite bands, but not too many people have heard of them.

"Sorry," Taylor says. "I was kind of hiding from someone."

"Skip?"

"How'd you know?"

The girl and Taylor trade places, but the girl lingers against the doorframe for a fraction. Her eyebrows disappear beneath her bangs and her teeth are bright white against the red of her lips as she smiles. "I noticed."

The door closes and Taylor leans against the wall, her cheeks flaming and her pulse racing, neither of which has happened to her in a very long time. She should go find Willa or Cam, but part of her wants to stay here until the girl comes out of the bathroom.

"Taylor!" Skip shoulders his way through a group of girls to where Taylor is standing. "There you are!"

Beside her, the door cracks open. The girl's hand reaches out, pulls Taylor into the bathroom, and slams the door in Skip's face.

"Thanks for the rescue," Taylor says.

"My pleasure. I'm Vanessa, by the way."

Vanessa's hazel eyes are ringed with dark, thick lashes, and her nose turns up a little at the tip. On her chin, near the bottom corner of her mouth, there are a couple of pale pimples covered with concealer, but they disappear when she smiles. The whole effect leaves Taylor feeling a tiny bit . . . breathless. "I'm Taylor."

They stand for a few awkward seconds, just looking at each other. Or maybe it's just awkward for Taylor, who is unsure how to handle being attracted to a girl who isn't Finley. It feels as if Taylor has a kick drum in her chest. She's about to suggest they go somewhere other than the bathroom when someone outside the door shouts, "Cops! It's the cops! Run!"

"Shit! Shit! Shit!" Vanessa exclaims. "I can't get busted for underage drinking. My parents will kill me." She pushes up the window, pops out the screen, and swings a leg over the windowsill. "Coming?"

Taylor follows Vanessa out the window and makes the short drop to the ground below. Vanessa scales the low chain-link fence at the back of the yard, and Taylor does the same.

"Over here," Vanessa says, beckoning her behind a hedge in the neighbor's yard. Taylor crouches beside her and they watch from between the leaves as people scatter in every direction. Taylor doesn't see Willa or Campbell anywhere, only the flashing blue and red lights of the police car and people scrambling to not be arrested.

"Do you live in Oswego?" Vanessa whispers.

"No. I'm from Ohio," Taylor whispers back. "I'm heading to Key West by sailboat. We start down the canal toward Albany tomorrow."

"Really? That's . . . incredibly cool."

There's something liberating about meeting someone who doesn't know the whole story, but at the same time it feels like a betrayal to leave Finley out. "There was supposed to be three of us," Taylor explains. "But our best friend died, so now it's just me and Willa."

"I'm sorry about your friend."

Vanessa's fingers brush the back of her hand, and Taylor feels too many things at once. She wishes she hadn't mentioned Finley, then feels immediately guilty. Vanessa is too close, but Taylor doesn't want her to go away, either. "I, um—I need to get to the park," she says. "We arranged to meet there if the party got busted."

"I'll walk with you, if you want."

"Yeah." Taylor nods. "Thanks."

They creep out from behind the hedge and skirt the neighbor's house in the shadows, emerging on the other side of the block, where there are no police cars. They walk in silence until they're across the next intersection.

"Have you seen Sister Kismet?" Taylor asks.

"Four times." Vanessa ticks off on her fingers. "Twice at Warped, once when they opened for The Joneses, and once at this all-ages show in the city. What about you?"

Taylor and Finley bought tickets to see Sister Kismet at the Agora Ballroom in Cleveland, but when Finley got sick again, it was clear she wouldn't be able to go. She died a few weeks before the concert and Taylor forgot all about it, until she found the unused tickets in her desk drawer. But to Vanessa, she just says, "Not yet."

"They're amazing live," Vanessa says. "Hayden's voice . . . that raspiness . . . well, I don't have to tell you, right? Sister Kismet is that one band that I want everyone to know about, but at the same time I don't want them to get so big that everyone knows about them."

Taylor smiles. "Same."

They talk about music the whole way to the park, comparing favorite bands, favorite concerts, favorite songs. Taylor is usually the playlist maker, the one who knows first about a band. But a Venn diagram of Vanessa's tastes and hers would overlap almost completely.

When they arrive at the park, it's deserted. No Willa. No Campbell.

"What if they got arrested?" she says as she texts her brother.

I'm at the park. Where are you?

"We probably shouldn't panic yet." Vanessa hoists herself onto the railing of the entrance to the playground. "Maybe we got here first."

"True."

Vanessa takes a pair of headphones from the pocket of her skirt and untangles them. She plugs the jack into her phone and offers one of the earbuds to Taylor. "Have you heard the new Shiri Gray album? It just came out this week."

Taylor leans against the railing, and Vanessa leans down to share the headphones. Her dark hair is soft against Taylor's temple. After the first three tracks, neither Willa nor Campbell has shown up yet.

"I'm starting to get a little worried," Taylor says.

She double-checks her phone, but Cam hasn't responded. She texts him again.

Are you okay? I'm still at the park.

Taylor watches for the reply bubbles, but they don't come. She and Vanessa listen to another song, but Taylor zones out, worrying that her brother and Willa are in jail. She has no idea how to get them out, or even if she has enough money for bail. "Maybe we should go back to the party."

"Sure," Vanessa says. "Whatever you want."

They take a more direct route back to the fraternity, but the crowd has thinned to just the guys who live in the house and a handful of guests. Taylor is relieved to see that Skip is not around, but she doesn't see Willa or Campbell, either. She shows a picture of Willa to the guy who looks the most sober. "Have you seen her?"

He shakes his head. "I wish. She's hot."

Taylor rolls her eyes and swipes through her photos until she finds a picture of Cam. "What about him?"

"Nope."

"Could they have been arrested?"

The guy laughs. "Everyone bolted. There was no one left to arrest."

"Maybe we crossed paths and they're at the park now," Vanessa suggests. "Do you want to go check it out?"

Taylor is not surprised that her brother is missing in action. He probably found a girl—or another party—but she doesn't know whether to be angry or concerned that Willa didn't show up at the park. Maybe both. Either way, Taylor decides that Willa is on her own. "I'm going back to the boat."

"I'm spending the weekend with my cousin, who lives near the marina," Vanessa says. "I'll come with you."

This time she turns up the volume on her phone so they can listen without headphones. The sound quality isn't quite as good, but Taylor likes listening to her favorite singer with someone who doesn't need an introduction. The time passes fast—too fast—and they reach the driveway to the marina.

"Taylor, can I ask you something?" Vanessa says.

"Sure."

"Do you, um—are you into girls? Because this whole night I've been getting this vibe, but I'm not sure if it's my imagination or wishful thinking or whatever."

Taylor pulls in a deep breath. She's never shared this secret with anyone except the neighbor's pigs, who live in a pen just over the property line between the two farms. The pigs don't judge and they never, ever tell. So telling a stranger is a leap of faith. "I, um—I'm pretty sure the answer is yes, but I've only ever loved one girl and she was my best friend."

"Oh . . . wow . . . okay," Vanessa says.

"I never told her because I knew she'd never love me back. At least not in the same way I loved her." Taylor's vision blurs and tears track down her cheeks. "And then she died."

"That must have been so painful." Vanessa offers her a tissue. "If I had known . . . God, my timing is terrible."

"I'm sorry."

"Don't be," Vanessa says. "But listen." She takes Taylor's phone and adds herself as a contact. "If you want to dial my number someday—when you're in a better place—I'll definitely answer." She lifts onto her tiptoes to kiss Taylor's cheek. "I had fun tonight."

"All I did was drag you around town looking for my stupid brother."

"If that bothered me . . . ," Vanessa says as she shuffles slowly backward toward the street, "I wouldn't have stayed."

Taylor watches as Vanessa walks away, tucking in her earbuds. A few yards down the street, she glances back and smiles—and it makes Taylor feel untethered. Like she might just float away.

Her thoughts are a jumble as she crosses the marina parking lot toward the dock. Taylor has never been interested in a girl—aside from Finley—but has had crushes on boys before Brady. She's suspected she is bisexual, but now it feels confirmed. *Am I okay with that? Is it okay that I'm attracted to someone so soon after Finley's death? Does that make me a jerk? What would Finley think? Would she be happy for me?*

Taylor reaches the boat, and Pumpkin is curled up on a cockpit bench. The companionway hatch is open and the twinkle lights are glowing. Taylor steps down into the cabin, where she finds Willa and Campbell tangled around each other on Taylor's bunk, sound asleep.

"What the hell . . . ?"

Their eyes fly open, and Campbell bolts upright, while

Willa scrambles to pull his shirt on over her lacy pink bralette. God, did they have sex in her *bed*?

"Shit." Campbell rakes his hand through his hair. "We forgot about you."

"I waited in the park because that was where we were supposed to meet." Taylor's hands clench into fists as she rages at them. "Did you even know the party got busted? Or did you deliberately abandon me at a frat house in a strange town?"

"We didn't mean—" Campbell begins, but Willa cuts him off.

"I'm sorry, Taylor. There's no excuse for leaving you behind."

"If you're waiting for me to say it's okay, you'll be waiting a long fucking time." Taylor turns and climbs out of the cabin. "You suck. Both of you."

She stalks to the head of the pier, trying to calm down, but she's buried beneath an avalanche of anger, unable to dig her way out. She wants to scream. She wants to hit something. Someone. Willa. Her brother. But at the same time she wishes one of them would come check on her. Taylor sinks down onto a park bench and sobs until her nose is congested and her eyelashes hurt. She hates that she doesn't know what she needs. She hates that life without Finley is so confusing.

When she finally returns to the boat, Campbell is crashed out in the v-berth while Willa is back sleeping in her own bunk.

She's wearing Cam's shirt and Taylor doesn't even have the energy to get angry again. She's just . . . exhausted . . . because she already knows how this ends. Willa and Campbell, as a word problem, would go something like: If a girl sailing from Sandusky to Key West at five knots per hour crashes into a guy who's redlining all the way to nowhere, into how many pieces will the girl's heart break?

Except Willa has made her bed—literally and figuratively—so Taylor decides she can find out the answer for herself.

43.4553° N, 76.5105° W
Time travel whenever possible.

Willa

WILLA WAKES UP WISHING SHE COULD TRAVEL BACK in time to relive last night. Campbell is still asleep just a couple of feet away, and her body feels . . . effervescent. They didn't have sex—Willa has lines she's not ready to cross just yet—but her memory still feels the warmth of his hands on her skin and the taste of his mouth. For a few moments she's content to watch him sleep, but then she glances across the cabin at Taylor, who is awake and scowling, and Willa wishes she could rewind to the point where they hadn't left Taylor behind at the party.

"I'm really sorry about last night," Willa whispers.

Taylor doesn't respond. She kicks away her comforter, gathers her shower gear, and walks off the boat without saying a word.

"I think she's still pretty pissed." Cam's voice is husky from sleep. He taps Willa's arm, and when she looks up, he beckons her to join him in the v-berth. "She'll get over it."

"You should go talk to her," Willa says.

"I can't go anywhere right now," he says. "I have a raging case of morning wood."

She laughs and throws her pillow at him. "Fine. I'll go."

"No," he groans. "Stay here with me."

Willa is so tempted to climb into the v-berth with him and make up for lost time. Except her relationship with Taylor is so fragile. So breakable. Instead, Willa walks up to the shower house and into the ladies' room. Only one shower is running and Taylor's striped towel hangs on the hook outside the curtain.

"Taylor? It's me."

Steam wisps out over the top of the shower curtain, but Taylor doesn't respond.

"I know there's no excuse for leaving you at the party," Willa continues. "I don't know what to say other than I'm sorry."

"You made a promise that my brother was off-limits."

"Seriously?" Willa is taken aback that of all the things Taylor could be upset about, *this* is the one. "You're holding me to a middle school pinkie swear? Do you know how ridiculous that sounds?"

"Yeah, ridiculous Taylor, not wanting people to use her to get to Cam."

"I never used you for anything," Willa says. "This has literally nothing to do with you."

For a prolonged moment, the rush of water echoing around the room is the only sound. Then Taylor says, "What about Finley?"

Even though Finley's feelings for Cam were delivered as punch lines, it doesn't make them any less valid. If she were here, she would be crushed. Willa's shoulders sag, and she leans her head back against the cool tile wall. Just *once* she'd like to be able to think about Campbell without having to factor Finley into the equation. She pushes off the wall and heads toward the door. "Maybe you should ask yourself why a dead girl's feelings are more important than mine."

Cam is dressed and sitting in the cockpit when Willa gets back to the boat.

"How'd it go?" he asks, shading his eyes with his hand to look at her.

"As well as you'd expect."

He laughs. "That good, huh?"

"In middle school she accused me of stealing Finley's friendship away from her," Willa says. "Now she thinks I stole you from Finley."

"I was never into Fin like that." Cam hauls Willa down beside him. He wraps an arm around her head and pulls her over to kiss her temple. She tickles his side, and he retaliates by kissing her neck, making her squirm. "You, on the other hand . . ."

A bubble of guilt threatens to break the surface of her happiness, but she presses her lips against Campbell's mouth and forgets all about Finley—just once.

Breakfast is an awkward combination of eggs, bacon, and silence, and afterward Cam retrieves a pair of wooden X-shaped supports from the back of his truck. The bridges spanning the Oswego River are too low for sailboats to pass under, so the marina crew removes the mast and cradles it on the supports, one on the bow of the boat, the other on the deck just behind the companionway.

"So what happens now?" Campbell asks.

The boat is ready to go, and their plan has always been that Cam would travel with them as far as Catskill, where the mast will go back up and he will get a ride to Oswego for his truck. But it's impossible to gauge what Taylor is thinking when she's been giving them the silent treatment all morning.

"Do whatever you want," Taylor says.

"Don't be like that." Willa gestures back and forth between the two of them. "This is *our* trip."

"So should I just pretend like last night never happened? Like it's totally cool that you abandoned me to hook up with my brother?"

Willa shrugs. "I've been pretending for years that you never called me trailer trash. Trust me, it gets easier with practice."

Cam's eyes go wide as Taylor's mouth drops open. She snaps it shut and looks down at her feet, her cheeks flushed pink with embarrassment, and mumbles, "Let's just go."

Campbell takes the helm as they motor south from Oswego. Willa is at loose ends without having to drive the boat, but she welcomes the break. After going through the first two canal locks—which are much smaller and easier than the ones on the Welland Canal—she sits beside him and pretends she's not on fire as he teases his finger along the hem of her cutoffs, tickling her thigh. Taylor moves as far away from them as possible, dangling her legs over the side of the bow while she reads *Outlander*. Willa pages through the Captain Norm book, trying to find the answer to Finley's time-travel clue. Upstate New York is brimming with history. Abandoned sanitariums. Crumbling mansions. Revolutionary War graveyards. But somehow she's sure that none of these things are what Finley had in mind.

Willa ducks under the mast and goes into the cabin, where she uses Taylor's laptop to pull up a satellite map of the area. Scrolling along the river, she notices a triangular-shaped clearing beside the main road. As she zooms closer, gravel lanes begin to appear. Then a building. Then a screen. She lets out a whoop of delight and scrambles back into the cockpit. "I found it! Taylor, I found it! There's a drive-in movie theater in Minetto!"

One night, back before they were old enough to drive, Taylor's dad was taking them to the Nicholsons' house for a sleepover when they passed the Sandusky Drive-In, which had been closed for all of their lives. The screen tower was falling apart, and chains were strung across the entrance to keep trespassers out, but it hadn't been torn down yet to make way for a sports complex.

Finley sighed. "I wish the drive-in was still open."

"Oh man. Did we ever have good times at that old place," Mr. Nicholson said. "When my friends and I were in high school, I'd park backward so we could sit in the bed of my pickup to watch the movie. We'd open up the cab's back window and crank the radio. One time I turned my truck box into a cooler and . . . I probably shouldn't tell you that story. After it closed down, Julie and I took the kids to the Star View Drive-In over in Norwalk once, but Campbell wandered off and we found him asleep in the back seat of someone else's car."

The girls laughed, but his story must have planted a seed in Finley's brain, because one of the first things they did after she got her driver's license was gather a bunch of people and caravan to the Star View. They parked their cars all in a row and sat in lawn chairs, and Finley opened the back hatch of her Fiat so they could listen to the movie with the volume maxed out.

"So we're going, right?" Cam looks from Willa to Taylor, who quickly turns back to her book as though she hadn't been paying attention. "We're literally minutes away from Minetto."

Willa nods. "I'm in. Taylor?"

"We don't have a car."

"No, but we have bikes," Cam points out.

"Two bikes."

"Willa can ride on my handlebars." He grins, and Willa can't stop herself from grinning back. In her head, she's been on approximately half a million dates with Campbell Nicholson, but none of them ever included sitting on the handlebars of a bike.

The fantasy is ruined when Taylor's lip curls. "Count me out."

"You *know* this is what Finley meant by time travel," Willa says. "You have to come. Please?"

Taylor is huddled miserably in the cockpit with her paperback and her cat as Willa and Campbell pedal away from the boat. While Willa was changing from shorts and a tank top into her favorite red floral sundress, she considered not going.

Even now, as she rides along the main road behind Cam with the breeze tickling the hairs on her neck, she feels a twinge of guilt for leaving Taylor behind. But going to the drive-in is what Finley intended for them, and Taylor had every chance to say yes. And Willa is not going to sacrifice the opportunity to be alone with the boy she likes. Not for Taylor.

It's hard to talk as they ride, but it takes only about ten minutes to reach the drive-in. Cam pays for their tickets, and they walk the bikes to an open spot in the front row. She spreads a blanket on the grass while he tunes the weather radio to the correct frequency.

"Taylor should be here," Willa says, sitting down on the blanket.

Cam drops down beside her and nuzzles the spot just below her ear. "I'm pretty good without her."

Willa's cheeks dimple as she smiles at him. His fingertips touch the back of her neck as he leans in to kiss her and she slips her fingers into his soft hair.

"Excuse me."

They stop kissing at the sound of a woman's voice. She's sitting in the car beside their spot with the window rolled down. In the back seat, two small faces are flattened against the window, watching them.

"You're not planning to have s-e-x, are you?" the woman asks. "Because I have kids in the car."

Willa and Cam look at each other and start laughing. He shakes his head. "No, but you might be concerned later. This movie gets pretty violent."

"Oh, I'm not worried about that," she says as her window slides upward. "They're just not ready for the *s-e-x*."

Cam falls back on the blanket, cracking up. Willa lies back beside him, giggling, and for a long time they don't do anything but laugh. Then he scrambles to his feet. "I'll go get us some popcorn. Butter?"

"Absolutely."

He kisses her quick. "Be right back."

Willa watches the light fade to twilight, and when the first star appears, she wishes for Campbell to be hers. He returns with one large tub of popcorn and a large drink with two straws, and her heart thumps like she's got an entire marching band in her chest. He sits down on the blanket. "Come here."

Willa settles between his thighs, leaning back against his chest, as the movie previews begin. He kisses her shoulder and she feeds him a piece of popcorn. "Keep rewarding me with popcorn every time I kiss you and I'll have to kiss you everywhere."

"Not *here*."

"Of course not here." He laughs softly. "Around these parts they're just not ready for the *s-e-x*."

Willa isn't sure she is ready for the *s-e-x* either. If the rumors about Cam are true, he's in a whole other world of experience. What if he has porn star expectations? What if she's bad in bed? She's not even sure how to be *good* in bed. But Cam doesn't mention sex again. He kisses the top of her head, the back of her neck, the palm of her hand—seemingly benign places that only make her want him more.

Campbell falls asleep during the second feature, sprawling out on his side. Willa lies facing him. She brushes his hair back from his face, and her breath catches in her chest as the lights of the movie play across his skin. Now she understands what it means to say you could stare at someone for hours. She could. She does.

He wakes when the car beside them revs up. He offers Willa a sleepy-eyed smile. "How long was I out?"

"Almost the whole movie."

"Sorry."

"It's okay."

He leans forward and kisses her. "When Taylor asked me to stay away from her friends, I should have said no."

"Well, I pinkie promised that I'd stay away from you."

Cam laughs. "That's serious business."

"In middle school? Hell yes it is."

As the cars line the lanes, all waiting their turn to leave the drive-in, he gathers Willa in his arms and they kiss until they're the only ones left. On the road back to Minetto, they pass a thicket of trees. Cam stops and swings off his bike, dropping it into the grass on the side of the road. Willa isn't sure what's happening, but she does the same and follows him past a NO TRESPASSING sign into the trees, where he catches her up and pulls her to him.

"I'm not ready to go back yet," he says against her mouth. "Let's spread the blanket out here and . . ."

She knows what his silence implies and a couple of hours hasn't suddenly made her brain ready, but her body knows what it wants. Cam turns on his phone flashlight so they're not fumbling around in total darkness as they spread the blanket.

Everything he does is gentle. The way he slides down the straps on her dress. The slow caress of his hand against her skin. The sweep of his tongue in her mouth. Except there's a twig poking her back under the blanket and they're making out on someone's private property. She hasn't been holding out for true love or even the perfect, romantic setting, but Willa feels more exposed than sexy. She wishes she could rewind a few hours and be Campbell's girlfriend for more than a minute before they have sex.

"Hey, um . . . can we take a break for a second?" Willa says. "Maybe we could just . . . talk a little."

Cam falls onto his back with a frustrated sigh and rubs a hand over his face. "Sure. I guess. What do you want to talk about?"

"I don't know. Things are moving kind of fast, don't you think?"

"With my sister around, we've gotta grab the time when we've got it," he says, leaning over to kiss her bare shoulder. Willa feels that pull inside her, magnetic and strong.

"I know, but—"

The sound of something rustling in the underbrush stops her short. An animal? A person? The rustling grows louder and closer—and a dog appears out of nowhere. Willa shrieks. The dog barks. And Campbell cracks up laughing.

"Otis!" a man's voice shouts from a distance as the dog barks and barks and barks. "Who's there? I'll call the police."

"We need to get out of here," Willa whispers, scrambling to her feet. Cam snatches up the blanket and they bolt out of the woods with the dog behind them. Their bike wheels kick up gravel as they pedal away, Otis giving half-hearted chase as far as the next driveway.

"Oh my God!" Willa laughs. "That was wild!"

"The best nights usually are."

They ride side by side back toward Minetto, and Willa works up the nerve to ask him why he dropped out of Cornell.

"It was boring, so I left."

Since graduation, Willa has been worried that college will be as exhausting as high school, but she never once considered it might be boring. This new fear crowds into her chest along with the cell phone at the bottom of Lake Erie and the broken taillight on the car, and she almost can't breathe. "Seriously?"

"I was surrounded by a bunch of overachievers knocking themselves out for . . . what?" Cam says. "A piece of paper and a mountain of debt? It's not worth it."

"So, do you have an alternate plan?"

He shrugs. "Just keep do what I'm doing."

Willa thought being a business major was the answer—she had a plan—but now doubt itches beneath her skin like an insect bite. She goes silent, wondering if she's made a mistake.

Cam laughs quietly. "You're thinking way too hard about this."

"But—"

"Relax, little Willa. College is made for people like you."

She's not sure what he means by that, but it doesn't sound like a compliment so she doesn't ask. Instead she pedals fast, then faster, making him race to catch up.

Taylor is asleep when they return to the boat. As they stand in the cockpit, Campbell picks a stray leaf out of Willa's hair, then takes a Sharpie from the back pocket of his jeans. In the dim light, she watches as he writes *not ready for the* s-e-x on her arm. She laughs softly, and he kisses her good night as though they're standing outside her apartment door. "Thanks for a fun time."

She smiles. "See you in the morning."

Taylor

TAYLOR WAKES TO FIND HER BROTHER AND ALL OF his belongings missing. It doesn't make sense that Campbell would leave. He was supposed to stay with them all the way to Catskill.

"What did you do?" she demands, shocking Willa out of sleep. She blinks as if Taylor is speaking gibberish.

"What are you talking about?" Willa asks.

"Cam is gone."

"Maybe he went for coffee or something."

"He took everything. Backpack. Wallet. Keys. Why would he just leave?"

Willa is still for a moment and her blinking picks up speed, as though she's trying to keep from crying. But Willa never cries.

"I don't know," she says. "I really don't know."

Taylor doesn't believe her. Especially since she slept in her dress and has bits of leaves stuck in her curls. Taylor notices a streak of black marker on the inside of Willa's forearm. "What's that?"

"Just a joke from last night. This woman thought . . ." Willa trails off. "Never mind. It's nothing important."

But as she scratches the back of her head, Taylor reads the words "not ready for the *s-e-x*." It seems more important than Willa lets on and Taylor guesses it's the reason why Cam left. Maybe he came, saw, and conquered. Or maybe—judging by the Sharpie tattoo on Willa's arm—he didn't.

Taylor texts Campbell. Where are you?

I forgot about some shit I had to do.

What shit?

The marina at Catskill will know what to do with the mast.

Is this about Willa?

The reply bubbles flash repeatedly, as though Campbell is typing and deleting his response. When it finally appears, it's only one word. **No.**

"I don't think he's coming back."

Taylor tries to read Willa's mood as she pushes back her comforter, but she's all business. No sign of tears. No hints at what might have transpired between her and Campbell. She's all locked up, as usual.

"We should go," Willa says, folding up her bedding. "Since

we traveled fast through the lakes, we don't have to rush the canal. We could stop at Fulton and Phoenix and maybe go to that little amusement park at Sylvan Beach."

Except last night—after Cam and Willa left for the drive-in—Taylor worked up the courage to call Vanessa. "It's um—it's Taylor. You put your number in my phone, but then I realized you didn't have mine."

"Hey! So glad to hear from you, Taylor," Vanessa said. "And I hope you don't think this is creepy, but I tracked down your Instagram so I could see pictures and follow your progress."

"It's only a little creepy." Vanessa's big laugh made Taylor smile. "So then you know we've only made it as far as Minetto."

"Yeah."

"We stopped for one of Finley's clues," she said. "But now my brother and Willa are on a date."

"Wait. What? Is that why they ditched you at the party?"

"Basically."

"So cold," Vanessa said. "I hope they crash and burn."

Last night Taylor laughed because she was still mad, but she knows what a broken heart feels like. She wouldn't wish that on anyone—not even Willa.

"Hey, did you see that Sister Kismet is playing in the city on the eighteenth at the Donut Hole?" Vanessa asked.

"Are you going?" Taylor asked in reply.

"Wouldn't miss it."

"Do, um—do you want to meet at the show?"

"Are you sure?"

"Honestly? I'm not sure of anything right now," Taylor said. "But maybe?"

Vanessa laughed. "Then *maybe* I'll see you there."

Taylor had been looking forward to a more leisurely pace of the canal system. The Captain Norm book described quaint little towns with restaurants and shops, and Taylor liked the idea of town-hopping, going for bike rides around the countryside, and taking nature photos. But now she doesn't want to linger *too* long in any one place. She wants to figure out Finley's next clue—'don't lose your head'—but she also wants to reach New York City in time to see her favorite band.

And Vanessa. Maybe.

They cast off from Minetto and spend a long day motoring the river. They pass through three locks, but now they're seasoned sailors when it comes to lock navigation. They don't need to discuss what to do anymore; they just do it.

Which is for the best since they're not really talking.

Each time they leave a lock in their wake, Taylor feels a little thrill of victory, and the last time she called home, her dad said he was proud of her—and that Granddad joined Instagram just to see her pictures.

They pass small towns and farmlands. Ducks paddle on the river with lines of downy babies behind them. Flocks of swallows wheel in the sky, swooping low over the boat. *Whiskey Tango Foxtrot* skims under fixed bridges so low it seems certain they'll bump their heads, and Taylor radios ahead for the lift bridges to open. Every now and then they're overtaken by a faster boat or they'll pass another heading in the opposite direction and they wave. Captain Norm said they might find themselves traveling with other boats heading in the same direction, but so far that hasn't happened.

"This would be a beautiful trip in the fall when the leaves are changing color," Taylor says, zooming in to snap a photo of a great blue heron standing on a half-submerged log, watching for fish.

Willa nods. "The cooler weather would be kind of nice too."

As hard as they've tried to keep the boat neat, neither of them have really made their beds since Cleveland. Dirty clothes are starting to spill out of the laundry basket. And the toilet smells bad. Taylor can't imagine having more gear on this small boat. Her heart feels tight when she thinks about how there's no room for Finley. "That means more clothes to pack, though."

Willa grimaces. "True."

They've passed each other water bottles and sunscreen and handed off information as they changed shifts at the helm, but this is their first casual conversation of the day. Really, their first since the fight. As always, they both seem to be pretending like nothing happened. Like everything is fine. Taylor knows friendships don't normally work this way, but she and Willa have never been normal friends.

On Willa's watch, Taylor goes below to update the website. She uploads a shot of Willa laughing as she plays beer pong. A group of frat boys doing Jell-O shots. Vanessa sitting on the railing at the park, singing along to Shiri Gray. It strikes Taylor that from the outside it appears they're having an amazing adventure. No one can tell they're struggling to keep the peace. No one sees the tears.

The engine goes silent, and Willa calls softly, "Taylor, bring your camera."

She climbs out on deck, and Willa points to the near shore, where a young deer stands motionless, except for the twitch of its tail as it watches at the boat. Taylor snaps several shots, including a profile portrait of Willa looking back at the deer. The tension in her face has relaxed and her smile is soft. They slowly, silently drift until something spooks the animal and it bounds off into the woods.

"That was cool," Taylor says. "Thanks."

Willa smiles as she starts the engine. "You're welcome."

The Oswego intersects the Erie Canal at Three River Junction, and they push their way across Oneida Lake, slipping into a dock at Sylvan Beach just before sunset. There is a rickety-looking amusement park at the edge of the lake, but they're sweaty and too tired to do more than sip bowls of soup before crashing out in their bunks. Taylor stretches out and looks across the narrow space at Willa, who is facing the wall. Closed off. No longer the girl who'd had such a great time in Niagara Falls. Taylor wonders if this trip will ever be that fun again.

41.0857° N, 73.8585° W

Don't lose your head.

Willa

WHAT DID I DO WRONG?

The question spins around in Willa's brain whenever she replays her time with Cam. He was sweet and romantic, and he kissed her like he meant it, but she wonders if "Thanks for a fun night" was Campbell Nicholson–speak for "See you later, loser." She worries she was too slutty. Or maybe not slutty enough. Maybe she was such dull company that stealing away in the night was the equivalent of gnawing off his own leg to escape a trap. Willa wants to believe Cam will come back. Even though there's no history to reinforce the claim, she refuses to be just another bug in his zapper.

Willa wishes she could analyze this with someone, but Taylor has zero objectivity when it comes to her brother and Willa would never have been able to talk to Finley about Cam. Willa's mom has had a series of dead-end relationships, so she's more cautionary tale than role model. The only person left is Campbell himself and he's in the wind.

"Can I borrow your laptop?" she asks Taylor, who shrugs rather than actually answering. "Thanks."

Willa logs into her e-mail account and finds an in-box full of messages from her mom. At least one a day, which is pretty impressive for someone who hates using the computer. E-mail is the deepest Willa's mom has ever delved into the Internet. She'll ask Willa to look things up for her and she refuses to use social media, calling it a "time suck" even though she wastes hours of her life watching decorating shows and cooking competitions on television. Willa has to admire her tenacity with these e-mails, though. There are only so many ways you can ask your daughter what the hell is wrong with her.

> To: Mom <colleen.ryan@email.com>
> From: Willa <willarryan@email.com>
> Subject: Re: I'm worried about you.
> I called from Cleveland, the night you blew off work
> to hang out with Steve. Maybe I'm not the one you
> should be worried about.

Willa hits send before she loses her nerve. She's not the kind of girl who acts out. She'd rather choke on her own tongue than sass her mother. But right now everything sucks.

Finley is dead, Taylor is mad, and Campbell is gone. Somehow they have to recapture the magic they had in Niagara Falls, otherwise this trip will be a complete bust. Willa closes the laptop and goes out into the cockpit.

"I'm really sorry I abandoned you at the party," she says. "It was a selfish, shitty thing to do and it won't happen again."

"Apology accepted," Taylor says, but she doesn't quite commit herself to a smile.

"I figured out the next clue. It's Sleepy Hollow."

"Cool."

"Actually, peak cool would be at Halloween, when they have midnight graveyard tours and haunted hayrides," Willa says. "But in June? I mean, there are a lot of historical sites we could visit, but nothing to lose your head over."

Taylor's brow furrows as the joke sails right past her. "Are you saying we should skip it?"

"Are you having fun?"

"I mean, this is better than working the farm stand all summer and we're *traveling*, but . . . I guess I thought it would be more exciting."

"Me too," Willa agrees. "Which is why I think we should skip Sleepy Hollow and focus on the next clue, which is obviously New York City. I mean, 'Take a bite out of life'? Finley really isn't bringing it with these clues."

Taylor snorts a laugh. "Okay."

"Really?" Willa had steeled herself for resistance, but this conversation has been unexpectedly smooth. "Okay, then."

Following a tip from Captain Norm, their next stop is Little Falls, where the free marina has a clubhouse equipped with showers and laundry. They spend the evening cleaning all the crumbly and sticky bits from the cabin and washing a mountain of dirty clothes. It's not the excitement they've been craving, but it's necessary and a clean boat feels like a fresh start.

"I've never been so happy to shave my legs." Willa sighs as she twists her damp hair into little buns on each side of her head.

Taylor laughs. "I was starting to worry someone would mistake me for Bigfoot."

Willa rummages through the storage box for something to eat, but her stomach revolts at the thought of rice, ramen, or soup. She sighs. "I would give my future firstborn child for a taco right now."

One of their favorite rituals when Finley was still alive was Taco Tuesday. Once in a while they'd meet up in a restaurant in town where the tacos were fifty cents on Tuesday nights, but mostly they did it themselves using kits from the grocery store. Either way, the three of them would get together, play Cards Against Humanity, and stuff themselves to bursting. Sometimes it feels to Willa that the only thing she and Taylor have in common—aside from Finley—is Taco Tuesday. Which might be a shaky foundation on which to rebuild a friendship. After all, everyone loves tacos.

Taylor groans. "Oh God. Yes. Let's go find some."

Most of the restaurants are buttoned up for the night as they walk down the main street of Little Falls, but they find an open grocery store and gather everything they need to make their own tacos. Willa grabs a bunch of cilantro in the produce department, and when Taylor laughs softly, Willa understands.

On their very first Taco Tuesday, Willa sprinkled a liberal amount of cilantro on her tacos. Finley, having never tried cilantro, did the same. But when she took her first bite, her mouth contorted and she spat the mouthful onto her plate. "Oh my God," she gasped, before taking a big swallow of Coke. "Why would you eat something that tastes like soap?"

"Most people taste deliciousness, not soap," Willa explained. "You're just a genetic misfit."

"I used to think leukemia was the worst thing that ever happened to me, but now . . ." She shuddered, and the three of them cracked up laughing.

Now Finley feels close and distant at the same time, and Willa wonders how that can be. She doesn't know how to be Taylor's friend without Finley. Or even if she wants to be. But here they are, buying taco fixings at Price Chopper.

They head back to the boat, where Taylor cues up Shiri Gray on her phone. Willa browns the meat as Taylor chops the veggies, and soon the scent of taco seasoning hangs in the air. Making small talk feels like scaling a cliff face without climbing gear, but they maintain an amiable silence as they work together to prepare a meal.

"How many days do you think it will take to get to New York City?" Taylor asks as she sits in the cockpit, balancing a plate on her knees.

Willa hangs an inflatable solar light from the boom. "A week, maybe six days."

"Sister Kismet is doing a show next Saturday. Do you want to go?"

The last time Willa and Taylor spent time alone together was in seventh grade, when Finley was away for the weekend, visiting her grandparents in Columbus. They met at the mall, where they shared a giant cookie from Mrs. Fields, spritzed perfume on themselves at the cosmetics counter at the department store, and tried on sneakers at the sporting goods store just because the guy who worked there was cute. Nothing earth-shattering, but fun is fun. And going to see Sister Kismet might be that kind of fun.

"Yeah, okay," Willa says. "Thanks for inviting me."

Instead of responding, Taylor crunches into her first taco and moans with happiness. "This was the best idea."

Willa laughs. "It's going to be so hard to go back to ramen after this."

"So maybe we should make it a regular thing."

"Taco Sunday?"

Taylor smiles, shrugging a little. "Maybe not a specific day. Just whenever we need them."

40.7128° N, 74.0059° W

Take a bite out of life.

Taylor

TAYLOR FEELS AS THOUGH SHE MIGHT BURST FROM excitement as the subway car sways, carrying them across lower Manhattan to the Donut Shop. Her insides are practically vibrating, and she wishes she were a fly, because two eyes aren't enough to see everything all at once. She drinks in the people riding the subway, staring at the woman who's been holding a wooden crucifix above her head since she boarded the train and the man clipping his fingernails onto the floor. Taylor glances around the subway car to see if she's the only one noticing these things and makes eye contact with a cute brown-skinned boy beside her. His short dreadlocks bobble as he shakes his head and grins. "You're not from around here, are you?"

"Is it that obvious?" Taylor asks.

"I mean . . . kinda," he says. "This is pretty normal compared to some of the strange things I've seen. One time, this guy sitting across from me reached into his coat and pulled out a slice of pizza, ate it, then pulled out a second slice. Another time this dude got on wearing a pink lace thong over his jeans, and I didn't want to judge his lifestyle, but it was *not* a look. Maybe keep 'em on the inside in public, is all I'm saying. And just the other day I saw a dead horseshoe crab lying on the floor, and I didn't even question it because *of course* there was a dead horseshoe crab on the subway."

Taylor laughs. "I feel so Midwestern right now."

"Is that where you're from?"

"Yeah. Ohio."

The boy nods a little. "Welcome to the city."

She smiles. "Thanks."

He gives her another grin before he looks back down at his phone and Taylor checks to see if the woman is still holding the crucifix above her head. She is.

The daylight was nearly gone when they motored into the anchorage at Pier 25. For Willa, navigating a darkened river full of tug-and-barge traffic and pleasure boats had been a white-knuckle ride. But the twinkling New York City skyline, towering up to the clouds was one of the most beautiful sights Taylor had ever seen. She was supposed to watching for boats that might be on a collision course with *Whiskey Tango Foxtrot*, but she couldn't stop gaping at the reflection of the skyscrapers sparkling across the Hudson in colorful streaks.

Taylor has always dreamed of coming to New York City. She wishes she'd been alive during the heyday of clubs like CBGB and Fillmore East, so she could have seen all the bands from the record collection her dad gave her. She might be decades late to the party, but she's here now and she wants to experience it all. "I'm so excited. Do I look okay?"

By the time they'd arrived at the Pier 25 mooring field, they barely had enough time to tie up the boat, pump up the dinghy, and row ashore to get ready for the concert. They'd encountered two days of solid rain traveling from Catskill— where they'd spent an entire day turning *Whiskey Tango Foxtrot* back into a sailboat—so everything Taylor owns is slightly damp and slightly wrinkled. But she managed to pull together an outfit of a black denim skirt that Finley had talked her into buying—"it makes your butt look amazing!"—and one of her dad's vintage Rolling Stones T-shirt. It's faded and paper thin after so many years of wear, but it's her favorite.

"Super cute," Willa says.

"You too."

Back when they were in middle school, it became a thing to collect Converse high-tops in as many colors as you could—the more unique, the better. Taylor doesn't remember how it even got started, but Finley had six pairs, including ones with Union Jacks on them. Taylor managed to sweet-talk her mother into buying her three pairs in fuchsia, orange, and yellow. Willa couldn't afford new Converse, but one day she showed up at school rocking a pair of black lows she'd found at the Goodwill. She'd drawn stars all over them with a bleach pen that turned the black to a shade of orange that looked almost tie-dyed, and everyone lost their minds over how cool they looked. Taylor had been so jealous of those shoes, so jealous of the way Willa was able to turn nothing into something.

Tonight, Willa is wearing a pink sequined skirt that she bought for two dollars on half-off Wednesday at the Salvation Army. Even though their outfits are similar—T-shirts and skirts—Willa belongs on the New York City subway. Her hair is piled on her head in a way that looks like it might tumble down at any second and her lips are painted red. The guy with the dreadlocks keeps stealing glances at her legs and Taylor can't really blame him. She doesn't really burn with a jealous rage anymore, but Taylor still kind of wishes she was as effortlessly cool as Willa.

They exit the subway at the Delancey Street station and round the corner to the Donut Shop. A line has already formed, and as they walk to the back, Taylor scans the faces, looking for Vanessa. Taylor texted her a few days ago—when they were in a town called Amsterdam—to let Vanessa know they'd make it to New York City in time for the concert.

Vanessa had replied that she'd be there, but none of the faces are hers and Taylor tries to squish her hope back into a more manageable size.

She gnaws on her thumbnail as the line moves slowly forward.

"Are you okay?" Willa asks. "You seem . . ."

"Sister Kismet is my all-time favorite," Taylor says quickly, technically not lying. "I just want to get inside."

The line shuffles forward, and she catches sight of Vanessa walking toward the club. Her pale skin has turned pink in the neon glow of the Donut Shop lights, and Taylor's fingers curl into her palms to keep from pulling Vanessa in line with them. But Taylor is still trying to find a place for everything in her head—and in her heart. She will always love Finley, but long days on the water have given her a lot of time to think. She's never used any specific words for herself. She loved Finley. She loved Brady. Now Taylor feels wings fluttering in her chest when she thinks about Vanessa. She's okay with being bisexual, but she's not ready for Willa to know just yet.

They pass through a cloud from the smokers gathered outside the front door and enter the club. The first floor is an actual storefront bakery/bar, but a narrow stairway leads down into the redbrick basement. Ahead, there's a small soundstage with a shimmering red and pink backdrop and speaker stacks at each corner. Behind are a couple of old leather couches and a few tables and chairs, but the rest is an open space for dancing. The warm-up band is doing their sound check.

"I'm going to the mosh pit," Taylor says. "Do you want to come?"

"I think I'll just stay here, if that's okay with you."

"Are you sure?"

"Go!" Willa motions Taylor away. "Have fun!"

She digs her phone from the front pocket of her skirt and hands it to Willa. "It's safer with you."

Taylor crosses the room and stands near the front of the stage. A few people have already started to congregate, staking their territory for when Sister Kismet comes on later. She feels a little awkward standing alone, until someone shoulder-bumps her and Vanessa says, "Hey, you."

Her bangs are caught back in a sparkly clip and she's wearing a sleeveless yellow dress with a black Peter Pan collar and black over-the-knee socks. Taylor's pulse ratchets up a notch as she smiles. "Hey back."

"It's so good to see you."

"You too."

Vanessa's eyebrows hitch up. "Yeah?"

"Definitely." Taylor smiles. "Yeah."

Vanessa opens her mouth to say something, but she is cut

off when the lead singer of the opening band shouts, "Hello, New York! We are the Tempura Shrimps!" and the band launches into their first song.

Taylor has never heard of the Tempura Shrimps, but their sound is catchy and fun for dancing. The music is too loud for talking, too loud even for sustained shouting, but she and Vanessa shimmy, bounce, and clap along through the entire set. Taylor's T-shirt is soaked with sweat, but she can't remember the last time she had this much fun at a show. Going to concerts with Finley and Willa was always a good time, but music was never their obsession.

"Let's go upstairs and get a drink," Vanessa suggests, pulling her damp dress away from her body.

"I don't want to lose our spot," Taylor says.

"We'll get it back. C'mon."

Taylor sees Willa perched on the arm of one of the leather couches, nodding as a guy talks at her. She doesn't look panicked, just bored, so Taylor opts not to rescue her. Only fair, all things considered. Instead, she follows Vanessa up the stairs.

Willa

A GUY WEARING A BLACK T-SHIRT WITH A FLORAL chest pocket cornered Willa, introduced himself as Jonathen—"with an *e*"—and launched into a no-reply-necessary monologue about how he's trying to launch his own line of homemade, organic men's grooming products.

"I make my own mustache wax using beeswax from my friend's hive," he says, twirling the skinny tip of his hipster villain mustache. "Want to touch it?"

"I, um—" From the corner of her eye, Willa catches sight of Taylor sneaking up the stairs and accepts this as her punishment for abandoning her at the frat party. "Not really. No."

"No problem." Jonathen shrugs it off. "You know, I've been sitting here trying to figure out what you are. Am I picking up a little African American maybe? Latina?" He waves his hand in front of her face, trying to conjure the answer without Willa even speaking.

She's pretty sure Jonathen "with an *e*" isn't actively trying to be offensive or creepy, but Willa has no desire to share her family history with a stranger she'll never see again, especially since he's too old to be hitting on her. So she smiles and shrugs. "Any or all of the above, I guess."

"Well, whatever it is, I'm digging it. Very sexy."

Gross.

"You know, I need to use the ladies' room," Willa says. "It's upstairs, right?"

"I'll save your seat," he calls after her.

She waves. "Sure. Thanks."

At the top of the stairs, she spots Campbell in the doorway, handing his ID to the bouncer. Willa's mouth spreads into a smile, and just as she's about to weave her way through the crowd, a blond girl slides her arms around Cam's waist from behind. He twists at the torso and his face lights up. When she tilts her chin, he lowers his head to drop a kiss on her lips.

Willa thinks her eyes must be playing tricks on her. This must be a guy who resembles Cam. She blinks, but the scene doesn't change. He is still here, at the same bar, in the same city, with a girl who is not her. She feels like a dropped glass, razor sharp and shattered.

"Shit." The need to flee claws inside her chest and she

looks around wildly for an escape. She can't look at Campbell. Can't speak to him. Or else she might really break.

Willa ducks down the hallway leading to the bathrooms and tugs open the door to the ladies' room, where a couple of girls are pressed against the graffitied wall, kissing. It's not desperate, no-coming-up-for-air making out, but tender kisses punctuated with smiles and inaudible words. The night takes an even more bizarre turn when Willa recognizes the blond French braid, the black denim skirt.

She stands there for a moment, her jaw somewhere in the vicinity of her shoes. Why is this something she doesn't know about Taylor? Has she always liked girls? Did Finley know? Willa stands until she realizes that she is invading their privacy, such that it is. Thrown for a loop by *both* Nicholsons, Willa slips quietly out of the restroom, walks down the hall, and shoulders her way out into the street. She takes Taylor's phone from her purse and texts Campbell.

It's Willa. I have Taylor's phone. Tell her I'm going back to the boat.

Where are you?

Just tell her.

As Willa rounds the corner toward the subway station, the air feels cooler than when they left the boat and clouds have filled in overhead, obscuring the stars. The wind tugs at her skirt and a soda cup rolls like a tumbleweed down the sidewalk. The first drops of rain fall heavy and she starts to run. She's not used to running in heels, so she grips the railing as she hurries down the steps to the subway.

Willa is drenched by the time she's rowed the dinghy out to *Whiskey Tango Foxtrot*. The rain is cold and relentless, the wind howling, and one of the boats has come free from its mooring and drifts dangerously close to the shore. Willa ties a double knot in the rope connecting the dinghy to the sailboat, then unlocks the cabin. Pumpkin jumps down off Taylor's bunk and threads herself through Willa's legs. Willa reaches down and strokes the cat's back, taking comfort in the fact that she's not completely alone. "It's you and me tonight, Pumpkin."

Once she's changed out of her wet clothes and donned her weather gear, she texts Campbell again.

The weather has gotten really bad. Tell Taylor she should not come back to the boat tonight.

A few seconds later, the phone rings.

"Hey, what's going on?" The concern in Cam's voice would make her cry if she had time for tears.

"One of the boats has broken away from the mooring and I'm afraid we'll do the same," she says. "It's grown too windy for me to row back for Taylor and I don't want to leave the boat, so tell her to find a place to spend the night."

"I'll come help you."

"There's nothing you can do," Willa says. *You can't help me.*

You can't make me want you, then just walk away. You can't prove me right about you. I don't want to be right. She wishes she had the nerve to say those things out loud, to shout them at him, but instead she says, "I got this."

In the background of Campbell's silence she can hear the distant sound of the band and people talking and laughing. Then, finally, he says, "Radio the Coast Guard if you need help."

She disconnects the call, steps out into the cockpit, and starts the engine. As Willa checks the anchor line, the wind rattles the rigging, but tonight it's less like music and more like a battle cry. The line to the mooring is secure, but as she watches the untethered sailboat swing in a wide arc, narrowly missing another boat, she knows there are no guarantees in sailing. She knows to expect the worst.

Even within the relatively protected water of the pier, *Whiskey Tango Foxtrot* bobs and pitches on the waves, and the wind sends all the boats in slow 360s around their moorings. Willa worries that the drifting boat will crash against the pier, but her priority is making sure her own boat stays safe. She spends the entire night standing watch, keeping the engine running in case she needs to cut the mooring line and motor away. She takes shelter from the weather only in tiny increments, only to get more coffee.

The rain stops at around four in the morning.

The wind takes another hour to taper off.

By the time the sun rises, the only sign of the storm is the loose boat, thumping against the pier. Willa kills the engine, peels off her wet gear, and falls into her bunk. She's nearly unconscious when Taylor's phone vibrates with an incoming text. **We're on our way.**

Willa groans. She just wants to sleep, but now she has to bail the rainwater from the dinghy and row ashore. As she pulls the oars through the water, she can see them—Taylor, Campbell, and Campbell's date—and Willa is tempted to row back to the boat, motor out of New York, and leave the Nicholsons standing right where they are. Instead, she tosses a line to Cam and climbs out of the dinghy.

"The weather radar was nearly purple last night!" Taylor throws her arms around Willa. "You . . . you are a big damn hero!"

She doesn't know how to respond to this strange new Taylor. Or how to act in front of Campbell and the girl clutching his hand. Willa has never believed that heartbreak is a physical phenomenon, but now, as she stands in the place where her head and her heart intersect, the pain is breathtakingly real. She masks it with a joke. "Throwing myself directly in the path of an oncoming thunderstorm was the only way I could get rid of Jonathen with an *e*."

Taylor laughs. "You mean Mr. Ironic Mustache?"

"There was no irony there," Willa says. "Did you find a place to stay, or did you party all night?"

"We shared a room at a hostel near the Donut Shop."

Taylor gestures at Campbell and the girl, forcing Willa to acknowledge them.

"This is Kaia," he says. "We went to Cornell together."

He is either completely oblivious or intentionally cruel. Either way, Willa doesn't want to know this girl's name. She doesn't want to know anything about her. She wishes she could rewind time and stop herself from kissing Campbell Nicholson at that fraternity party, but the only direction she can go now is forward. Willa curls her hands into fists to keep from slapping the smug little grin from his face, then turns to Taylor. "So, what are we doing today?"

"We were thinking about getting something to eat and then—"

Willa cuts her off. "You should do that. I'm going to crash for a couple of hours and maybe hit up some thrift stores."

In the two days down from Catskill, they discussed all the things they could do in New York. Explore Central Park. Take an Alexander Hamilton tour of the city. Visit museums and art galleries. Ride the ferry to see the Statue of Liberty. Willa still wants to do some of these things—but absolutely *not* with Campbell and Kaia.

Confusion etches a line in the gap between Taylor's eyebrows. "I thought we—"

"I was awake all night," Willa says. "So you just go do your thing and I'll do mine."

Taylor

THIS IS A WATERSHED MOMENT FOR TAYLOR NICHOLSON. She can choose to spend the day in New York City with her brother and a girl whose presence is causing Willa pain—or not. The fearless girl who defeated a thunderstorm is lost inside someone small and diminished, and Taylor is embarrassed that her brother is responsible for it.

"I can upload some pictures while you sleep," she says. "Then we'll do stuff together, okay?" Taylor turns to Cam. "I'm staying with Willa."

He shrugs. "We're going to find early brunch."

As he leaves with Kaia in tow, Taylor rolls her eyes and calls after him, "Early brunch is *breakfast*, you ass."

She'd hoped to make Willa laugh, but Willa just stands there, her expression hollow, as Campbell walks away.

"I don't think he means to be cruel," Taylor offers, even

though she knows her words are unhelpful. "He's just—"

"Let's not do this now."

Taylor does the rowing as they return to the sailboat. She makes them bagels with cream cheese for breakfast, which they eat in silence. The way Willa stares into the middle distance is unsettling, but there is nothing Taylor can say—nothing she thinks Willa will want to hear—that will make her feel better. Willa curls up on her bunk, and Taylor uploads the photos from the concert that she took with Vanessa's phone. She smiles as she scrolls through images of the Donut Shop, of her all-time favorite band, and especially of Vanessa. Taylor feels guilty, but last night was one of the best nights of her life. Her feelings for Vanessa make Taylor's sexuality feel more solid. She has a word for it now that she's never used before.

Her parents wouldn't freak out if they knew. Taylor's dad has so much chill that he'd say he loves *her* no matter who *she* loves. And her mom would probably turn into the LGBT version of a soccer mom—in a good way. Taylor knows she's lucky, and it's a comfort to know that when she's ready to come out to them, she won't have to fear for her safety. But she's not ready yet. She's still adjusting to the thrill of being able to fantasize about kissing a girl who actually wants to kiss her back.

———

Willa seems a little more cheerful as she rummages through the racks at a thrift shop only a few blocks from the pier. She slips her arms into a raspberry-colored faux-fur jacket. Taylor would look like an overgrown Muppet wearing something so fluffy, but Willa can pull it off. Taylor snaps a picture with her instant. "That's super adorable. You should buy it."

Willa glances at the price tag and gnaws her lower lip. "It's more than I'd normally spend."

"Okay, but where will you find something this cute in Ohio? And don't forget how cold it gets in Cleveland during the winter."

Willa smiles. "I do kinda love it."

"Cam will take it back home for you," Taylor says, and Willa crinkles her nose at the mention of his name. "I know, but it's the least he can do after being such a dick."

"Thanks," Willa says quietly, as she drapes the coat over her arm and moves on to browse the next rack. "For spending the day with me, I mean. And adding some thrift shops to the itinerary."

Taylor had planned the day while Willa was sleeping, so Willa has no idea where they're going next. Taylor likes being the expert for a change.

They visit three more thrifts, where she watches as Willa ferrets out a pair of skinny black pants, a gray mohair cardigan, and a red velvet slip dress that would look awesome with black ankle boots. In the last shop, Taylor finds a Rough Trade T-shirt. As they wait their turn at the cash register, she says, "You have the coolest fashion sense. When did that even happen? How did I not notice?"

"We had a jeans day in sixth grade and I wore a T-shirt that my mom bought at the Goodwill," Willa says. "When I got to school, Madelyn Davies told me it used to be her shirt and pointed out a little mustard stain on the sleeve to prove it. She and her friends spent the rest of the day laughing at me."

Taylor's whole body flushes with shame for having ever made fun of Willa, for calling her trailer trash. This new knowledge doesn't excuse the way she behaved back then, but the middle of a thrift store doesn't feel like the right place to apologize. Or maybe she's too embarrassed to do it.

"Madelyn Davies is the worst," Taylor says instead.

Willa laughs. "Right? But that's not really the point. I hated the way people talked about me—as though being poor is the most awful thing you can be—so I decided to give them something else to talk about. If I always looked great and my clothes were on-point, they couldn't laugh anymore."

"A very good strategy," says the white-haired lady behind the cash register. She's rocking a buzz cut with red Harry Potter–style glasses and a giant silver stag's head pendant. She reminds Taylor of her maternal grandma, whose favorite saying is from a Dylan Thomas poem that goes "Do not go gentle into that good night. Rage, rage against the dying of the light." Grandma drives a Corvette convertible and takes her miniature schnauzer nearly everywhere she goes, even to places where no dogs are allowed.

"You wear this dress, darling," the shop lady says to Willa. "And I guarantee no one will be laughing."

"Thank you." Willa's cheeks dimple as she smiles, then turns to Taylor. "So, what's for lunch?"

"It's Sunday, so . . ."

"Please say tacos, please say tacos, please say tacos."

Taylor laughs as they head to the door with their purchases. "I'm thinking . . . tacos."

"It's like you read my mind."

They find a hole-in-the-wall taqueria selling dollar tacos—crunchy chicken for Taylor, soft al pastor for Willa—which they eat while walking up Broadway. Taylor takes pictures of the Empire State Building and the triangle-shaped Flatiron. They snap a touristy selfie in Times Square, then window-shop their way along Seventh Avenue to Central Park. They pass a line of horse-drawn carriages waiting for fares and take pictures with a white horse named Rosie. Inside the park, Taylor sinks down on the grass beneath the shade of a leafy tree and kicks off her shoes. "My feet are killing me. I'm definitely taking my bike to Kent so I don't have to walk across campus."

Willa stretches out on her stomach, propping her chin on her hand. "Have you gotten your housing assignment yet?"

"They're supposed to be out in the next couple of weeks," Taylor says. "What about you?"

"Not yet, but I haven't checked my mail since Oswego, so . . ."

"You don't sound very excited."

Willa shrugs. "I guess I am."

"But you've been working your whole life for this."

"That's kind of the problem." Willa stands and slips her feet back into her shoes. "We should take the subway when we go back to the boat."

Taylor wonders why Willa doesn't want to talk about college, why she's not more excited about being accepted into one of the best colleges in Ohio. Or maybe she just doesn't want to talk to *Taylor* about these things. Maybe it only seemed like their friendship was starting to have legs.

"Definitely," Taylor says. "But we're not done with Central Park yet."

As they continue, their pace is slower. Ambling. They pause to watch the little kids playing in the playground. The clank of baseballs against metal bats rings out as they pass the ball fields. They stop to ride the carousel, where Taylor chooses a tawny horse with a wheat-colored mane and Willa climbs astride a brown horse wearing battle armor. Taylor snaps an instant shot and hands the photo to her as the carousel begins to turn. "Willa Rose Ryan, First of her Name, Queen of Goodwill, Seducer of Coasties, Conqueror of Thunderstorms."

Willa laughs. "Okay, give me that camera."

She takes a picture of Taylor and hands it back. "Taylor Marie Nicholson, First of her Name, Chronicler of Watery Road Trips, Vanquisher of Locks, Ruler of the Mosh Pit."

Taylor looks down at the image of a girl on a horse whose mane matches her own, then smiles at Willa. "Those are good titles. Thanks."

"You're welcome."

They visit the John Lennon Memorial, where Taylor takes a photo of them lying on the ground with the word IMAGINE above their heads. They take turns sitting beside Hans Christian Andersen and scaling the *Alice in Wonderland* statue. When she runs out of instant film, Taylor switches to the camera on her phone. They stop at a gift shop to buy a New York City snow globe to go with the one from Niagara Falls. Finally, they end up at the Metropolitan Museum of Art, where they sit on the steps and people-watch until the sun begins to fade.

"This has been an awesome day," Willa says as they ride the subway back to the mooring field. "I needed it. Thanks."

"You're welcome."

Taylor considers telling her about Vanessa. Maybe she

can trust Willa with this secret. She sits up a little taller in her seat, summoning her courage. She can almost taste the words in her mouth. Then Willa's eyes flutter closed and Taylor loses her nerve. In the end, she swallows what she was going to say and looks out the window into the subterranean darkness.

Willa

TAYLOR IS STILL ASLEEP WHEN WILLA FIRES UP THE engine and unties the boat from its mooring. They hadn't planned on leaving New York City this early, but she woke before dawn with anticipation fizzing in her chest. The ocean is so close that the yearning for the feel of salt air on her skin is almost more than Willa can bear. When the boat is clear of the mooring field, she turns it into the wind, shifts the engine to neutral, and climbs on deck to raise the mainsail.

Willa is sailing past the Statue of Liberty when Taylor emerges from the cabin, still wearing her pajamas. Her eyes bug out and she dives back through the companionway, returning with both of her cameras—and her cell phone. After Taylor snaps dozens of shots of the statue, she settles on the cockpit bench with her phone. Willa watches the way she smiles at the screen, wondering if Taylor is texting the girl from the concert. She looks happier than she has in a long time. Certainly since before Finley died.

New York Harbor reminds Willa of a huge-scale version of Sandusky Bay—more tankers, more ferries, more skyline— and as *Whiskey Tango Foxtrot* skims across the water, she is proud of how far they've come. She smiles to herself, thinking, *I've got this.*

Except when they sail beyond the mouth of the harbor into the Atlantic Ocean, everything changes. The protective arms of New York and New Jersey are gone. The ocean waves are higher and more rolling than anything she's ever experienced. The boat pounds through the crests and valleys, and Willa is eleven years old again, afraid to sail a dinghy to Kelleys Island. But this time she doesn't have Finley to reassure her that she can do it.

Taylor drops her phone and grabs for the bucket, retching into it. Down in the cabin, Pumpkin leaps into the sink.

"I'm so sorry," Willa says. "I don't know what to do to make this easier for you. I guess I could put a reef in the main to reduce the sail area. . . ." She stops because at this point she's just spouting words. The truth is that Willa is afraid to climb on deck on an unpredictable sea. If she's thrown into the ocean, Taylor wouldn't know how to rescue her. Even worse, Willa is embarrassed by her fear. She's supposed to be a sailor. "Maybe we should call your dad."

Taylor hands over her phone and throws up as Willa hits the speed dial for Mr. Nicholson.

"We've just sailed into the Atlantic and it's pounding out here," she explains. "I thought maybe I could reef the main—"

"Turn on the engine and motor sail," he interrupts. "It'll keep the boat more stable through the waves."

"That feels like cheating."

Taylor's dad chuckles a little, but it's the laugh of someone who has forgotten more about sailing than Willa will probably ever know. "Unless you're racing, there's no reason to torture yourself. Use the engine and save the sailing for a better day."

Being given his blessing to be a fair-weather sailor is a relief to Willa. "Thank you."

"Anytime," Mr. Nicholson says. "Put Taylor on the line, okay?"

Willa hands the phone to Taylor, then starts the engine and rolls in the jib. Doing these things doesn't change the nature of the wind and waves, but the boat stops pounding so hard and she feels more in control.

Taylor disconnects the call and offers her a grim smile.

"Everything okay?" Willa asks.

"My mom looked at her credit card statement," Taylor says. "And she saw the charge for the room in Niagara Falls."

"Oh, shit."

"Exactly. She basically cut off the card, so if we have an actual emergency, she'll handle it."

"Is she really pissed?"

"Disappointed."

Willa winces. "God, that's the worst, isn't it?"

"At least when they're mad you know it won't last forever," Taylor says.

Willa wants to ask her why she did it, why Taylor would book a hotel room overlooking Niagara Falls when she knew her parents would be disappointed. But Willa is pretty sure she knows why and doesn't know how to say thank you, so she says, "They love you, Taylor. Their disappointment won't last forever."

After eight hours of sailing, both girls have found their sea legs. Taylor has been fortified by a steady stream of saltines and ginger ale, and Willa has lost her fear of the waves. Even Pumpkin has ventured out of the sink to sit on Taylor's lap. They reach Manasquan Inlet after lunch.

"Maybe we could keep going," Taylor says, flipping through the pages of the Captain Norm book. "I haven't gotten sick since this morning, and the book says it's only fifty-two miles to Atlantic City."

"That's *only* another ten or eleven hours," Willa points out. "We'd have to sail all night."

"Captain Norm says if we stay offshore, there are no obstacles to worry about. We can break the night into shifts so you don't have to do all the work."

Willa's eyebrows hitch up at Taylor's sudden faith in the advice of an elderly Looper who published his own book. "Are you absolutely sure about this? Because once we commit, turning back would be a huge waste of time."

Taylor closes the book. "Let's do it."

Willa unfurls the jib and kills the motor on her first watch, and *Whiskey Tango Foxtrot* finds a six-knot groove, soaring down the Atlantic coast. The rush of the waves along the length of the boat is music. This has always been Willa's favorite part of sailing, when wind and water come together like a song. Her heart aches that Finley is not here for this. She aches for everything Finley has missed and all that she'll miss as Willa's life goes on without her. Ever since Finley's leukemia returned, ever since she died, Willa has kept a lock on her emotions. She wants to howl and rage, scream and cry, and she knows it's not healthy to keep it bottled up. But she's afraid if she lets her emotions out, she'll never be able to put them back in the bottle again.

Taylor comes out on deck wearing her inflatable life vest and seasickness bands on each wrist—just in case. She salutes Willa. "Nicholson reporting for duty."

Willa laughs. "Ms. Nicholson, you have the con."

She crashes out in her bunk, and when she wakes, she's confused because through the companionway she can see the sky behind Taylor—and it's blue. Daytime blue. Willa climbs out on deck and looks around. Stretched along the Jersey shore are high-rise buildings, including one that's mirrored to reflect the sky. "Where— Is that . . . *Atlantic City*?"

Taylor's smile stretches wide as she nods. "Yep."

"Wait. You sailed all night?"

"Well, Pumpkin and I *motor-sailed* all night."

"Taylor! This is huge!" Willa jumps down into the cabin and grabs Taylor's instant. She snaps a picture of Taylor holding both the tiller and her cat with Atlantic City over her shoulder.

"I'm adding this to your list of titles," Willa says. "Sailor of the Darkened Seas."

She didn't know Taylor's smile could get wider than it already is, but it does. Then Taylor says quietly, "I didn't think I could be a sailor."

"Well, let me be the first to tell you," Willa says, as the instant photo blooms into focus. "You are."

39.3643° N, 74.4229° W

Make your own luck.

Taylor

"DO YOU THINK FINLEY MEANT FOR US TO GAMBLE?" Taylor asks as she and Willa pedal their bikes down New Hampshire Avenue. There are no casinos yet, just rows of newer-looking town houses, churches, and corner shops. When Taylor thought about Atlantic City, she never considered garbage trucks or nail salons, never considered that there are people who actually live there.

"Maybe," Willa says, as they ramp up onto the wooden boardwalk. It's still early, so there aren't many tourists out yet. Only power walkers, a couple of homeless men, and a handful of other people on bikes. "I mean 'Make your own luck' seems pretty obvious in a town full of casinos."

"I can see her wanting to sneak in, even for just one pull on a slot machine."

"We have the fake IDs," Willa says. "Do you think we should try?"

Taylor has always had to be coaxed into Finley's more reckless schemes—jumping off the Cedar Point Causeway Bridge comes to mind—and now she sometimes wonders if that made her the boring friend. Willa and Finley came back from regattas with tales about how they "borrowed" an FJ at two in the morning so they could night sail on Indian Lake. Or how they had to drink water out of an old sailing boot as their initiation into the junior race team. The whole ordeal had made Willa vomit, but they'd still laughed like it was the coolest thing that had ever happened. The thing is, they'd never been caught, prompting Taylor to believe Finley was charmed and her good luck surrounded them like a bubble. Now that Finley is dead, Taylor can't be sure she's still protected.

"I don't know," she says finally.

They ride past a stretch of abandoned casinos, including the huge glass structure that seems to melt into the sky and the one that resembles the Taj Mahal, which strikes Taylor as odd, considering the real thing is a mausoleum. This end of the boardwalk creeps her out, and Taylor is relieved when they start seeing shops that are open and casinos lit up and ready for action.

Now the boardwalk reminds her of a permanent carnival midway with restaurants, souvenir stands, psychics, tattoo parlors, art galleries, and strip clubs (gross). There are shops selling "world-famous" fudge and saltwater taffy, and three piers jut out into the ocean—one with amusement park rides, one with arcade games, and even one with a shopping mall. Everything on the boardwalk is layered with age and wear, but through the lens of Taylor's camera it's all beautiful.

"You're really good," Willa says, watching a shot of the grand carousel develop.

"It's the instant. The old-school border makes everything special."

"Stop," Willa says. "You have a good eye."

Taylor's cheeks warm at the compliment. Her parents are always heaping praise on her work and they have a couple of framed shots hanging in the living room. But they brought her into the world, so they're predisposed to love everything she does. From Willa, it feels earned. "Thanks."

She could spend the whole day taking pictures, but Taylor can tell Willa is getting restless to do something else. "Should we go on some of the rides?"

"Everything is so expensive." Willa tugs at her lower lip as they look at the admission prices. The rides are priced by tickets, and some of the more thrilling rides cost seven tickets or more. "I left most of my money on the boat, and I don't really want to pay ten bucks to ride one thing."

"We could go to the beach. That's free."

They chain their bikes to a nearby rack and claim a bit of real estate on the Atlantic City Beach, where they lounge on the sand for a couple of hours. Taylor takes photos of the surf, a few seagulls, and she and Willa take turns posing beside the Atlantic City Beach lifeguard boat. Taylor scrolls through their Instagram feed from the beginning of the trip, watching their tans grow darker and their faces more relaxed. Taylor still wishes Finley were here, but spending the summer with Willa hasn't been as bad as she'd expected.

A Frisbee skids into the sand beside her towel, and Taylor looks up to see a boy wearing red swim trunks approaching fast. He looks to be around her age. "Hey," he says. "Sorry about that."

"It's no problem," Taylor says.

Beside her, Willa lifts her head and shades her eyes to get a look at him. His white skin is starting to turn pink in the sun and his bony shoulders are crowded with freckles. He sweeps his floppy hair off his forehead and smiles with teeth too big for his mouth, first at Taylor, then at Willa.

"I'm Jake, and over there is Peyton and Dale." He gestures toward two white boys standing with their hands on their hips as they wait for Jake to fetch the Frisbee. "Want to play?"

Taylor swings a glance at Willa, who is already pushing off the towel to stand. "Sure."

"So, we road-tripped down from Philly," he says as

they walk across the sand toward the others. "Are you from around here?"

"Actually, we sailed from Ohio," Taylor says.

Jake spins the disc upward into the air and catches it on the way down. "With your family or something?"

"No, just us," Willa says. "We're on our way to Key West."

"Really?"

Taylor nods. "Yep."

"I'm impressed," he says. "And now our hour-long road trip seems super weak. So thanks for that."

"Our pleasure," Willa says, making him laugh.

Jake introduces them to Dale—blond hair, named after a race car driver—and Peyton—also blond hair, definitely *not* named after a quarterback—and the five form a circle on the beach. For a while they throw the Frisbee to one another randomly and without warning. Then they play a rowdy game called JackPot in which Willa, Peyton, Jake, and Taylor bunch up and compete to catch Dale's throws, not unlike bridesmaids at a wedding. The game ends when Jake and Peyton accidentally knock heads, sending both of them sprawling on the sand in pain.

When the sun is high and scorching—especially on poor Jake's milky skin—they take refuge in the shops. They scavenger hunt for the funniest T-shirt on the boardwalk— tie-dyed with a pug wearing sunglasses and a hoodie that says PUG LIFE—which Jake is obligated to buy and wear. They take pictures of themselves pretending to do shots from I ♥ ATLANTIC CITY glasses. Willa buys a postcard for her mom and Taylor considers a snow globe, but she doesn't want to buy it in front of the boys. They stop to watch the pulling machine as it stretches saltwater taffy and they take more than their share of the free samples. Peyton springs for corn dogs, which they eat sitting on a bench overlooking the ocean, arguing over whether ketchup or mustard is the best condiment for corn dogs. Taylor and Willa both vote for ketchup, but mustard wins.

Dale is the first to finish eating. He lets out a long, rolling burp, then, "Okay. Now it's time to hit the casino."

"Dude, you have to be twenty-one," Jake says.

And from Peyton, "Don't they card at the door?"

"I have it on good authority that they do not," Dale says. "Casinos are busy places. They won't even know we're there."

Peyton pulls a skeptical face. "Who's your good authority?"

"My cousin Jeff."

Jake leans into Taylor and whispers, "Jeff is an ass."

"Come on, you guys," Dale says. "What's the worst that can happen?"

"We go to jail," Willa says.

"We'd probably just get kicked out," Peyton says. "The police department is too busy for small-time shit like that."

"Look," Dale says, "the whole *point* of Atlantic City is gambling, so are we doing this or not?"

Taylor thinks about night sailing, bridge jumping, drinking boot water, and 'Make your own luck.' She answers without hesitation. "We're in."

Willa's eyebrows hitch up over the top of her sunglasses. "We are?"

"It's what Finley would do."

"Okay." Willa's sigh is skeptical, but she nods her assent. "We're in."

Dale chooses the next casino on the boardwalk and leads the way inside. The atmosphere is busy, it's noisy, and there are people everywhere. Families pass through from the boardwalk to the hotel. Poker and roulette players cluster around the gaming tables. And there is an army of slot machines lined up in rows. No one asks to see their IDs. No one even seems to notice them at all.

"We should probably avoid the tables." Willa keeps her voice low. "Too many people and too much time for them to realize we're not legal."

Taylor feels a tiny twist in her stomach, but she ignores it. "Good point. So maybe we should try the slots?"

Except the machines are loud, flashy, and kind of complicated. And there doesn't seem to be a good place on the casino floor for a group of teenagers to remain invisible. After the boys have chosen their machines, Willa splits away to a different row and Taylor follows.

"What do we do now?" she asks.

Willa feeds a five-dollar bill into one of the machines. "I have no idea."

Taylor chooses the slot machine beside Willa's and puts in ten dollars, which gives her one thousand credits. She follows the instructions on the screen, making bets on each spin, but she's reckless and before long all her credits are gone. The novelty has worn off and she's about to suggest they go look for the boys when Willa's machine goes crazy. Jaunty music plays and WINNER flashes on the screen above a total of $751.76.

"Oh my God!" Willa looks a little dazed. "I think I just won."

"You think?" Taylor laughs and snaps a quick photo of the machine. She tucks her phone into her pocket as the slot attendant comes over to verify the win. Taylor stands as tall as she can, trying to look older, more . . . legal.

"I'll just need to see your ID," the man says to Willa.

She hands him her fake license. He studies it for a long moment, then glances up, comparing the ID photo to the girl standing in front of him. Taylor's heart climbs into her throat and sticks there as she waits for his verdict.

"I'll be back shortly," the attendant says, and walks away, taking Willa's ID with him.

"I'm starting to think this was a bad idea," Taylor whispers as a bead of sweat trickles down her spine. Across the room, the slot attendant is talking to another hotel employee. He gestures in their direction. "Maybe we should leave."

"You can't be serious," Willa says. "I just won seven hundred and fifty bucks, and that ID worked just fine in Canada."

"I know, but my parents are already upset about the credit card thing. If we get caught—"

"This was your idea," Willa says as the slot attendant and the other man disappear through a door marked CASINO STAFF ONLY. "It's what Finley would do, remember?" She gives Taylor a bitter look. "Maybe it's no big deal to you, but I could buy a decent laptop for college. I can't just walk away from that kind of money."

"If you get arrested, do you honestly think Case Western is going to let you in?" Taylor says. "I'm still a minor, Willa, but you're not. So take those odds if you want, but I'm getting out of here."

Willa is still standing beside the slot machine as Taylor walks away. She moves toward the exit quickly, trying hard not to break into a run, trying not to draw attention to herself. Taylor doesn't stop until she is out in the warmth of the summer evening, down the boardwalk. She goes into a souvenir shop to buy a bottle of water. Despite the icy chill of the casino, her underarms are sweaty and her heart rate has not returned to normal.

Along the boardwalk, the lights are starting to come up as the day fades into night. The amusement park rides are outlined in light and Taylor thinks about how pretty the grand carousel will look in the dark. Alone, she walks down to the Steel Pier and buys a ticket.

Taylor climbs the stairs to the carousel's upper deck and chooses a brown horse with a black flowing mane and a saddle painted with flowers. The carousel begins to turn, and with each revolution, the foolishness of the casino recedes, until Taylor feels more like herself again.

The ride slows to a halt and Taylor leaves the Steel Pier, backtracking for her bike. She wonders if she will always be the boring friend, if she's immature for preferring carousels to illegal gambling. Except today wasn't boring. They were having fun until they went to the casino and Willa turned into someone Taylor didn't recognize.

She arrives at the marina to find Willa's bike lashed to the bow of the sailboat. The engine is running, the mainsail cover has been removed, and the winch handles are tucked in their pockets in the cockpit—all things they do when they're preparing to leave.

"Were you going to leave without me?" Taylor demands as Willa comes up from the cabin.

"Of course not."

Taylor maneuvers her bike aboard. "What happened at the casino?"

"Nothing," Willa says. "When you're done stowing your bike, would you untie the spring line, please."

"The police aren't after you, are they?"

"Don't be dense."

Taylor has so many questions, but Willa is coiled so tightly she looks like she might explode. Taylor secures her bike to the lifelines, then goes back to untie the rope that connects the middle of the boat to the dock. "Where are we going?"

"Away from here."

"What happened to the boys?"

"Could you get the bow line now?"

"Are you mad at me for leaving the casino?"

"God, Taylor, is it not obvious that I don't want to talk about this right now?" Willa shouts. "I just want to get the hell out of this place!"

Taylor scurries up on deck and removes the bow line. Willa backs the boat slowly out of the dock. With a cloud of weirdness hanging over the boat, they motor silently down the Absecon Inlet. Past the breakwall. Out into the dark ocean.

Willa

ATLANTIC CITY SHOOK WILLA TO THE CORE AND SHE ran from it, putting distance between herself and the monster who'd stood in the casino, snarling and greedy for something that didn't really belong to her. They sailed all night to Cape May, topped off the gas cans at first light, and sailed up Delaware Bay to the eastern end of the Chesapeake & Delaware Canal. They divided their days into four-hour shifts, and Willa's interactions with Taylor were of the ships-in-the-night variety, sharing information about weather and wind conditions. Never anything personal. And certainly not what happened in Atlantic City.

Now the boat is tied to a dock at the Delaware City marina, and Willa doesn't want to confess that she watched the CASINO STAFF ONLY door with the unwavering stare of a junkyard Doberman. That when the slot attendant came out, he brought a security guard. That Peyton was correct about what happens to underage gamblers. That being escorted to the front door and told never to return was the single-most embarrassing moment of Willa's life. That she'd left her fake ID and most of her dignity at the Tropicana.

So she says nothing. Instead, Willa puts out fenders and double-checks Taylor's knots. Docked in front of *Whiskey Tango Foxtrot* is a big bulky trawler called *What's Next* with a Great Loop flag fluttering on the bow. An older woman with a tiny Yorkshire terrier waves. "Hello! Are you Loopers, too?"

"Um, sort of . . . ," Willa says. "We're on our way to Key West from Ohio, but we've basically been following the Great Loop route."

The woman's cheeks form plump dumplings as she smiles. "I'd say that's close enough to count."

It isn't strictly true—only people who have completed the entire loop get a flag—but if this lady is a typical Looper, then Captain Norm wasn't wrong about them being friendly people. She has happy eyes and her hair color matches her dog's. Willa wonders if it's deliberate, like Finley's neighbor who dyes her hair exactly the same tawny gold shade as her Afghan hounds.

Taylor comes up on the bow as the woman asks, "Are you girls making this trip all by yourselves?"

"Yep," Willa says. "We can't do the whole loop because

we start college in the fall." She doesn't want this lady to feel sorry for them, so she omits the part about Finley.

"A few years back we met a couple of gals who were sailing the loop together, but they were older than you," the woman says, then speaks into a two-way radio. "Norm, honey . . ."

Taylor's eyebrows shoot up and she whispers, "*Norm?*"

Statistically speaking, there are thousands of men in the United States named Norm, but this is the Great Loop, which means the probability of this Norm being *the* Captain Norm is higher than in the ordinary world.

". . . what were the names of those two gals who sailed the loop?" the woman says into the radio. "The ones who were interviewed by all the magazines."

Norm's reply is inaudible, but the lady nods.

"That's it. Katie and Jessie. They were from Michigan, as I recall," she tells Willa and Taylor. "Anyway, I admire you young women who do brave things like this. I couldn't go without air-con—oh, good heavens, where are my manners? I'm Amy." She switches to the kind of baby talk people reserve for toddlers and pets. "And this little schweetie is Sunshine."

For the first time in days, Willa's heart feels light and she dimples into a smile. "I'm Willa . . . and this little schweetie is Taylor."

Amy has a hooting laugh, which cracks them up. Willa hopes she doesn't think they're laughing at her, but she smiles again as she says, "Aren't y'all just the cutest things? Listen, would you like to join us for dinner?"

The thought of having a home-cooked meal is almost enough to make Willa cry, especially after two days of nearly nonstop sailing. Taylor's head practically nods off her neck as she answers for them. "We'd love that. Thank you."

"Come on over in an hour," Amy says. "We're having lasagna with salad and garlic bread."

"Can we bring anything?" Willa asks.

"Just yourselves."

"So . . . are we ever going to talk about Atlantic City?" Taylor asks as they clean the cabin and gather their dirty laundry. "Are you okay?"

"They threw me out of the casino," Willa says, folding her comforter.

Taylor blinks. "Wait. That's it?"

"I've never been thrown out of anywhere in my life!" Willa exclaims. "The security guard led me out by the arm like I was some sort of criminal, and the boys . . . They took off running. The guard told me if I ever come back—like *ever*—they'll have me arrested."

"Which is better than actually *being* arrested," Taylor points out.

"I know. It's just—I've spent the past two days dying of

embarrassment. I knew you were right to leave, but the idea of having that much money prickled under my skin like a fever and . . . I was awful."

"You were a little awful."

Willa tries not to laugh, but when Taylor crinkles up her nose and smiles, Willa knows all is forgiven. Still, she apologizes. "I'm really sorry."

"The good thing about being alone was that I had some time to think," Taylor says. "Finley talked me into doing a lot of things I might not have done, but I think—well, I want to have my *own* adventures now, even if they're boring by her standards."

Willa nods. "So maybe we need to stop trying to figure out what Finley would do and just do what *we* want to do."

"And if one of us feels uncomfortable, we talk about it," Taylor says. "Agreed?"

"Agreed."

"Right now I'm asking myself what Taylor wants, and Taylor wants lasagna."

Willa cracks up laughing. "Come on, schweetie. Let's go eat dinner with Captain Norm."

"Hang on. There's something I want to do first."

While Taylor is gone, Willa empties Pumpkin's litter box—something she swore she'd never do, but it's the last thing left to clean—and a few minutes later Taylor returns with a small bouquet of red tea roses.

"Where'd you get those?" Willa asks.

"I might have taken them off a bush in someone's yard."

"You know that's something Finley would totally do, right?"

"We shouldn't go empty-handed. It's bad manners." Taylor has the same mischievous grin as her brother, but Willa can't help laughing.

"I love how you justify theft with proper etiquette."

"Hey," Taylor says. "My mom raised me right."

Willa is still giggling as they approach the trawler. A man with a white Hemingway beard comes out onto the back deck and waves a hand in greeting.

"Do you think he looks like the guy in the book?"

"Not sure," Taylor whispers back. "Maybe."

Norm opens a little gate to let them onto the boat. Through an open double doorway, the cabin looks as if a Cracker Barrel gift shop exploded. Candles. Antiqued bird knickknacks. A galvanized tray full of shells. Paneled walls are covered with framed pictures of smiling children and vintage-look wooden signs that say things like BETTER TOGETHER and BLESS THIS BOAT. Country plaid cushions adorn the settee. It's not really Willa's style, but she has to admire Amy's commitment to the theme.

Amy stands at a counter, chopping yellow peppers in a galley with a proper oven, a small fridge, and even a microwave. After a month of food unevenly warmed on the camp stove—or just eating meals cold—Willa would sell her soul for a microwave.

TRISH DOLLER

"Come on in," Amy says, gesturing at the large U-shaped settee with a table in the middle, as Norm settles in a recliner and picks up the remote for a full-size TV. Sunshine runs over to sniff the girls' ankles. "Make yourselves at home."

"These are for you." Taylor offers Amy the roses.

"Oh, you didn't have to do that," she says. "But they're beautiful. Thank you. Norm, honey, will you fetch me the short vase?"

Even though he hasn't been in the recliner long enough to get comfortable, he puts down the remote and joins her in the galley. Norm opens a high cupboard, takes down a clear plastic vase, fills it with water, and even arranges the flowers.

"Thank you." Amy kisses his cheek. "You're the best."

He grumbles, but Willa catches a hint of a smile before he returns to his chair.

"So, um—where are you from?" Willa asks.

"I'm originally from outside Nashville," Amy says. "And Norm is from Baltimore. We met out here on the loop several years ago, and the four of us—including our former spouses—became great friends. After my husband and I divorced and Norm's wife lost a battle with pancreatic cancer, we kinda fell for each other."

"That's sad," Taylor says. "And romantic."

Amy nods. "It's both. But I love the stuffin' outta him."

Norm just shakes his head as he changes the channel. "Same here."

A timer *ding*s and Amy pulls a pan from the oven, sending the scent of meat and tomato sauce wafting through the boat. Willa's stomach rumbles.

"Taylor," Amy says, "if you wouldn't mind grabbing the salad . . . and Willa, hon, would you bring the garlic bread? It's right there in the basket on the counter."

Soon they're all settled around the table with plates of steaming lasagna. Actual plates, not plastic. Silverware that matches. Drinking glasses with—sweet Jesus!—ice cubes.

"What we need is a trawler," Willa says.

"Or maybe you could just adopt us," Taylor suggests, making Amy hoot. Then, "Okay, I have to know. Are you *the* Captain Norm? The one who wrote *Getting Loopy with Captain Norm*?"

Amy claps her hand together and beams. "See, Norm, I told you people would buy your book. You have fans!"

"I knew it!" Taylor exclaims. "Your book is super helpful. We use it every day."

"No exaggeration," Willa agrees.

Norm's face is flushed as he offers them a closemouthed smile. "Thanks."

"Maybe after dinner we can get a picture of you with the girls," Amy suggests.

He rolls his eyes, but after Willa and Taylor help with the dishes, Amy pulls out her digital camera. Norm is patient as his wife snaps what feels like a hundred photos, each time saying, "Oh, that is just precious. Let me get another one."

"Would you mind if I run back to the boat to get the book for you to sign?" Taylor asks.

"I s'pose that would be all right," he says.

Willa waits until Taylor is off the boat, then says, "Tomorrow is Taylor's eighteenth birthday. Would you be willing to let me borrow your oven to bake her a cake? We only have a camp stove and—"

"Oh, honey, of course," Amy interrupts. "Do you need a cake mix because I have cake and frosting and—we'll throw her a party. What's her favorite kind of food?"

"She loves tacos."

"Okay, so tomorrow morning we'll have Norm keep her busy while you and I run to the grocery store for taco fixings and balloons and such." Amy wanders toward the galley, talking more to herself than to anyone else. "We'll need candles, I think."

"Now you've gone and revved her up," Norm says.

"How can you tell?"

He sniffs a laugh. "Good point. Taylor can help me scrub the hull."

"I'm sad to miss out on that."

He cracks an actual smile, which feels hard-earned. He levels a finger at Willa. "I like you, kid."

"Thanks." She laughs. "I like you, too."

Taylor

HER BIRTHDAY ARRIVES AS UNCEREMONIOUSLY AS every other day of the year, and as they eat breakfast, Taylor wonders if Willa even remembers. But before Taylor has time to read too much into it, a gruff voice calls out, "Hey, Taylor. I need you to come help me scrub the hull."

Taylor puts down her bowl of cereal and climbs out on deck. Captain Norm is standing on the dock beside *Whiskey Tango Foxtrot* with a bucket and a long-handled brush. "Me?"

"Yes, you."

"Why?"

"I don't have time for questions. Just come on."

"Um ... okay," she says, scratching the back of her head in confusion. "Let me get my shoes."

Taylor returns to the cabin and slips on her flip-flops. "Apparently I'm going to help Norm wash his boat."

Willa's eyebrows pull together. "Why?"

Taylor lifts her shoulders in an I-have-no-idea shrug. "But they've been so nice to us. How can I say no?"

After dinner, Amy invited Taylor and Willa to stay for a movie and made a giant batch of her special rosemary Parmesan popcorn with garlic and lots of butter. The large television and country decorations were a little slice of home, and it had been hard for Taylor to leave. If Amy had suggested a sleepover, Taylor would have said yes in a heartbeat. So even though she's not sure why Norm needs *her* to help him scrub the hull of his boat, there is no other answer but yes.

"Have fun with that." Willa yawns. "I'm going back to bed."

Taylor scratches her nose with her middle finger, then goes out to meet Captain Norm. He has her climb down into his dinghy, then hands her the scrub brush and the bucket of soapy water.

"Just do along the waterline," he instructs. "Call me when you finish this side and I'll come loosen the dock lines so you can get the other."

Taylor wonders if doing all the work is still considered helping, but she doesn't say it out loud. She snaps a picture of the brush and bucket, posting them to Instagram as she mutters, "Happy birthday to me."

She's cleaning an area near the back of the boat when

Willa comes off the sailboat wearing shorts and a cute floral tank top. Her hair is twisted up in two little buns on the back of her head. "Amy invited me to go to town with her," she says. "Since you're stuck scrubbing, I'll pick up some groceries. Is there anything special you want?"

A German chocolate birthday cake with coconut-pecan frosting, Taylor says in her head, but in real life she splashes the brush into the bucket and says, "No."

"Okay, well, I'll see you later."

Finley would have done something special for Taylor's birthday. Finley would have at least *remembered.* Taylor scrubs ferociously until Norm comes out on the back deck. "You don't need to take off the paint job."

"Sorry," she says. "I'm just frustrated because it's my birthday and Willa didn't remember."

Norm crosses his arms over his chest. "Of course she did. Why do you think you're washing my boat?"

"Wait." The brush goes still against the side of the boat. "Seriously?"

"You better act surprised or Amy will have my hide."

"Oh, I'm surprised," Taylor says. "But do I have to keep scrubbing?"

He chuckles. "Nah. But I'm s'posed to keep you busy, so you can come with me to the service department up at the marina."

As they walk, Taylor finds herself telling Norm the real story of *Whiskey Tango Foxtrot*. She talks about Finley. She talks about everything, even the part about Vanessa, even though she's not sure how open-minded he is about girls kissing girls.

"I'm really sorry to hear about your friend," he says, when she finishes. "But this is a good thing you're doing. I don't know that I believe in magic, but out here in the loop . . . Well, I think it's about as close as you can get."

She smiles. "Thanks."

Norm nods, but he doesn't speak, and Taylor thinks maybe he's used up all his words for the day. They walk in comfortable silence the rest of the distance to the marina. Taylor and Willa have put so much faith into his book—into his words—that she has to believe that what Captain Norm says is true.

"Good morning, Captain," the service manager says as Norm leads Taylor into the service department. The name tag on his blue polo shirt says DOUG. "What can I do for you today?"

"Looking for a small outboard. Four-horse or less. And I don't want to spend more than two hundred bucks."

"You're not going to find anything that cheap," Doug says. "Least not that runs."

"Then sell me one that doesn't run."

"I've got an old Johnson that needs a carburetor gasket."

Norm scratches his beard. "Okay. So throw in a carburetor gasket and we've got a deal."

Doug looks a little dazed, as though he's not sure how he ended up on the losing end of this negotiation, but as Taylor and Norm follow him into the service bay—toward a row of used outboard motors on stands—Taylor leans over and in a low voice says, "That was pretty Jedi."

Norm winks at her. "Damn straight."

He installs the new carburetor gasket right there in the service bay, working slowly and methodically, as Taylor watches. When he finishes, Norm carries the engine down to the dock.

"I'm going to need you to inflate your dinghy," he says.

"What? Why?"

"Because this outboard ain't going to mount itself."

"Wait. Did you buy that motor for . . . us?"

"Consider it a birthday gift."

"But why would you do that? You don't even know us."

"I've met just about every kind of person there is," Norm says. "I know you and Spitfire are good girls, and I want you to make it to Key West. A sturdy outboard'll help."

"I just—"Tears prickle in Taylor's eyes. She never expected so much generosity from strangers, least of all a gruff old salt like Captain Norm. "It's too much."

He waves her off. "Just go inflate the dinghy, will ya?"

When the outboard is in place, Norm tells Taylor he'll be right back. He goes aboard his own boat for a couple of minutes and returns with a pair of fishing rods and a small bait bucket. "You like to fish?"

Taylor's granddad would try to take her and her brothers fishing when they were little, but Granddad liked to go out before the sun was even up. Carter would complain that the fish didn't start biting until sunrise and Campbell would fall asleep on the ride out to Granddad's favorite fishing spot, but Taylor loved zipping across the quiet bay in the dark. She didn't mind waiting for the fish to bite. And she loved how Granddad would let her reel her catches all the way to the boat on her own, without taking over. "I do."

"Let's take your dinghy out for a spin."

Later, as Taylor and Norm step aboard *What's Next*, he shoots her a warning glance. "Remember what I said. Surprised."

Except when he slides open the door, Taylor's surprise is authentic. She has to duck beneath a garland of blue pompoms to enter the cabin, where a cluster of multicolored helium balloons sits in the middle of the table with a birthday cake—German chocolate—and a couple of small gift bags with tissue paper poking out.

"Happy Birthday, Taylor!" Willa shouts, as Amy begins

singing the birthday song. For the second time in a day, Taylor feels tears welling up. She laughs at Amy's off-key delivery—to be fair, no one ever sings the birthday song well—and sniffles as Willa pulls her into a hug.

"I know it's not what Finley would do," Willa says.

"No," Taylor says. "But it's still pretty perfect."

In true Amy fashion, dinner is not simply tacos, but a smorgasbord of taco fixings, including chicken *and* beef, black *and* pinto beans, and homemade guacamole that's better than Taylor's mom's recipe. Taylor is touched that Willa remembered her favorite kind of cake and baked it for her. And she laughs when Willa presents her with a black gift bag that says OVER THE HILL on it. Inside, is a snow globe from Atlantic City—featuring the Ferris wheel and grand carousel from the Steel Pier—and a couple of scratch-off lottery tickets.

Taylor rolls her eyes, but she's smiling. "This is a terrible gift."

Willa grins. "I know, right?"

"I love it. Thanks . . . for all of this."

"It's probably weird to be here with me instead of home with your family on a milestone birthday," Willa says. "For what it's worth, I'm glad you're here."

"Me too."

Amy's gift is a silver bracelet with a dangling compass charm. "A friend gave me this after my husband walked out on me and the kids. You know what she said to me? She said,

'Amy, it's okay to feel lost for a while, but this is to remind you that you don't have to stay lost.' And . . . well, I just think it's time to pass it on."

"You've both been so kind to us." Taylor looks to Norm and back to Amy. "I don't know what to say, other than thank you."

"That's plenty, Twigs," Norm says.

"Wait . . . *Twigs*? You call her Spitfire and me Twigs?"

Norm shrugs. "Suits you."

"Because I'm tall," she says flatly.

"Because one day you'll be so strong and deep-rooted that nothing will knock you down." He crosses his arms over his chest. "Now. As pleasant as this has been, if you two are not away from the dock at first light tomorrow, I'm cutting your lines."

This birthday was not one Taylor could have ever anticipated, but it might just go down as one of the best. She smiles at Norm. "Yes, Captain."

36.8508° N, 76.2859° W

Give a "ship."

Willa

IT DOESN'T TAKE LONG FOR THEM TO UNDERSTAND what Finley might have been thinking when she created the "Give a 'ship'" clue. Entering the harbor at Norfolk, they pass a massive naval base filled with aircraft carriers and destroyers. A three-masted schooner sails past *Whiskey Tango Foxtrot* as the sun dips toward the horizon. And not far from their marina is the USS *Wisconsin*, a huge World War II battleship. There are ships *everywhere*.

"What do you think she meant for us to do?" Taylor asks as they sit in the cockpit eating bowls of macaroni and cheese. "Take a tour? Join the navy? Become pirates?"

"I thought we were going to stop worrying about what Finley would do."

"We can still try to decipher the clues."

"Okay, so—" Willa sits back down and takes up her bowl.

"I think what's significant about this clue is that the word 'ship' is in quotes, which turns it into a pun. A bad pun, but this *is* Finley we're talking about. Maybe she meant for us to do something that would make a difference. Maybe she wants us to give a *shit*."

"About what?"

"Not sure," Willa says. "Do you mind if I use your computer to do a little research?"

"Go for it."

Before she begins looking for answers to Finley's clue, Willa logs into her e-mail account, where she finds a note from her mom, her official dorm assignment from Case Western, and an e-mail with the subject line: "Roommates!" Willa opens that one first.

> To: Willa Ryan <willarryan@email.com>
> From: Olivia Szymanski <pinkstarburst451@email.com>
> Subject: Roommates!
>
> Hi Willa,
> My name is Olivia Szymanski and I'm your new roommate. I just sat here for 15 minutes trying to think of something to say that was clever and cool, so I guess I'll give you the quick facts instead. I live in Niles, Ohio (near Youngstown), and I'm planning to major in genetics. I'm also the middle kid of three, which means I'm good

at sharing. My sister handed down her microwave and dorm fridge when she moved off-campus, so you don't have to worry about getting those things. If you're interested in coordinating our bedding and stuff, I made a pinboard of my dream dorm, but if you'd rather do your own thing, that's fine too. I hope you don't mind that I already google-stalked you and I'm totally in awe of your sailing trip. I can't wait to meet you in person and hear all about it!

–Olivia

Willa clicks the link leading to Olivia's pinboard, which is filled with images of matching headboards, wall monograms, and lilac-colored bedding sets in mixes of florals and stripes. One picture has a chandelier and another has a flokati rug. It's all very pretty, but Willa's heart feels heavy because it reminds her of how Finley's bedroom looked before the hospital bed and round-the-clock nursing care. Before her leukemia returned, Finley had dared to dream about going to college.

"I don't think I'm smart enough to get into Case Western," she said once when they were sophomores. "But if I get into Ursuline and you're at Case, maybe we could get an apartment together in Cleveland."

Back then, college had seemed so far away, but now the weeks are passing fast and Willa feels a fish of anxiety swimming in her chest.

She closes the window on Olivia's dream dorm and looks her up on social media, where Willa discovers Olivia was a cheerleader, honors student, and state champion in singles tennis. There are pictures of Olivia with her friends at parties, church, football games, school dances, and even building a Habitat for Humanity home. There are pictures of her boyfriend, Jack. Of Olivia with her sisters, Chloe and Sophia—all three of them were adopted from China, according to one of the photo captions. Hashtag "blessed." Of Olivia at her high school graduation with her white parents, Craig and Robyn.

By most metrics Olivia Szymanski seems like the ideal roommate. But Willa would rather live with someone who secretly smokes or listens to death metal or keeps her toenails in a jar than one who reminds her so much—too much—of Finley Donoghue. Willa is not ready for that kind of friend again.

She's not ready for any of it.

Leaving Olivia's e-mail unanswered, she returns to her in-box to read the response from her mother.

To: Willa <willarryan@email.com>
From: Mom <colleen.ryan@email.com>
Subject: Re: Re: I'm worried about you.

I love you very much, but my personal life is not up for debate. I hope you can respect that.

The fish in Willa's chest gets bigger, and she wishes her mom could understand that it's not just about her personal life. Colleen Ryan is a smart woman who is quick to learn new things, and Willa knows her mother could do anything she set her mind to do. If only she would set her mind.

> To: Mom <colleen.ryan@email.com>
> From: Willa <willarryan@email.com>
> Subject: Re: Re: Re: I'm worried about you.
>
> I didn't drop my phone in the lake. I threw it, because I was angry and frustrated and so, so tired of constantly worrying about *you*. You deserve better–and I'm not just talking about Steve. I want you to have a secure job, a car that doesn't come with a laundry list of problems, and, yeah, someone who wants you to be his one and only. I can't force you to do any of these things, but I hope you'll at least think about it. I love you, do you love me?

Willa hits the send button before she loses her nerve. She doesn't feel like trying to answer Finley's clue anymore, so she does a generic Internet search for things to do in Norfolk. They could tour the naval base or the USS *Wisconsin*, but Willa is no more interested in warships than Taylor would be. As she scrolls through the list of suggestions, Willa comes across an art studio called the Mermaid Factory.

"I found something we could do," she tells Taylor, who comes down into the cabin. "You know how Sandusky had those lighthouses all over downtown that were painted by different local artists?"

"My grandma bought one at an auction," Taylor says. "The artist painted it in kind of a van Gogh style."

"Norfolk's thing is mermaids, and there's this place where you can buy and decorate your own mermaid on a smaller scale," Willa explains. "And part of the money they make goes to benefit the arts in the Norfolk area."

She clicks on the gallery pages so Taylor can see sample photos of Red Hat Society mermaids, military-themed mermaids, seasonal mermaids, and even Disney princess mermaids.

"This is it," Taylor say, excitement building in her voice. "This is the answer to the clue."

"Wait. Really?"

"When we were little, like five or six, we would spend hours pretending to be mythical creatures," Taylor says. "Most of the time I would be a fairy, but Finley *always* wanted to be a mermaid."

Willa is stabbed with jealousy that Taylor's history with Finley goes back farther than her own. She feels left out of this clue—the way she'd felt left out with Captain Norm—even though Finley never promised that every clue was meant for both of them. Her smile is forced as she says, "Then we should make Finley a mermaid."

The next day, they ride their bikes to the Mermaid Factory, where they join a group decorating session. Along with Willa and Taylor, there are three elderly women in town for their upcoming sixtieth class reunion. They joke and laugh a lot, and Willa can't help wondering if she and Taylor and Finley would have been like that when they were old. Would they have forgiven old hurts? Would they have remained friends?

"I'm going to paint a mermaid that looks like Queen Elsa," says a little voice beside Willa, snapping her out of her thoughts.

"No, I am," a second voice says. "Mommy, tell her I get to paint Queen Elsa."

The two little girls are sisters on vacation from Michigan with their parents, and their mother looks frazzled before the actual decorating has even begun. "You *both* can paint Elsa."

The last of their group is a young newlywed couple from Florida, who are taking a honeymoon road trip up the East Coast. He doesn't seem super thrilled about decorating a mermaid, but he watches his wife choose paint and glitter with a raw, unguarded expression Willa has never seen. The kind of love her mother deserves.

Most of the members of the group choose to decorate

small ceramic figures mounted on stands, but Willa and Taylor opt for a larger wooden mermaid they can hang on the wall of the boat.

"We could paint the *Whiskey Tango Foxtrot* flags on her tail," Taylor suggests, as they stand before a cabinet filled with decorating supplies. There are paints in every shade imaginable. A rainbow of glitter-filled jars. Shells. Rhinestones, Decals. Raffia. Flowers. Feathers. Mosaic tiles. Bits of fabric. The possibilities are endless. "Or, maybe we could paint her wearing Finley's cheerleading uniform with some blue and gold fabric."

"We could," Willa says carefully, not wanting to start an argument. Especially since the little girls from Michigan have moved on to bickering over whose Queen Elsa is going to look the prettiest. When it comes to fighting, she and Taylor could easily give them a run for their money. "But what do you think about mosaic? We could make her tail different shades of pink and—"

"Yes," Taylor interrupts. "Let's do that."

Willa blinks. "Really?"

"Really."

Together, they plot out a pattern for their mermaid's tail and gather shades from deep fuchsia to light pink. They choose a variety of browns for the hair and the palest tans and pinks for the mermaid's skin. Two hours later, Taylor glues the final mosaic tile in place as Willa fastens a compass charm to the mermaid's hand.

"She's so beautiful," Taylor says, her eyes shining with tears. "What are we going to do when the trip is over? We should have made two."

For two hours Willa's mind had been blissfully blank, but now she wants to lay claim to Mermaid Finley, to snatch her up the way Taylor snatched Finley's list of clues before the trip even began. But they'd collaborated instead of arguing. They'd had fun. Willa doesn't want to be the one to ruin it, even though she *wants* to ruin it. "You can have her."

Taylor gnaws her lower lip. "Are you sure?"

Willa nods, but as she pedals back to the boat with the mermaid sparkling in the front basket of her bike, she thinks about the way the pendulum has swung in the opposite direction from where they started. Now they're being deferential to each other. Extra nice. But it feels every bit as false as the way they'd once tolerated each other for Finley's sake. Like their friendship will never be real.

"Do you think we should take the Dismal Swamp or the Virginia Cut into North Carolina?" Taylor asks.

"I don't care," Willa says dully.

"Are you okay?"

"I'm fine," Willa says, but it's not true at all. Her skin feels tight, like she's wearing it incorrectly. Like her life no longer fits properly and she doesn't know how to fix it. But instead of telling Taylor any of this, she deflects. "What does Captain Norm say?"

Now that Taylor has a direct line to the author, she's taken to texting Norm instead of referring to the book.

"He says the Dismal Swamp Canal is peaceful and more protected," Taylor says, and Willa likes the sound of peace and protection since right now she's feeling neither. "But the Virginia Cut comes out near the Currituck National Wildlife Refuge, where—" Taylor stops abruptly. "I think I found the answer to the next clue. 'Get a little wild.' Currituck is a refuge for a herd of wild horses."

Willa wants to be more excited about the next stop, but she can't muster any enthusiasm at all. Instead she just says, "Then I guess that's where we're going."

Across the gap between their bunks, Taylor snores softly, but an idea grips Willa's mind in a way that won't let her sleep. She takes the laptop and climbs out onto the foredeck to do . . . what? She's not sure yet. She tries to sit and listen to the breeze in the rigging, but the thought prods at her. What if? What if? What if? She opens a blank Word document and writes a letter. Rewrites. Edits. Rewrites it again. Finally, she copies the letter into the body of an e-mail addressed to the director of admissions at Case Western. Next she replies to Olivia.

To: Olivia Szymanski <pinkstarburst451@email.com>
From: Willa Ryan <willarryan@email.com>
Subject: Re: Roommates!

Hi Olivia,
I just wanted to let you know that I won't be your
roommate this fall. I've decided to withdraw my
enrollment and take a gap year so I can finish the Great
Loop route that my friend and I started this summer.
You seem like a really nice person, so I'm sure your next
roommate will be lucky to have you.
Wishing you all the best
–Willa

Taylor

WILLA HAS BEEN QUIET SINCE THEY STARTED DOWN the Virginia Cut. Scratch that—she's been quiet since they decorated Mermaid Finley, which now hangs on the bulkhead above the sink. Taylor is sitting on her bunk, uploading new pictures from Norfolk, when she hears the whine of an outboard motor excessively close to *Whiskey Tango Foxtrot*.

"Hey. How you doing?" a male voice drawls.

"Fine, thanks." Willa's response is overly polite as she reaches for her balled-up tank top lying on the cockpit bench and pulls it on over her bikini.

"Name's Glenn. What's yours?"

"Nice to meet you, but we're kind of in a hurry to make the next bridge opening, so if you wouldn't mind moving along . . ."

"Aw, come on, now," he says. "It's a beautiful day to party and I've got plenty of beer."

At the metallic *thump* of cans against fiberglass, Taylor climbs out into the cockpit to make sure Willa is okay.

"Well, hello." Glenn is standing in a camouflage-colored aluminum fishing boat with his fist curled around one of their lifelines. He's older than them by at least a decade, maybe more, and he's wearing a dirty trucker cap that matches his boat. A six-pack of Budweiser sits on the gunwale, as though he's about to invite himself aboard. He grins at Taylor. "There's two of you."

"We really don't have time to party," Willa says, a note of desperation in her voice. "But thanks anyway."

Glenn doesn't release his hold on the lifeline, and Taylor can see his mind working on his next sales pitch. He's not an unattractive guy, but he doesn't seem to understand that he's not welcome here. "Aw, come on. I'm a nice guy."

Taylor flings open the cockpit locker and pulls out the speargun that Campbell stashed away. The one Taylor couldn't imagine ever needing. Now she aims it at Glenn, whose blue eyes go wide as she says, "My friend told you to keep moving."

"Hey, now," he says. "I didn't mean any harm. I was only looking for a little fun with two pretty ladies."

"Don't care what you meant. Don't care what you want," Taylor says. "And you're gonna have a whole lot less fun if you don't take your hands *off this boat*."

Glenn lets go of the lifeline, but when he reaches for his

Budweiser, Taylor lowers the point of the speargun toward his hand. "We'll be keeping that."

"Couple of crazy bitches," he says as he sits down in his boat. "That's what you are."

"All I'm hearing right now is *wah*, *wah*, *wah*," Taylor says. "Move along."

He flips his middle finger at them as he motors away, but she grabs the six-pack, snaps a can out of its plastic loop, cracks it open, and takes a slurpy drink. "Thanks for the beer, asshole!"

Taylor is still cracking up when she looks back at Willa, expecting her to be laughing too. Except Willa is sobbing, her shoulders shaking violently as tears stream down her face. Taylor puts the speargun away and touches Willa's arm. "Hey," she says softly. "It's okay. He's gone."

Willa screams, a furious sound that rips through the trees on either side of the river. Her hands are clenched so tight it's a wonder her fingers don't break.

"It's not okay! Nothing is okay!" Her words scrape against her throat as she sobs them out. "Why do we live in a world where that *asshole* thinks doing shit like that is acceptable . . . where your brother can fuck with people's feelings and get away with it . . . where my mom is so broken she can't hold a job . . . where I have to be perfect all the goddamn time so no one will think I'm trailer trash?"

She screams until her voice gives out. Willa rages her fists at the sky, as if doing battle with God. "Why the fuck are we allowed to even be alive in a world where Finley Donoghue is *dead*?"

Taylor's skin burns hot as she's forced to face the role she played in Willa's pain. She takes over the tiller, keeping the boat steady in the channel while Willa's tears fall faster than the hem of her tank top can handle. Taylor wishes she could pull over to the side of the river—like she would if they were in a car—because her own vision is blurred with tears. But they are in a remote stretch where there are no towns, no docks. They have no choice but to keep traveling forward.

"I wish I could rewind time to that day at the sailing club and take it all back," she says. "I was so jealous that it was easier to hate you than admit I understood why Finley wanted to be your friend. She was right about you. You're the coolest person I know, and I'm sorry. For everything."

Willa pushes the heels of her hands against her eyes to stanch the flow of tears and sniffles wetly. "If I'm the coolest person you know, you really need to meet more people."

"Well, that was a lie anyway. Captain Norm is way cooler than you."

The corners of Willa's mouth quiver. Not *quite* a smile, but almost. "Obviously."

She goes down into the cabin to use the bathroom, and

when she comes back out on deck, she is wearing a dry tank top and her hair is damp around her face. Her eyes are still kind of puffy as she sits down. Taylor takes a drink of the Budweiser, then passes the can to her. Willa takes a sip, then crinkles her nose.

"I know," Taylor says. "It's not fine Canadian hockey-flavored beer."

Willa's smile is cheerier this time, and she laughs a little. Taylor adjusts course slightly. "So . . . can we unpack the rest of your meltdown?"

"Do we have to?" Willa sounds congested from crying. "Maybe we can pretend I didn't just lose my shit in the middle of the Intracoastal Waterway."

"Whether he meant it or not, Cam *was* cruel to you, and I'm sorry."

"I keep wondering what I did wrong," Willa says. "Like, was I so boring that running away was his only option?"

"You're the one sailing to Key West. If anyone is boring, it's Campbell," Taylor says. "It's one thing to get accepted into an Ivy League school, but another to flunk out because you never go to class."

"Wait . . . that's what happened? He told me he left."

Taylor shakes her head like the lie doesn't even come as a surprise. "Maybe someday my brother won't suck, but until then you deserve so much better than him."

Willa is silent for a beat, then rests her head on her knees. "I am such a hypocrite." When she looks up, there are fresh tears in her eyes. "I've been pissed at my mom for believing Steve will break up with his girlfriend for her, but I've been the same way with Campbell. I really thought I was different. That I'd be special enough to change him."

"Maybe your mom feels the same way about Steve," Taylor says. "Or maybe she knows and doesn't care. I know you love her, but it's kinda not your business."

"She said the same thing." Willa sighs. "I have to apologize to her."

"You can use my phone whenever you're ready."

"Thanks," Willa says. "Can I ask you something?"

"Sure."

Willa shifts to sit cross-legged on the cockpit bench, and Pumpkin creeps up from the cabin to curl in her lap. Willa leans in, like she's about to dish gossip at a sleepover. "Why didn't you tell me about the girl in New York?"

Taylor blinks. It wasn't as if she hadn't already been planning to tell Willa about Vanessa, but she's a little thrown that Willa already knows—and slightly worried that her sexuality might never have been a secret. What if Finley knew too? "How did you find out?"

"I saw you kissing in the bathroom at the Donut Shop," Willa says, her dimples popping as she smiles. "And I've been

239

trying not to pry, but oh my God, Taylor, I need whatever details you're willing to share. Or, you can tell me to mind my own business."

"No. It's cool. Her name is Vanessa." It feels good to finally share her feelings, and Taylor is relieved that Willa isn't being judgmental. Not that Taylor expected her to be, but it's nice to have support. "I met her at the party in Oswego. We bonded over Sister Kismet while hiding from the cops."

"Total meet-cute," Willa says, nodding.

Taylor's skin warms, and she can't stop herself from smiling. "I know, right?"

"Are you going to see her again?"

"I don't know," she says. "There's the whole long-distance thing and we're both going to be in college. And it feels a little . . . I don't know . . . soon."

"I totally get that, but don't forget that Finley would want you to be happy. And if Vanessa does that for you—" Willa stops abruptly. "Did Finley know you like girls?"

Taylor shakes her head. "I wasn't even sure myself because the only girl I ever liked was her."

"Wait. Are you saying you had feelings for her?"

"Basically for as long as I knew her."

"Whoa," Willa says softly. "That kind of brings that day at the sailing club into perspective. I mean, it's still not okay that you called me trailer trash, but I couldn't figure out why you were so mad at me when you didn't even like sailing."

"Oh, it gets weirder," Taylor says. "I was also mad that Campbell chose you over Finley."

Willa scratches behind Pumpkin's ears. "That shouldn't make sense, but I guess it does. You wanted Finley's happiness, even if it wasn't with you. And if she wanted Campbell . . ."

"Exactly."

"Well, the bright side is that he never got the chance to break *her* heart," Willa says wistfully. Then, "So how does Brady fit into the picture?"

"I loved him too."

Willa's eyebrows lift. "How . . . *interesting*."

"I was going to tell you when we were in New York City, but kissing a girl was brand-new for me, and I just wanted to keep it private a little while longer."

"I shouldn't have asked. I'm sorry."

"It's totally fine," Taylor says. "I'm glad you know."

"I know it's not the same as being able to tell Finley," Willa says. "She was your best friend."

"It would have been unfair to dump my unrequited love on her, so this isn't something I could have talked to her about. Thanks for listening."

"You're welcome."

"I haven't said anything to my parents yet, so . . ."

"Hey, what happens on the boat stays on the boat, okay?"

Taylor nods. "Agreed."

Willa slides on her sunglasses and makes a locking motion over her lips. "Now, give me that tiller. We've got wild horses to see."

36.5141° N, 75.8653° W

Get a little wild.

Willa

"THERE IS LITERALLY NO WAY WE CAN GET TO COROLLA in this boat," Willa says as she studies the depth chart of Currituck Sound. "This whole bay is practically shallow enough to walk across without getting your hair wet; our keel would get stuck in the mud in a hot minute."

Taylor strokes a bit of navy-blue polish on her big toe. "Is there a ferry?"

"Nope."

"Could we take the dinghy?"

"We could, but it would probably be a two- or three-hour trip each way, and then we'd have to find a safe place to beach it," Willa says. "There are other places in the Outer Banks where we could see wild horses, but this is really the only place where they're not penned."

"So how are we going to make this happen?"

245

Willa steps into her flip-flops. Her ruby polish has chipped down to tiny bits of color and she thinks maybe she should paint her own toenails. "I'm going to ask the people who work at the marina. Maybe someone will have a suggestion."

The marina manager is standing on the fuel dock when Willa walks up, but it's the guy in the skiff that's tied to a piling who catches her attention. He has reddish-blond hair, sun-stained skin, and dimples—*oh my!*—but it's his faded brown T-shirt that makes the hair prickle on the back of her neck. Because across his chest it says GET A LITTLE WILD.

"Where did you get that shirt?" she asks, only vaguely aware that she's interrupted their conversation.

"It's my work shirt," he says. "I run wild horse tours over in Corolla."

"Oh my God." Willa barks out a laugh. "This is just—Finley had to have something to do with this."

"Sorry, but you're not making any sense at all."

"No. I know," she says. "But my friend and I were just trying to figure out how to get to Corolla"—she makes an effort to pronounce it *kuh-RAW-luh*, the way he just did—"and now here you are, wearing those exact words on your shirt, and there's no way this is a coincidence."

"Nope. Still not making sense," he says. "But if what you're getting at is that you want me to ferry you across the sound to see wild horses, then heck yeah, I'm gonna do that. Because I'd be six sorts of stupid to say no to a girl that looks like you."

Her cheeks are sunburn-hot as she smiles at him. "I'm Willa."

"Just in case it matters to you at all, I'm Wyatt."

Willa and Wyatt. It's toothache-sweet, and she can already hear Taylor teasing her about it. What's more, it's ridiculous to even let her thoughts run that far ahead, but his eyes are the color of the ocean and Willa can't stop looking at him. "It definitely matters."

Completely squeezed out of the conversation, the marina manager walks away, shaking his head and chuckling.

"When do you want to leave?" Wyatt asks.

"As soon as Taylor's nails are dry."

"If Taylor is your boyfriend, the whole deal is off."

"*She* is not my boyfriend *or* my girlfriend."

His dimples deepen. "Then I'll wait right here while you go get her."

Taylor is wiggling her toes in an effort to help the polish dry faster when Willa returns to the boat. "So the weirdest thing just happened," she says. "I met a boy."

"I hate to break this to you," Taylor says. "But meeting boys is not weird. There are hundreds, probably thousands, who would love to meet you."

"Maybe so, but *this* boy is going to take us in his boat to see wild horses."

"His name better not be Glenn."

Willa laughs. "Actually, his name is Wyatt, and Taylor . . . ? He's wearing a T-shirt that says 'Get a little wild.'"

Taylor is silent for a beat, then, "That just gave me chills."

"I know, right? But there's no way Finley could have planned this. She couldn't have known."

"No," Taylor agrees. "But that doesn't mean it's not fate."

They quickly load a tote bag with bottles of water, sunscreen, towels, and all of Taylor's cameras before heading to Wyatt's skiff. He's talking on the phone as they approach.

"He is seriously cute," Taylor whispers.

"Dibs," Willa whispers back.

Taylor laughs. "Easy tiger. I'm just enjoying the scenery."

"Gotta go," Wyatt says into the phone, then disconnects the call. He looks a little surprised, as if he didn't expect Willa to come back. He smiles at her, then aims his attention at Taylor. Willa gnaws the end of her thumbnail. It hadn't occurred to her that he might prefer tall and blond to short and brown, but now she can't unthink it.

"You must be Taylor," he says.

"That's me." Taylor steps down into the boat. "But before we go anywhere with you, I'm going to need to see your driver's license."

He digs into the back pocket of his striped tan board shorts and hands over his wallet. "Of course you are."

"Thanks for humoring her," Willa says as Wyatt helps her into the skiff. He gives her hand a gentle squeeze, and the butterflies in her stomach go a little crazy. He doesn't throw her off-kilter the way Campbell did. Mostly because when Wyatt smiles, he's all dimples and sincerity.

"He has a library card," Taylor announces. "No condoms. Ooh! Who's the beautiful girl in this picture?"

Willa's heart does an elevator drop, but he just dimples up and rolls his eyes. "That's my nana."

Taylor laughs as she hands back the wallet. "It's a little weird that you keep a picture of your grandma in your wallet, but it's also very sweet. Which is good news for you, Wyatt James Kennedy. Unless you have a girlfriend."

His eyes meet Willa's. "I don't."

"Perfect," Taylor says, claiming the bench in front of the steering console so Willa can sit beside the cute boy. "Just be warned—the last guy who messed with us was introduced to the business end of speargun."

Willa covers her face with her hands, trying not to laugh. She loves this Taylor, who is funny and protective at the same time. She feels like a friend. Maybe like a best friend.

"Not gonna lie," Wyatt says. "I'm a little scared of you right now."

"We're harmless," Willa says. "Mostly. It's a long story."

He shrugs one shoulder as he turns the key to start the engine. "I've got all day."

Wyatt pulls the skiff alongside a small pier that juts out from an empty lot covered with grass-speckled sand and shrubby pines. The trip across the bay was fast, windy, and too loud to talk, but here it's quiet, except for the birds singing in the trees. He leads the girls across the property to a topless black Jeep. "My parents own this land. Eventually they're going to build a summer rental here, but for now . . ."

"It's beautiful." Willa climbs into the back of the Jeep and sits on an upturned five-gallon bucket so Taylor can have the front-seat legroom.

Wyatt grins at Willa in the rearview mirror. "It gets better."

He backs off the lot and heads down an unpaved sand road, past an elevated rental house with multiple wraparound decks. An SUV is parked under the stilts, and a bunch of kids are splashing around in a pool behind the house. "So right now we are just north of Corolla in Carova, which is basically the end of civilization on the Outer Banks," Wyatt explains. "We don't have any shops or restaurants or even roads up here. Just miles of beach and our herd of wild horses."

At the corner, he turns north. The houses to their right are closest to the beach, separated from the ocean by dunes.

Every now and then, Willa catches a glimpse of blue water between the hills of sand.

"The first appearance of the wild colonial Spanish mustangs dates back about five hundred years," Wyatt says. "One theory is that they were abandoned by Spanish explorers who tried to settle the area but were chased out by the local natives. Another is that they swam ashore during a shipwreck of an English cargo ship on its way to the colonies from the Caribbean."

He pulls into a sand "driveway" toward a three-level house sided with brown wooden shingles. It's not as huge as some of the beachfront houses they passed, but it has the same wrap-around decks on every level.

"Either way, most of the horses on the Outer Banks are descendants of those mustangs," Wyatt continues. "But the Corolla herd has reproduced almost exclusively within the herd for nearly five centuries, so they're genetically closest to the originals."

They climb a flight of wooden steps to the elevated front porch, and Wyatt pushes open the door.

"This is my house," he says, dropping his car keys on a table beside the door. The open living room is painted sunshine yellow, except for one wall filled with windows overlooking the ocean. "And today it's the perfect place to see the horses for two reasons. First, the wind is blowing in the right direction to bring them to the beach. And second . . ."

Wyatt opens a glass door leading out onto the back deck. Behind the house, almost close enough to touch, are six mustangs, grazing on sea oats. Willa's breath catches in her throat and Taylor gasps.

". . . they love our backyard."

Taylor dives for her digital camera from the bottom of the beach bag as Willa rests her elbows on the deck railing. The horses are varying shades of brown—tawny, chestnut, russet, and chocolate. Small and stocky and shaggy and utterly gorgeous.

"Finley would be losing her mind right now," she says.

Finley always loved animals, but after she was confined to a hospital bed, she spent hours watching videos of baby sloths getting baths and rescue dogs finding their forever homes. She'd laughed for *days* over a video of a horse squeaking a rubber chicken. Taylor glances at Willa, and they exchange a knowing smile.

"I could give you the full tour spiel, but it's actually my day off," Wyatt says. "And watching is better than talking."

"Does this happen a lot?" Willa asks.

"Yep."

"Does it ever get old?"

"My mom is a vet who works with the Corolla Wild Horse Fund," Wyatt says. "And my dad owns the tour company I work for, so we'd be in big trouble if it got old. But it really doesn't. The mustangs don't belong to us, but they're ours . . . if that makes sense. We love them."

The tenderness in his voice makes Willa's heart thump extra hard, makes her want to reach for him. But that would be silly when she's only just met him. Instead, she curls her fingers into her palms and watches the horses shuffle slowly over the dune, nickering softly as they munch sea oats and fallen persimmons from the Kennedys' tree.

Wyatt leans on the railing, his elbow resting lightly against hers. His voice is soft, with a note of wonder, as he says, "Where did you come from?"

Willa tells him the whole story, beginning with their promise to Finley and the list of clues. She omits the part about Campbell. He's not irrelevant—after all, if he hadn't pushed her away, she might not be here right now—but maybe he doesn't deserve to be part of the story anymore. She talks about the Hurricane Deck at Niagara Falls, the storm in New York City, nearly getting arrested in Atlantic City, and the speargun incident on their way from Norfolk. She even tells Wyatt about meeting Captain Norm.

"The next clue on Finley's list was 'Get a little wild,'" Willa explains. "We have no idea if she picked that phrase to reference wild horses, or if she researched tour companies and found yours, but when I saw your shirt . . ."

"I'm definitely okay with giving Finley credit," he says,

beckoning the girls to follow him down the narrow board-walk built over the dune that leads down to the beach. "How long are you staying?"

"We're leaving in the morn—"

"What do you do around here for the Fourth of July?" Taylor interrupts.

"We're having a barbecue here at the house tomorrow," he says. "My friends and I usually set up a Slip 'N Slide on the beach and surf if there's decent swell. At dusk, we'll take boats down the sound to see the fireworks at Corolla. We have a guest room, and I'm pretty sure my parents wouldn't mind if you joined us."

"We haven't slept in real beds since Niagara Falls," Taylor points out as they kick off their flip-flops at the end of the boardwalk. "So you can count me in."

Before Willa can say yes, a chocolate-brown horse drops onto the sand and rolls around on its back, just a few yards away from where a family has set up their lounge chairs for a day at the beach. Even though she knows Finley had nothing to do with it, being here seems magical. Fated. Willa looks up at Wyatt and smiles. "We're definitely staying."

Taylor crouches low, like a real photographer, her camera whirring with every shot. They're quiet as the horses in the water come out and shake, sending spray into the air around them. At moments like this Willa wishes she hadn't thrown her phone into Lake Erie. She could be taking pictures of wild mustangs. She could be putting Wyatt's phone number in her contacts for later, when she's in South Carolina or Tennessee or Michigan. Because Wyatt seems like the kind of boy you keep.

"Willa," he says. "I would really like to take you out on a date."

The last word has barely left his lips when she says, "I'd love that."

Taylor

Brady: How's it going, stranger?

Taylor: Hey, hi!

Brady: Your pictures today are incredible.

Taylor: Thanks.

Brady: How's the trip going? Are you figuring out how life works without Finley?

Taylor: Slowly, but yeah.

Brady: It doesn't look like you and Willa have gone full Hunger Games yet.

Taylor: Ha! We've discovered that we actually kind of like each other.

Brady: That's good.

Taylor: It is. How are you?

Brady: I'm figuring out how life works without Taylor.

Taylor: And?

Brady: I have a date tomorrow night.

Taylor: Good. I hope she deserves you.

Brady: Thanks. Night, Tay.

Taylor: Night, B.

Vanessa: Those horse pictures are so gorgeous. I almost feel like I'm there.

Taylor: Willa's on a date right now, so I kinda wish you were.

Vanessa: Did she ditch you again!?

Taylor: This time it's cool. Pumpkin and I are lying on a giant porch swing overlooking the ocean. And Willa is out with a guy who won't break her heart.

Vanessa: It sounds like the two of you are in a better place.

Taylor: Definitely. I'll call you in a few minutes.

Campbell: Where are you?

Taylor: Outer Banks

Campbell: I was thinking about hopping a ride. What's the closest airport?

Taylor: Why?

Campbell: Why what?

Taylor: Why do you want to hop a ride with us?

Campbell: Cabin fever. And I wouldn't mind seeing Willa again.

Taylor: Nope. You had your chance and you blew it.

Campbell: What do you mean?

Taylor: You took advantage of her feelings and then hurt her by showing up in NY with another girl. Willa really liked you.

Campbell: Past tense?

Taylor: Right now she's on a date with a guy who is worthy of her.

Campbell: That's kind of harsh. You're my sister.

Taylor: That's why they call it tough love.

Willa

WYATT PULLS A WIRE MESH TRAP OUT OF THE WATER at the end of his parents' pier on the Currituck Sound side of Carova. Inside are at least a dozen crabs. Willa is wearing the same red sundress she wore to the drive-in with Campbell—hoping to attach a better memory to it—but now she wonders if she might be overdressed for this date. "What exactly are we doing?"

"The market price for blue crabs is really high in restaurants this time of year," Wyatt says, tossing one of the animals back into the water. "So we're going to bring a few of these guys to my friend, who will cook them for us."

Wyatt keeps nine of the crabs, putting them in a red plastic bucket he stows in the back of his Jeep. They drive down the beach until they reach the paved road marking the end of the protected area for the wild mustangs. The beginning of civilization. The beach houses in Corolla are closer together, and they pass boutique shops and a few restaurants before Wyatt turns onto a smaller road. He parks in front of a shabby-looking red wooden shack called Number One Jimmies.

Beside the restaurant is a handful of picnic tables with strings of lights crisscrossing overhead that will be prettier when it's dark. Beach music spills out through the front screen door as Wyatt holds it open for Willa.

"This place is so great," she says.

"It gets better."

Inside, the walls are painted white and hung with old sepia photos of crabbers and their boats. There are no tables, only a blackboard menu featuring nothing but seafood and an order window.

Willa smiles. "You've said that before."

"And I was right, wasn't I?" Wyatt says. "So trust me on this."

A white guy comes out of the kitchen wearing a red Number One Jimmies T-shirt with a dirty apron double-tied around his waist. He's a few years older than Willa, and Wyatt introduces him as Mike. After the nice-to-meet-you pleasantries, Mike asks, "What'd you bring me?"

"Half a dozen jimmies and a couple of sooks that'll be good for cakes," Wyatt says, handing him the bucket. "Steam up the four fattest for us, and you can keep the rest."

"You want some shrimp?"

"That'd be great. Thanks."

"Was that English you were speaking?" Willa asks as she follows Wyatt to a table outside. "Because I couldn't understand a word of it."

"Jimmies are male crabs," he explains, sitting down across from her. "Sooks are females. And the number is the size equivalent. So, number one jimmies are the biggest, meatiest males. Number twos are smaller males that are less meaty, but still desirable. Threes are the smallest, usually female."

"That sounds sexist."

Wyatt waves his white paper napkin like a surrender flag. "No social implications here. Just crab physiology."

In the hours since they met this morning, Willa has discovered there's more to this boy than a handsome face. She likes the way his brain works and his sense of humor, and the way he seems completely at ease with his place in the world. Still, she really likes his face a whole lot. "What happens now?"

"Mike's going to steam our jimmies with shrimp, red potatoes, corn on the cob, sweet onions, and some andouille sausage," he says. "And then we're going to eat ourselves into a coma."

"After a month of living mostly on rice, Top Ramen, and instant mac and cheese, I am down for this," she says. "I almost feel bad for leaving Taylor behind."

"I don't feel bad at all."

Willa falters as she realizes she had a similar conversation with Campbell when they went to the movies in Minetto, but she reminds herself that this is not the same. Taylor practically pushed her out the door—and Wyatt is nothing like Campbell.

She smiles. "I said almost."

"Willa," he says. "Would you mind if I move to that side of the table so I can kiss you?"

"How fast can you get over here?"

Wyatt drops backward onto the bench beside her and leans over, touching his fingertips to the baby curls at the nape of her neck as their lips meet. The first kiss is fleeting, barely a kiss at all, but his mouth immediately returns for a second. Then a third.

"I'm glad you showed up on the gas dock this morning and confused me into hanging out with you," he says, touching his forehead against hers.

"It really was some of my best work."

He drags his teeth across his lower lip as though he's deciding whether to kiss her again. When he does, the tip of his tongue teases her mouth, and she parts her lips to deepen the kiss. She ignores the quiet niggling thought that they should not be making out at a restaurant, but kissing Wyatt Kennedy might just be her new favorite thing. When he pulls back, he grins. "I used to think it was weird when couples sat on the same side of the table, but I get it now." He pivots on the bench so they're facing the same direction. "I'm looking forward to elbowing you while we eat."

"I don't know how I've lived eighteen years without blue crabs in my life," Willa says as they lay side by side on a plaid blanket. She was a little nervous when Wyatt took the blanket from the back of his Jeep and spread it on the ground in the middle of his parents' empty lot, but this is not half naked in the woods; this is looking at the stars in a sky untouched by light pollution. "I will never forget that dinner."

Mike had come out of the shack with a stainless-steel pot and upended the contents onto the butcher paper-covered table. No plates. No utensils, except for a wooden mallet. Willa and Wyatt had dug into the pile, smashing open the crabs to pick out the sweet meat, peeling the skins off the shrimp with their fingers, and challenging each other to see how fast they could eat the corn off the cob. They'd laughed a lot. Talked more. Kissed each other with buttery lips.

And now that they're alone beneath the cloudless night sky, Willa feels secure knowing that holding this boy's hand is enough for both of them.

"I told you it got better," Wyatt says.

"I'm going to have to introduce you to Lake Erie perch," she says.

"Are you inviting me to Ohio on the first date?"

She laughs. "Maybe . . . although I might not be back there for a while."

"Why not?"

"A few days ago I e-mailed Case Western to withdraw my enrollment so I can finish the Great Loop on my own."

"I can't really say whether that's a good idea or not, considering I've opted out of the whole college experience," he says. "But what made you decide to withdraw?"

"It kind of started at graduation when I realized there was nothing all that special about being valedictorian," Willa says. "And then I got an e-mail from my assigned roommate. She was so excited and it hit me that I'm just . . . not . . . excited, I mean. I chose Case because studying business is practical and smart, but what I really want is to go to Kenyon and learn how to write."

"Is it too late to do that?"

"For this year it is," she says. "So I figured I would use the next year to finish doing the loop and write about my experiences and then reapply to Kenyon."

They fall into silence for a few beats; then Wyatt releases her hand. "Come 'ere." He lifts his arm for her to move closer, and she does, scooting against his side with her head on his shoulder. "We've known each other for only . . . what? Twelve hours? But I already know you've got this."

Somewhere in the back of her mind, Willa is aware that their relationship is progressing at an unnatural pace, but Wyatt is as familiar to her as brand-new, as comfortable as exciting. Sailing away from Corolla—away from *him*—is going to hurt.

"I don't think I've ever seen this many stars in my life."

Stars that aren't usually visible to the eye are tiny pinpricks and the rest seem close enough to touch. A comet streaks across the sky, but this time Willa can't form a wish fast enough because she wants so many things.

Taylor

IT'S BEEN A LONG TIME SINCE TAYLOR HAS SEEN WILLA without that tiny crease of worry between her eyebrows. But as Taylor makes a video of Willa sliding down a long sheet of plastic tarp toward the ocean, she's laughing. She hits the water, and Wyatt scoops her up and tosses her into an oncoming wave. When Willa comes up, she fake punches him in the stomach and he leans down to kiss her nose.

It was a good decision to stay in Carova for the night. They both needed a break from the boat, and it wasn't as weird as Taylor expected to eat dinner alone with Wyatt's parents—*John and Beth, please*—last night. Over plates of shrimp Alfredo, they'd asked Taylor a ton of questions about the trip, and after dinner they drove down the beach to Corolla for ice cream. They reminded her of her own parents, which made Taylor feel both at home and a little homesick.

Now, John has set up a gas grill loaded with ribs and barbecued chicken, which he mops with homemade sauce. Beth's filled a folding table with potluck side dishes from the neighbors—both local and summer people—who have congregated in lawn chairs and beach loungers. They dip into giant coolers stocked with beer and soda, and their laughter drifts on the air. The younger kids are building sandcastles and looking for shells, while the teenagers are gathered along the edges of a homemade Slip 'N Slide.

"Seeing Wyatt with a girl is kind of weird," says Corinne, a summer girl who has been coming with her family to Carova Beach from New Mexico for most of her life. Her blond hair hangs over her shoulders in two long braids.

"Really?" Taylor says.

Heidi, one of the local girls, joins the conversation, passing her red party cup to Corinne, who takes a sniff, then drinks. "I think all of us have had a crush on him at some point," Heidi says. "He's such a sweetheart—"

"And hot," Corinne adds.

Heidi nods in agreement. "Everyone is so spread out around here that it's not easy to date, but Wyatt has always been kind of oblivious. He's always been way more into surfing than girls."

Corinne laughs as they watch him drop a kiss on the top of Willa's head. "Apparently not anymore."

"We're leaving tomorrow morning," Taylor says.

"Ouch." Heidi shakes her head sadly. "Wyatt's initiation into the summer-vacation heartbreak club is going to be brutal."

Willa runs over, her curls dripping wet and sand stuck to the side of her forehead. Taylor wants to warn her to keep her heart safe, to protect her from getting hurt again. Saying goodbye to Vanessa was hard enough and Taylor hadn't been in over her head. But Willa's stress is completely erased. She's *happy*. "Hand over the cell phone, Nicholson," she says. "It's your turn to slide."

As she walks to the head of the Slip 'N Slide, Taylor wonders how they never thought to do this on Cedar Point Beach. Finley would have loved this. Sadness punches the tender place beneath her rib cage, but the pain of missing her best friend doesn't feel quite so bottomless anymore. But before she can feel guilty about that, Wyatt's friend Shaun jogs toward her, dumping biodegradable soap-water onto the plastic, making the surface more slick. When he reaches Taylor, he leans in and softly chants her name, the volume building until everyone is shouting. "Tay-lor! Tay-lor! Tay-lor!"

She kisses her knuckles and fist-bumps the sky. Takes a running start. Then launches herself onto her stomach, zooming face-first into the salty sea.

Later, following an afternoon of learning—well, *trying*—to surf and eating plates of barbecue, Taylor, Willa, and all of Wyatt's friends are gathered downwind from the adults, drinking stealth beers and sharing the weed from Willa's stash. Taylor's hair is crunchy from the salt water and her bikini bottoms itch with sand, but she feels mellow enough to try a hit. She watches Willa first, then pinches the joint between her fingers.

"Just hold it in your lungs, if you can," Corinne says. "You might cough at first, but you'll get used to it."

The sweet smoke tickles her throat and Taylor coughs a little, but no one makes fun of her. She passes the joint to Heidi, who says, "You two are officially invited to all our parties, forever."

Taylor laughs. "But only if we bring the weed?"

"I mean, no," Heidi says. "But also yes?"

"I'm trying to talk Willa into coming back up here after she finishes her trip," Wyatt says. "Or maybe for the winter."

"What, like during Christmas break?" Taylor asks.

"No," Willa says. "I, um—I haven't had a chance to mention it yet, but I'm not going to Case. I'm going to take a year to finish the Great Loop on my own."

Taylor's anger doesn't even know where to begin with all this new information. Withdrawing from college? Finishing the Great Loop? Or the fact that the first person Willa told was a boy she met *yesterday*. Sharing the truth about her feelings for Finley with Willa was deliberate—Willa hadn't been a default confidante—so it hurts that Willa would make such a huge decision without saying anything at all. "When did you do this?"

"Norfolk."

"So you had lots of chances to tell me. You just didn't," Taylor says. "Not even during your emotional breakdown in the middle of the ICW."

Willa's stare is hard, even as her eyes brim with tears, and Taylor instantly regrets every single word. Not only because she's torn Willa down in front of a group of friends—again— but because Taylor violated the "what happens on the boat stays on the boat" agreement they made outside Norfolk. Taylor is still free to come out to her parents whenever she sees fit, while Willa's private business is out in the open for everyone to wonder about.

"I really thought you'd changed," Willa says, getting to her feet. She dusts the sand off her hands like she's done with this conversation. Done with Taylor. "I thought we were actually starting to be friends, but you're still the same old leopard with the same old spots. Fuck you."

All this time, Taylor had been worried that one gust of wind would knock down their house-of-cards friendship. Instead, she blew it over herself like the big bad wolf.

Around them, confused glances bounce back and forth, and an awkward silence falls over the group. No one moves as Willa stalks up the beach toward the house, until Wyatt scrambles to his feet and chases after her. Leaving Taylor to think maybe Willa chose to tell the right person after all.

Taylor wipes her tears with the back of her hand, sniffling as she pushes up from the blanket. "I'm sorry I ruined everything."

"Stay here," Corinne says. "Wyatt's got this."

Heidi nods in agreement. "Willa's your best friend, right? She'll get over it."

The lump in Taylor's throat is lodged so tightly that she can't tell Heidi that she's already lost her best friend. Or that she doesn't want to lose the only other person who knows how that feels. She wouldn't blame Willa for hating her. She wouldn't even blame her if she packed up her suitcase and left Taylor behind. Gnawing her lower lip, Taylor glances back at the house, but Heidi tugs her hand.

"Taylor, sit. Let Willa cool off a little bit first."

Pushing against the instinct to go apologize, Taylor sits. And when Corinne hands her the charred stub of the last joint, Taylor takes the hit. She laughs when everyone laughs at something Shaun says, but her mind is elsewhere. Taylor doesn't want to be the crappy friend anymore, but she doesn't know how to undo the damage she's done.

Everyone is getting ready to go watch the fireworks when Willa and Wyatt return. They're holding hands and Willa is smiling, which Taylor takes as a good sign.

"Hey, um—" she begins.

"I just want to have fun tonight," Willa interrupts, her words as cold and sharp as the icicles that dangle from the roof of the Nicholsons' garage in the winter. Taylor's face heats at the understanding that *fun* does not include *her*. She gets into a skiff with Shaun and Corinne and someone's parents, and as they caravan down the sound to Corolla, Willa feels so far away. Too far away. And as the first rocket bursts into bloom in the fading daylight, Taylor is certain this is the worst Fourth of July ever.

Taylor

"SO, THIS IS HOW IT'S GOING TO GO," WILLA SAYS AS she stuffs clothes into her duffel bag. Even if Taylor were unable to hear the anger in her voice, she can see it in the way Willa packs. Her hairbrush clatters against a bottle of shampoo, and nothing is neatly folded. "We get to Key West as fast as we can. No more clues. No more pretending that we're ever going to be friends. We finish this and get on with our lives."

Taylor doesn't know what to say because how do you argue with someone who has already made up her mind? So she says what Willa wants to hear.

"Fine."

Willa

NOT LONG AFTER THEY MOTORED AWAY FROM THE
marina where they'd first met Wyatt, the radio chatter began.
A tropical depression had developed off the coast of Africa
and was projected to build into a major hurricane as it traveled across the southwestern Atlantic. Dorian—the fourth
named storm of the season—was predicted to make landfall
somewhere around Cocoa Beach.

"Should we be worried about that?" Taylor asked, her
mouth full of crunchy sour cream and onion chips. The
noise dragged up Willa's spine and she clenched her teeth
against it.

"By the time we get to Florida, the storm will be long
gone," she said, then put in her earbuds, blocking out the
sound. Blocking out Taylor.

Taylor tried to apologize that morning, but Willa was still

too angry to listen. Ever since, they've been skirting around each other in the cabin, and when they stop to refuel, do laundry, or buy groceries, they split up until it's time to start moving again. As though they're taking separate trips aboard the same boat. They have no lasting memories of South Carolina. No adventures. No Taco Sundays. The silence has grown, brick by brick, into a solid wall. Willa knows this is not what Finley had imagined, but maybe she and Taylor just aren't meant to be friends.

Now, a third of the way through Georgia, Willa's phone vibrates on the cockpit bench beside her. Wyatt gave her one of his old smartphones, and even with a spiderweb crack in the corner of the glass, it's still nicer than the one she threw in Lake Erie. She's been able to take pictures and text them to him—and seeing his dimples on the lock screen makes her smile every time.

His text says: **Are you listening to the weather right now?**

Not at the moment.

Where are you?

Middle of nowhere, Georgia. Population: 2.

Across the cockpit, Taylor's phone starts blowing up with incoming texts. Willa glances up in time to see Taylor's mouth fall open. Her eyes are huge and round and scared. "Captain Norm says the tropical storm made a sharp swing north."

Dorian has been upgraded to a cat 3, expected to hit between Savannah and Charleston. Seriously, Willa, where are you?

Willa catapults through the companionway and cranks up the volume on the radio.

"... maximum sustained winds have increased to near 115 miles per hour with higher gusts. Little change in strength is expected before the center reaches the coast, then weakening after the center moves inland. Hurricane-force winds extend outward up to twenty-five miles from the center and tropical-storm-force winds extend outward up to one hundred miles ..."

The forecast makes it official. Dorian is heading toward land, and *Whiskey Tango Foxtrot* is in its path. As Willa's internal organs rush headlong into panic mode, her brain freezes. She's always known a hurricane was possible, but she figured it wasn't probable. She has no survival plan for this.

"The governor of South Carolina has issued a mandatory evacuation order for coastal areas," Taylor says. "And the governor of Georgia is recommending the same. Willa ... what are we going to do?"

Returning to Savannah would be putting themselves directly in Dorian's path. They could try to make it to Brunswick, but they've been fighting gusty winds and a strong current all day—and there are only a few hours before dark.

"Norm wants to know our exact location," Taylor continues.

Willa presses the heel of her hand to her forehead, trying to wake up her brain. They need to find a safe place. But where? She'd meant her text as a joke, but it's also terribly true. With sparsely populated barrier islands to the east and swamps to the west, they are literally in the middle of nowhere.

"Willa!"

Taylor's shout jolts her back to reality. "Sorry. What did you say?"

"He wants to talk to you."

Willa's hand is shaking as she takes the phone. "I don't know what to do. Please tell me what to do."

"Start by taking a deep breath." The steady deepness of Captain Norm's voice is an oasis of calm. "Now, tell me where you are."

"We've just reached the north end of Sapelo Island, but we're still about a day out from Brunswick. Maybe more with the current."

"Well . . ." Norm is quiet for a beat. "There's no shortage of little creeks around those parts, so grab your chart book and find yourself a safe place to tie up. A floating dock would be ideal—especially if you get a tidal surge—and if you can take shelter on land, do that. Otherwise, button up and say inside unless the boat is sinking."

"I can't do this."

"Sure you can," he says. "How many dock lines ya got?"

"Too many."

Norm's deep chuckle is another shot of calm. "Good. You'll probably want to use about eight. And even at a dock, you should put out an anchor."

"Okay."

"Don't forget to strip the sails, and you'll wanna tie down anything that might blow away."

"Okay."

"Once you've settled on a spot, text the coordinates to your family and to me," Norm says. The idea that these might be her last-known whereabouts punches a giant hole in her wobbly confidence. She draws in another deep breath, but it isn't enough to still the erratic beat of her heart.

"What if—" she ventures, but he cuts her off.

"Don't even let your mind go there," he says. "Focus on what needs doing and do it."

"Okay."

She disconnects, then sends a quick text to Wyatt. **We're looking for shelter around Sapelo Island. I'll let you know when we've found a place.**

Wish you were here.

Me too. But I'll see you again soon.

Counting on it, so stay safe.

She smiles at the little red crab that has become his signature at the end of every text conversation. They haven't reached heart emoji status yet, but crab emoji status might actually be better. Willa tucks her phone in the pocket of her weather jacket and opens the chart book.

On deck, Taylor has the tiller trapped between her knees as her thumbs fly over the keyboard of her phone. Behind her, the wind ripples across the water and her hair is tied up in a knot to keep it from blowing in her face.

"Would you mind driving while I take off the sails?" Willa asks.

"Yeah, of course. Which way are we headed?"

"Inland. There's a shrimp dock where we might be able to tie up."

Willa removes the jib and mainsail, folding them into their canvas bags and stacking them in the v-berth. She removes the boom and lashes it to the deck. She ties extra lines around their bikes so they won't blow away and brings the gas cans into the cockpit. Down in the cabin, Willa rinses the dishes and stows away anything that could become a projectile in a storm, including the Finley mermaid and Taylor's snow globes. She puts fresh batteries in the flashlight.

"We're coming up on the shrimp docks," Taylor calls. "It looks like most of them are taken by shrimp boats."

There are a few shrimpers on deck here and there, prepping the boats for the coming storm. They pause to stare as the girls motor past, their expressions curious or surprised or *interested* in a way that makes Willa feel naked. She knows she shouldn't assume the worst about strangers, but there's nothing comforting about docking here.

"I don't like this," Taylor says, her voice low. "I mean, I'm already worried about the hurricane."

Willa nods. "We'll find another place."

But as they follow the bends and curves, there are no homes with docks like in South Carolina or town docks. There aren't any towns. Willa consults the chart book again. "We're running out of real estate. The only thing I see between here and the Atlantic is the Sapelo Island ferry dock."

"It will be dark soon," Taylor says. "Let's just go there."

The sun is nearing the horizon when they arrive at the south end of the island. The ferry pier is empty and the ticket office windows are boarded with plywood. There are a handful of cars in the parking lot, but no one is around. It reminds Willa of something out of a zombie movie, and she half expects the undead to come shambling out of the trees.

"We're closer to the ocean than we should be," she says. "But hopefully we'll be protected in the lee of the island."

Taylor looks doubtful. "Hopefully."

They're somber as they tie up to the innermost dock, stretching lines out in every direction until it looks like *Whiskey Tango Foxtrot* is caught in a spiderweb. Willa uses the dinghy to set the anchor in the marshy shallows near shore. Once she's back on board, they deflate the little boat and stow the outboard in a cockpit locker. Taylor takes out the spear-gun. "Just in case."

They walk a little way up the road to have a look around, but there's nothing to see. There are no houses or shops or restaurants. The people who live on the island have either evacuated or are holed up in their homes, making it feel as though Willa and Taylor are utterly alone. The air is hot and dense in anticipation of the oncoming storm, and the first raindrops fall like tiny bombs. They run back to the boat as the drops turn to a downpour, soaking through to their skin.

31.4178° N, 81.2958° W

Believe the unbelievable.

Taylor

EVERY TIME SHE THINKS THIS IS THE HARDEST RAIN she's ever experienced, Mother Nature—well, Hurricane Dorian—seems to prove Taylor wrong. For a while they were able to keep the hatches cracked to let the air circulate, but the cabin has become a sauna and they've stripped down to their bathing suits, trying to stay cool.

Now the rain is coming down sideways and working really hard to get into the boat. It drips from windows they thought were watertight. Drips from the bolts on the ceiling where the mast connects to the deck. It vibrates the companionway hatch boards and sprays through the cracks between. All this, and the hurricane hasn't even hit yet. Taylor peers out her (leaking) window into utter blackness and it feels like the world has vanished. She looks away, hating the feel of being so alone.

"I figured out 'Believe the unbelievable,'" she says, dropping onto her bunk, avoiding the growing damp spot.

"Yeah?"

It's weird to actually be talking to Willa again. She wonders if this is temporary. "I think Finley wanted us to take a ghost tour of Charleston, or maybe Savannah."

They didn't do anything noteworthy in either city—just docked, slept, ate, and kept on moving south. Taylor bought snow globes, but there aren't any memories attached to them. They haven't done anything memorable since North Carolina. It's her own fault, and Taylor's pretty sure getting caught in a hurricane is at least half her fault too. She should have been paying better attention to the weather instead of feeling sorry for herself. She feels a tiny surge of relief when the corner of Willa's mouth hitches up and she nods.

"That makes total sense. Finley always liked creepy, oddball stuff."

Finley had loved being scared. Stephen King. Horror movies. Even in elementary school her favorite books were the Goosebumps series. In middle school, Finley's dad gave her a book called *Weird Ohio*, filled with scary urban myths. She wore out the pages—until she was old enough to drag her friends to find the actual places.

"This one time we drove all the way to Cincinnati to see this tombstone." Taylor rearranges herself on her bunk, trying to get more comfortable. "The story goes that when this man died, he wanted his eyes removed and put into the eye sockets of his bust."

"That's . . . not possible."

Taylor rolls her eyes. "Urban myths can't be killed with logic."

"Right," Willa says, peeling the seal on a can of Pringles. She tilts it in Taylor's direction, offering her the first chip. "I forgot you need salt, fire, and your dad's old Impala."

Taylor barks a laugh at the reference to *Supernatural*, another of Finley's favorite obsessions, along with any TV show about ghost hunters. "Anyway, the bust is supposed to watch you, and some say it will turn its head and even talk."

"Of course."

"So we found the grave," Taylor continues. "The bust was made out of black stone, but the eyes looked super real. They were probably made of glass or something, but I swear to God it seemed like they were following us around the cemetery. It was so creepy."

"That's how it was the time I went with her to Hell Town," Willa says. "I think you were at your grandma's house for the weekend, but we drove to Boston Mills to see this deserted town surrounded by a whole bunch of ridiculous myths. Like, one of the stories was that there had been a chemical spill and the people who refused to leave turned into mutants. Finley went there expecting to see disfigured people or evidence of a satanic ritual. Instead, it's a bunch of old houses that were abandoned when they expanded the state park. It was kind of eerie, but that's all."

Taylor nods. "Like Gore Orphanage."

"Or the time she made us wait all night to see the headless motorcyclist."

A gust of wind grabs the boat and shakes it, making them scream—and then crack up laughing. Outside the wind has started to howl, and it rattles the rigging so hard it sounds like a helicopter is hovering above the boat. As their laughter subsides, Willa's expression turns serious. "I never believed any of that stuff, but if we make it through a hurricane, I might just believe the unbelievable."

Taylor's smile fades and fear creeps back in. "If . . . ?"

"We've done everything we can," Willa says. "But what if it's not enough? There are lots of things that could go wrong, and I'm afraid of them all."

Taylor has never heard Willa admit that she is scared, and it makes her wonder if she's not frightened enough. "Should we go back to the shrimp docks? Or try to find something more inland?"

"I don't think we'd make it in time."

"Okay, so . . ." She tries to think like Willa. "Maybe we need to focus on what we can control. Are you hungry? We have tortillas, a can of chicken, some shredded cheese, and a tomato about to go bad. We could make Hurricane Tacos."

Willa's smile is grim, but it's still a smile. "Yeah, okay."

Taylor puts on a playlist of Finley's favorite songs to drown out the howl of the wind, then braves the hatch board spray to get tortillas and chicken from the cupboard as Willa gets the tomato and a bag of cheese from the cooler. The wind strengthens outside, making the boat shudder violently, like an angry hand is trying to snatch *Whiskey Tango Foxtrot* from the dock and throw it out to sea. Taylor grabs for the overhead rail, and Willa grips the edge of the counter, her knuckles going white until the turbulence subsides.

Cooking becomes a slower-than-normal process, but in the calm moments, they manage to assemble a dinner of chicken tacos. As they sit at the table to eat, it feels a tiny bit back to normal. Taylor takes a bite of her taco. The chicken is too salty, the cheese is bland, and the flour tortilla sticks so tightly to the roof of her mouth that she has to pry it free with her finger.

"Gross." She and Willa say the word at the same time, and when their eyes meet, they burst out laughing. They don't speak; they just laugh until tears trickle from the corners of their eyes. Taylor's sides feel like they might split apart and Willa is trying to catch her breath, but whenever they look at each other, it starts all over again.

The boat heels over hard and the saucepan slides off the stove, splattering chicken all over the cabin floor. The sail bags slide around the v-berth, startling Pumpkin, who tries to jump in a sink full of soapy water. Their laughter dies as they're reminded where they are, what is happening. "Are we going to be okay?"

The roar of the storm nearly drowns out Willa's voice as she says, "I don't know."

"If, um—if we don't—" Taylor doesn't want to think about death, but she's seen pictures of the aftermath of a hurricane. Flattened trees. Boats blown on land. Houses flattened into a pile of boards. "I just want you to know how sorry I am for what happened in North Carolina."

Willa doesn't respond right away, and Taylor worries her apology is no longer good enough. If Willa can't forgive her, she won't be surprised.

"I wonder why Finley thought we could be friends without her," Willa says finally. "She was the glue. But there have been moments on this trip—lots of them, actually—when it seemed like she might have been right. It's just—sometimes it feels like I'm Charlie Brown and you're Lucy, and I never know when you're going to pull the football away."

A tear trickles down Taylor's nose, but this time it's not from laughing. "I guess I was just hurt that you shared something that big with a stranger instead of me."

"But see, even now it's not about you," Willa points out. "I was planning to tell you, but I ended up telling Wyatt first. It wasn't a deliberate choice, but it was *my* business and I shouldn't have to defend it. You embarrassed me for no reason, Taylor, so what reason do I have to believe you won't do it again?"

Willa grabs a towel and wipes up the mess on the floor, leaving Taylor to wonder if their hurricane truce has been broken. Taylor washes the dishes, then makes a couple of peanut butter and jelly sandwiches as a replacement meal.

"So . . . I think Finley hoped that the things we experienced on this trip would become the glue." She hands Willa one of the sandwiches. "But maybe she also wanted us to have another person in the world who knows how it feels to miss her. If we have each other, we'll never really be alone."

Willa takes a bite and just chews, not giving anything away. It's torture not knowing what she's thinking—and Taylor finds herself needing Willa's forgiveness. "I guess what I'm saying is that I don't want to be Lucy anymore. I'd kind of like to be Linus, but he's the smart one like you. In reality, I'm probably the Charlie Brown."

Willa rolls her eyes, but there's a hint of a smile on her lips. "If we don't die out here in the middle of nowhere, I suppose I can give you one more chance."

"Hey, Taylor, can I ask you something?"

The girls are huddled between the sail bags in the

v-berth since the windows have leaked all over their beds. They should be trying to sleep, but the wind is screaming and the turbulence is almost constant. Pumpkin has taken refuge behind Taylor's knees, and the weather radio jabbers in the background as Dorian closes in on the Atlantic coast. The storm is still predicted to make landfall north of Savannah, but the boat is within the wingspan. The worst is yet to come.

"Yeah, I guess."

"What's it like kissing a girl?"

Taylor's face flushes as she remembers how effortless it was to kiss Vanessa. She didn't have to pull back to keep from getting too much tongue, and Vanessa did this sexy, teasing thing against Taylor's upper lip that made her kind of dizzy. "It was . . . Okay, so this might not make any sense at all, but it was kind of like kissing myself."

Willa's eyebrows pull together. "What?"

"With Brady, I sort of had to teach him what to do, but Vanessa just seemed to know exactly what I liked," Taylor says. "Maybe it's because we're both girls—"

"Maybe it's because Brady Guerra kisses like a golden retriever."

"Wait." Taylor's eyebrows come together in confusion. "How do you know?"

"Eighth grade. Your birthday party. In your mom's closet,"

292

Willa says. "Seven minutes of . . . well, heaven isn't exactly the word I'd use."

"He got a little better."

"How much better?"

Taylor laughs. "Probably not much."

"Have you ever wanted to kiss me?"

"Are you flirting with me?"

Willa laughs as she props her chin on her knees. "I'm just curious. I mean, why Finley? Why not me?"

"Have you even seen yourself? You're way too short."

"Hey!" Willa smacks Taylor with a throw cushion, sending the cat scampering. "I am adorable."

"You are," Taylor agrees. "But I have never wanted to kiss you."

Willa sniffs. "Whatever. It's your loss, really."

Taylor laughs, but in the quiet moment that follows, she tries to find the right words to answer the real question. Why Finley? Why not someone else? "From the very first day, Finley made me feel safe and special . . . and loved."

Willa nods. "Yeah. It was impossible not to love her back."

Pumpkin creeps back into the v-berth. Taylor rests her chin on her knees, mirroring Willa. "Why did you decide to withdraw from Case?"

"I thought studying business was the smart thing to do," Willa says. "I'd get a good job, make a lot of money, and would never have to worry about paying the electric bill. But now . . . I guess this trip made me realize that's not what I want. I mean, I'd rather not be poor, but I want to see the world. Live in it. And . . . I want to write about it."

"So, are you really going to finish the loop alone?"

Willa nods. "My plan is to spend the winter in Florida and get a job. I could wait tables, or there's a pirate ship in Fort Myers. Maybe I can be a deckhand."

"You'd probably get hired in a hot minute," Taylor says. "And you'd make a great pirate."

"You think?"

"I mean, you're a little short, but—" Willa smacks her again with the pillow. "I figured you'd go back to North Carolina to spend the winter with Wyatt."

"It's super tempting," Willa says. "But I have to keep my priorities straight if I'm going to reapply to Kenyon next fall. I'm kind of hoping he'll do some of the loop with me."

"See . . . this is why I never wanted to kiss you. You're way too cool for me."

Willa laughs. "Shut up."

"I've been doing a lot of thinking, too," Taylor says. "And I've decided on a major."

"Really?"

Taylor has spent most of her life flying by the seat of her pants. She earned a solid B average in school and had no clear idea of what she wanted to do with her life. She applied to colleges along with everyone else, then crossed her fingers. Getting accepted into Kent State was good enough. It still is, but spending the summer behind the lens of her camera has given her a new perspective. "I'm going to study photography."

Willa nods like a bobblehead. "Yes! If your work is great now, just imagine how amazing you're going to be. Someday you'll be famous!"

"Calm down. I haven't even started college yet."

"Once this storm is over—"

Whatever Willa was going to say is swallowed when another huge gust slams into the boat. The boat tilts, and Taylor falls against Willa. This time, *Whiskey Tango Foxtrot* does not right itself.

"What just happened?"

"The storm must be getting close," Willa says, easing herself carefully out of the berth. The slant of the floor makes it difficult for her to walk as she reaches for her weather jacket. "The water level has dropped. We're sitting on bottom."

"Where are you going?"

"I need to make sure all of the lines are still holding."

Taylor's eyes go wide. *"Now?"*

"Unfortunately."

"Do you need help?"

"Maybe sit in the cockpit . . . just in case."

Rain pours into the cabin as Willa slides back the companionway hatch. They're not even in the cockpit before they're smacked in the face by wind and water, making it difficult to see.

"Wait here!" Taylor shouts. "I have an idea."

Willa

WILLA FEELS RIDICULOUS WEARING A DIVE MASK, but the rain is coming down so hard that she would be blind otherwise. And Taylor is a genius for coming up with the idea.

Whiskey Tango Foxtrot is leaning 45 degrees toward the dock and the lines on that side of the boat have gone slack. Leaving Taylor in the cockpit, she creeps slowly along the tilted deck, stopping with every gust of wind that threatens to send her over the edge. She holds tight to the lifeline until it's safe to move again. The rain stings her exposed skin and soaks through her weather jacket. It's almost six in the morning, but the clouds make it seem like it's still night.

At the bow, Willa discovers that the bikes are still secure, but the dock line running from the boat to the ferry pier has broken. Captain Norm warned them to stay on the boat, so she considers ignoring the problem. Except it needs to be fixed.

"We need another dock line!" she yells back at Taylor, but her words get swept away.

Willa slowly works her way back to the cockpit, where she rummages through the storage locker for one more length of rope.

"A line snapped and we need to replace it," she yells to Taylor. "Do you want to stay on the boat or go up on the pier?"

Taylor points to the pier, and Willa gives her the okay sign. Taylor shimmies beneath the lifeline on the low side of the boat and steps onto the floating dock. The wind tries to push her backward as Taylor forces herself forward. Her hood flies back, making her hair whip wildly around her face.

Both of them fight their way into position. Willa ties off one end of the rope, then tosses the other end to Taylor. The wind snatches it away, and Willa has to gather it back up to try again. On her next attempt, she tries to factor in the wind, but again they miss. Three times. Four times. The rope is heavy with muddy water. Five times. Six times. Willa can barely see through the rain-splattered mask.

"Fuck you, Dorian!" she screams, heaving the coiled rope.

This time Taylor catches it.

Back inside the cabin, they collapse on their bunks, still wearing their weather jackets. It doesn't matter that the cushions are wet because they could not possibly be any more soaked than they are right now.

". . . the center of Dorian," the weather forecaster says, "will approach the coasts of South Carolina and Georgia later today . . ."

This time Willa is too exhausted to scream. She just lifts her arm up off the bunk and extends her middle finger at the radio.

The water returns first, flooding the sound and all the little creeks, lapping at the windows on the low side of the boat. Making it feel like they're underwater. Like they're sinking. Willa waits for the boat to right itself, but it doesn't happen.

We should be floating. Why aren't we floating?

"Something's wrong," she says, moving as fast as she can manage to the companionway. She shoves open the hatch and sticks her head out into the battering rain. Water is spilling over the low side of the boat, trickling into the cockpit. Her mind shifts into overdrive, listing the things they'll need for a quick getaway and assessing where they'd find shelter if the boat sinks. *We might be able to pry the plywood off one of the ticket office windows and smash the glass,* Willa thinks, *but what if we can't? Then what?*

"The water is coming up over the low side," she says, closing the hatch. "If the cockpit fills, the boat won't float and the flood water will sink us. We may have to consider abandoning ship."

"Where are we going to go?"

"I don't know," Willa says. "But we should pack ditch bags just in case. Take only what you can't live without."

As Willa packs her duffel with the flashlight, a change of clothes, her wallet, and Wyatt's GET A LITTLE WILD T-shirt, she touches the faded Campbell drawing. "Though she be but little, she is fierce." Willa doesn't feel fierce at all. She feels helpless and utterly swamped with sorrow at the thought of losing the boat. Taylor is crying as they climb back into the v-berth with the VHF and the cat.

"Ten hours into this trip, I wanted to go home," Taylor says. "But now this boat feels like home. It can't end like this."

Willa puts her arms around her friend, hugging her tight. If she had any words of comfort, she'd offer them, but she doesn't know what to say. Instead they cling to each other as the forecaster announces that Hurricane Dorian has made landfall at Hilton Head, South Carolina. Flying debris crashes against the hull. Lightning illuminates the cabin as bright as daylight. Less than a second later, thunder booms, shaking the boat. The rain sounds like machine-gun fire. Like they're caught in the middle of a war without any weapons of their own. Willa closes her eyes and hopes that dying won't hurt too much . . . and that's when she feels the boat begin to rise.

The sky is overcast as Willa slides back the companionway hatch, but there is a bright spot where the sun is hidden behind the clouds. The water is muddy, like coffee with cream, and the trees along the shoreline are all leaning in the same direction. A car in the ferry lot has been stabbed through the windshield by a tree branch. And the wind indicator at the top of the mast has blown away. But the rain has passed and *Whiskey Tango Foxtrot* is still caught in its web of dock lines. Still floating.

"We made it," Taylor says as they step out into the cockpit. Sodden leaves are wedged in every nook and cranny, and there is sand packed into even the smallest cracks. "We survived a hurricane."

Willa sits down to steady herself as tears of relief track down her cheeks, and Taylor goes back into the cabin for a moment and returns with the pirate flag. She runs it up into the rigging, where it flutters in the breeze. NO QUARTER. NO SURRENDER.

"I'm going to call Captain Norm and my parents," Taylor says. "Do you want me to have them pass a message to your mom?"

"No," she says, taking her phone from the pocket of her jacket. "I need to do this myself."

Taylor walks out onto the bow to give Willa some privacy.

"Hi, Mom."

"Willa. Oh God. Willa." The tears in her mother's voice make her cry harder. "I've been worried sick and I'm furious with you, but right now I have never been happier to hear your voice. Are you okay?"

"I'm sorry I threw my phone in the lake," Willa says. "I'm sorry I didn't call. I'm sorry I judged you and demanded you change your life because I didn't like your choices. I'm just . . . so sorry."

"Where are you right now? Are you in a safe place?"

"We're still tied to the ferry dock at Sapelo Island in Georgia," Willa says. "But we'll be heading for Brunswick tomorrow morning. We got thumped pretty hard by the outer bands of the hurricane, but the boat is fine. Taylor and I are fine."

"Good. Now . . ." The strength has returned to her mom's voice, and Willa braces for a different kind of storm. "Don't you *ever* ignore me like that again."

"I promise."

"From now until you reach Key West, I expect regular updates. From you, not your Instagram."

"Yes, ma'am."

"And another thing . . ." In the pause that follows, Willa racks her brain to think of what else she's done wrong, but she draws a blank. "I broke up with Steve and on Monday morning I start as a teller at Civista Bank."

"Wait . . . what?"

"You were out of line, but you were also not wrong," her mom says. "My choices affected you in ways you didn't deserve. I should have been your role model, not the other way around, and I'm sorry for that."

"Hey, Mom? I love you, do you love me?"

"Yes, I love you, do you love me?" her mom replies, and Willa's smile reaches all the way down to her heart.

As her mom fills in the details about how Mrs. Donoghue helped her get the job and let her borrow a pantsuit for the interview, Willa thinks about all the unbelievable things that have happened in the past twenty-four hours and how this—her mother—might be the most unbelievable thing of all.

Taylor

WILLA STANDS ON THE BOW AS TAYLOR DRIVES *Whiskey Tango Foxtrot* toward a slip in the marina. She's never actually done this before—that's always been Willa's job—but if the boat can survive a hurricane, it can survive Taylor learning to dock. She tries to envision herself gliding neatly into the dock, hoping that if she can imagine it, she can do it. In reality, Taylor turns the tiller too soon, bumps the piling, and kind of bounces into the slip. She feels like she might die of embarrassment, but Willa gives her a thumbs-up. "You did it!"

"That sucked."

"Well, yeah," Willa says as she positions a fender between the boat and the dock. "But the next time you'll do it better, so who cares?"

Their original plan had been to spend a single night in Brunswick and keep moving, but as they carry the wet cushions out into the sun, it's clear they're going to need more time. The boat is disgusting, they haven't bathed in three days, and they're in desperate need of some time on dry land. Taylor is tempted to suggest they blow off the work and do something fun first, but their habits are ingrained now. They clean the boat, empty the toilet, put the sails back on, and make a shopping list. When Taylor finally gets to take a shower, it's well earned and quite possibly the best shower of her life.

"I think I want to cut my hair," she says as they ride their bikes toward downtown Brunswick. Over the past two months it has gotten noticeably longer, hanging almost to the small of her back. When Finley's hair fell out during chemotherapy, she consoled herself by braiding, curling, and styling Taylor's hair. Taylor didn't mind—she would have done anything to make her best friend happy—but now Finley is gone and even washing this much hair has become a pain.

"Like how short?" Willa asks.

"Super short. Chopped off."

"Are you sure? That's a pretty drastic change."

"I feel like my life has been a series of drastic changes lately," Taylor says. "And it's bugging the crap out me."

Willa laughs. "Do you want me to come with you for moral support?"

"You can go do the boring grocery shopping while I have someone massage my scalp and make me look amazing."

Willa pushes up the tip of her nose with her middle finger, then pedals off in the direction of the Winn-Dixie, while Taylor pauses to look up hair salons on her phone. The closest place is less than a quarter mile away, so she rides up, parks her bike, and steps inside.

On her way back to the marina, Taylor can't stop looking at herself in store windows, can't stop running her fingers through her hair. It no longer flutters out behind her, and the air touches the back of her neck in a way it never has before. But Taylor didn't just get a haircut; she had her hair color lightened to a pale blond, which makes her look like a completely different person—maybe the person she wants to be.

She's almost at the marina when her phone vibrates with a text. **Hey, it's Wyatt. I'm on a layover in Atlanta on my way to Brunswick. I'll be there in a couple of hours and I want to surprise Willa. Can you help me?**

She stops to reply in front of a live music venue. A signboard beside the front door advertises a band called the Freecoasters. Tonight only. Taylor could call it divine providence or the hand of fate—or even belief in the unbelievable—but her heart feels as light as her hair as she texts Wyatt back. I have an idea.

Once their plans are in place, Taylor returns to the marina. She's walking up the dock when Willa spies her. She sits up to get a better look and her eyes bug out. "Oh my God, Taylor!" she cries. "You *do* look amazing. I had no idea you were planning to bleach it too."

"I wasn't," Taylor admits, stepping aboard the boat. "But the stylist talked me into it."

"That was such a good call. I love it."

"Thank you. Me too." Unable to help herself, Taylor runs her fingers through her hair again. "Anyway, there's a show tonight at a live music club in town. We're going."

"I don't know," Willa says. "I'm exhausted and kinda just want to go check out the marina's book exchange library."

Taylor shakes her head. "Did I mention we're going to see a band tonight? Because that's what we're doing. We'll have not-Hurricane Tacos here first, and we only have to stay for one set."

"God. Fine." Willa sighs. "Did you pay the salon extra for the bossy attitude?"

Taylor laughs. "They threw it in for free."

A couple of hours later, the girls are finished with dinner and dressed for a night out. Taylor is recycling the outfit she wore to the Sister Kismet concert and Willa's wearing the red slip dress she bought at the thrift store in New York City. With her hair done up in a curly bun, she is absolutely beautiful, and if Wyatt's mouth doesn't hit the floor when he sees her, Taylor is going to kick his ass all the way back to North Carolina.

She snaps a photo of Willa as she perches on the seat of her old battered cruiser bike wearing her dress and heels. Everything about the picture is perfect. The composition. The juxtaposition of glamorous and shabby. The rosy quality of the fading light. As Taylor uploads it to their Instagram, she knows this one will be off-the-charts popular.

In town, they lock their bikes to a street sign in front of the club, where Wyatt is waiting outside. There are enough people milling around that Willa doesn't see him at first. But when it hits her that Wyatt is standing in front of her in downtown Brunswick, she *launches* herself at him. He catches her up in his arms, holding her tight. With her face buried in his neck, Willa can't see the expression on his face—like everything in his world is *right*—but Taylor can, and it makes her smile. This is a boy who is going to be a part of Willa's life for a good long while—maybe even longer.

As they enter the club, Willa and Wyatt are in their own little bubble, oblivious to everyone around them, including Taylor. She feels a tiny bit like a third wheel, but it's a temporary condition. In just a few weeks, she'll be at Kent State, where she might meet someone special. Or maybe not. But one of the things *Whiskey Tango Foxtrot* has taught her is that you get there when you get there. Leaving Willa and Wyatt in their love bubble, she moves toward the stage.

The band comes out and takes up their instruments, and

the lead singer is a blond woman wearing a tank top that says I'M NOT BOSSY, I'M THE BOSS. She straps on her guitar and steps up to the microphone.

"Hello, Brunswick!" she says. "We are the Freecoasters from Fort Myers, Florida, and we waited out a hurricane to be with you tonight, so I'm going to need you to get out on the dance floor and show me your moves."

Taylor stakes her claim on a solo piece of dance floor until Willa takes her by the arm and pulls her right into the middle of the crowd.

29.9012° N, 81.3124° W

Stay young.

Willa

EVERYTHING IN WILLA'S WORLD IS *RIGHT*. EVEN though Wyatt has gone back to North Carolina, she had the chance to spend four whole days with him. They danced to the ska band in Brunswick. Sailed outside the ICW along Jekyll Island. Anchored inside Cumberland Island, where they camped overnight on the beach. And bodysurfed Atlantic Beach before Wyatt left from Jacksonville to go home. It wasn't enough time, but it was better than no time at all.

Now she and Taylor are back on their own, motoring steadily toward Finley's next clue—"Stay young"—which can only mean the Fountain of Youth in St. Augustine. Except the closer they get, the more Taylor withdraws, and Willa has no idea why. "Are you mad at me?"

"No."

"Then what's wrong?"

"I don't want to go to the Fountain of Youth," Taylor snaps.

"Okay, so—"

"And I'm angry that Finley would even make it a clue." Taylor slides her fingertips beneath the bottom rim of her sunglasses to wipe her eyes. "She's dead so she gets to stay seventeen forever, but we have to keep getting older and someday we'll run out of memories of her. We *can't* stay young, so I don't want to go to some stupid tourist trap and pretend like it's possible."

"Do you think it was intentional?"

"I don't know," Taylor says. "Maybe she was just being cute, but I feel kind of manipulated. Like she came up with this whole list because she didn't even trust us to grieve without her help."

"But here's the thing . . . I read the same clue and it never occurred to me that our memories of Finley are finite," Willa says. "It's possible you're giving her the credit for the work you're doing."

Taylor's mouth opens and closes as if she was going to speak and changed her mind. Then, "I didn't think of that."

"Finley was a pretty insightful person, but she couldn't actually see the future. Maybe we shouldn't give her list that much power."

"I still don't want to go to the Fountain of Youth."

"Yeah, it's kind of gone cold for me too," Willa says. "Do you want to skip St. Augustine and keep going?"

She holds her breath as she waits for the answer. Willa would never force Taylor to visit a place that makes her uncomfortable, but Willa has been excited about St. Augustine since they first started talking about the trip.

"No, it's cool," Taylor says. "I'd like to see the rest of the city. Just not the fountain."

They pick up a mooring ball in the harbor, and in the morning they take the dinghy ashore so they can explore St. Augustine. Willa and Taylor join the other tourists, wandering along St. George Street, a narrow pedestrian walkway that was once the main street of the old city. They poke around in gift shops, snap pictures of themselves in front of the oldest wooden schoolhouse in the United States, and eat empanadas on the grass beside the old city gates.

As they walk down one of the side streets that border the old part of the city, Willa notices a small purple clapboard house with yellow trim and flower boxes brimming with red flowers. It looks like it should be an antique shop or a teahouse, but a painted sign hanging over the porch steps, rimmed with a string of white lights, says SWEET MISERY TATTOOS. An older white woman with a thick bundle of dreadlocks comes out onto the front porch and waves at the girls as she waters the flowers. As they pass, Willa feels a pull in her belly, an inexplicable call to walk up the porch steps.

"Have you ever thought about getting a tattoo?" she asks Taylor.

"Not really. I mean, one time Finley decided that when we were all eighteen we were going to get Whiskey Tango Foxtrot signal flag tattoos." Willa makes a horrified face and Taylor laughs. "I know, right? And at the time, all I could think about was how the tattoos would bind you and me together forever, which was unthinkably terrible. No offense."

"No, I understand."

"But we *are* bound together," Taylor says. "By Finley, by this trip . . . by a freakin' hurricane."

"Do you want to get a tattoo?"

"What? Now?"

"I mean, think about it. If we can survive a hurricane, we can survive anything . . . even losing Finley," Willa says. "The tattoo will be a permanent reminder that there's someone else out there in the world who knows how those things feel. That you're not alone."

Taylor smiles as Willa throws her own words back at her, then gives her a hug. "I hate you."

"I know."

"Let's go get a tattoo."

They turn back toward Sweet Misery, where the woman is

still watering her flower boxes. Willa notices that she's wearing at least a dozen bangles on her right arm. Like a warrior's gauntlet of silver. Like armor.

"I had a feeling you might be back," the woman says as they climb the stairs. "Come on in."

Bells jingle on the front door handle as they step into a living room that's been converted to a waiting room, with a brown leather couch dotted with a rainbow of furry throw pillows, a cash register counter filled with body jewelry, and a coffee table swallowed up by tattoo magazines. The woman turns around, her patchouli scent enveloping them, making Willa's nose twitch. "I'm Ellen. How can I help you, my darlings?"

"We're interested in getting tattoos," Taylor says.

"Will you need some time to look at the flash?" Ellen asks. "Or maybe you have a design in mind."

"We were in northern Georgia aboard a twenty-five-foot sailboat when Hurricane Dorian hit," Willa says. "So we're thinking something hurricane related, but we're not really sure what."

"I've had clients who've gotten hurricane vectors or even the colored radar imaging," Ellen says. "So, I suppose the next question is what you want the tattoo to convey. Do you want a conversation piece? Or something more personal."

"Personal," Taylor says quickly. "A reminder that we survived."

"A moment in time." Ellen cocks her head and touches her fingertips to her lips. She's wearing an enormous silver skull on her index finger. She reminds Willa of a pirate. "Or a place."

Her words spark an idea in Willa's mind. "What about the coordinates of Sapelo Island?"

Ellen nods. "Coordinates are popular, but they can be very personal."

"Are they very expensive?" Willa asks, only just realizing that they're going to have to *pay* for the tattoos.

"What day is it?"

"Thursday," Taylor offers.

"Ah, Thursday!" Ellen taps her knuckle to the middle of her forehead. "Today is buy one tattoo, get a second for half the price."

"Why do I feel like you just made that up?" Willa says.

Ellen lifts her arms like a game-show hostess, her bangles clanking. "I own the place, darling. And it's clear you girls have a story to tell. I would be honored to hear it."

"You have a deal."

"Wonderful. Who would like to go first?"

Taylor—the girl most likely to chicken out—opts to get the first tattoo, but Willa goes along for moral support. They look up the coordinates for the ferry dock online, and as Ellen slips on a pair of black latex gloves, Willa begins telling the story, starting with a deathbed promise and ending with a hurricane. By the time she reaches the end, they have matching tattoos—Taylor's on her inner wrist and Willa's on her inner arm just above her elbow.

"The lovely thing about these particular coordinates is that it's unlikely you will ever regret them," Ellen says. "After all, they mark the spot where you learned exactly how strong you are."

25.7255° N, 79.2968° W

Reach for the stars.

Taylor

THE INTRACOASTAL WATERWAY IN FLORIDA IS different from that in every other state they've traveled. Less wild, more populated, and really . . . really . . . *long*. The farther south they go, the heavier the boat traffic. They see fewer tugboats and shrimpers, more sport fishing boats and mega yachts. The waterfront homes grow bigger and fancier as they pass though Palm Beach and Boca Raton. And there is a ridiculous number of bridges. Most are tall enough for *Whiskey Tango Foxtrot* to pass beneath, but they have to rearrange their schedule to wait for the drawbridges to open. It takes them an entire week to reach the northern outskirts of Miami.

"Where do you want to stay tonight?" Willa is lying on the cockpit bench with her feet propped on the cabin top, flipping the pages of *Getting Loopy*. "There's a good anchorage at Dinner Key that's closish to downtown, or we could go to No Name Harbor, which is kind of remote, but a good jumping-off point for heading south."

Taylor is in a weird place emotionally because she's sick of Florida, but she also isn't ready to run the final lap. The breeze ruffles the chart book on the seat beside her and the pages settle on a different chart. It feels like a sign.

"Let's not stay in Miami tonight," Taylor says. "Let's make a detour east."

"There's nothing to the east except the Bahamas."

"Exactly."

"Are you serious?"

"In just a few days this will all be over," Taylor says. "And this is the chance of a lifetime."

Willa looks into the distance at the last two bridges before Dinner Key, then picks up the chart book. "If we leave right now and sail all night, we'll be in Bimini by morning."

Taylor pushes the tiller and the boat makes a hard left, turning into the deep channel that runs along the Port of Miami—where a line of enormous cruise ships waits to sail—and out into the ocean. Once they've cleared land, Willa raises the sails and Taylor turns off the engine. Her stomach flutters with an excitement she would have never expected.

While they still have daylight and Wi-Fi, they quickly look up the immigration and customs regulations and where they are allowed to anchor. As much as they love Captain

Norm, his book has no information for an unauthorized detour to the Bahamas. They have to do this without him.

Taylor texts her dad. Willa and I are going to Bimini.

I don't remember this being part of the original plan.

A lot of things aren't part of the original plan.

True, but . . .

If you were 18 and the Bahamas were only 50 miles away, what would you do?

Have fun, Taylor.

They're not far out from Miami when a pod of bottlenose dolphins appears near the boat and swims alongside them. A couple of the dolphins show off for each other, leaping high out of the water and doing flips. Willa manages to catch a flip on video, but Taylor's favorite subject is the baby dolphin drafting along in its mother's wake as she swims beside the boat. Taylor can hear the little puff of air from its blowhole whenever it surfaces. The pod stays with them for more than an hour, playing in the waves that break from the bow, then leave just as suddenly as they arrive, peeling away to go where dolphins go.

"That was incredible," Willa says.

It's on the tip of her tongue to say *Finley would love this*, but Taylor is learning that it's okay to experience things without running it through that particular filter. Finley *would* love this, but what really matters is that *Taylor* loves it.

Willa

WILLA HAD BEEN EXCITED ABOUT GOING TO CANADA, but crossing part of an *ocean* to reach a tropical island is almost more than she can stand. As *Whiskey Tango Foxtrot* passes into inky-blue water, the depth gauge goes bananas, flashing 9999 and 6666 and—inexplicably—LOL. Even as she and Taylor crack up laughing, Willa understands what the depth gauge is experiencing. The idea of thousands of feet of water below the keel has scrambled her programming too.

Not long after, they enter the Gulf Stream, a current that runs north like a river through the ocean, and smooth sailing turns a little bit choppy. Before they left Miami, Willa plotted a course for a point south of Bimini, counting on the Gulf Stream to push them exactly where they want to go.

"I think we should motor sail for a while," she says. "The stream has slowed our progress, and I'm worried we're going to get pushed past the Bahamas and end up in the middle of the Atlantic."

They leave the mainsail up and the engine helps the boat cut through the current, but it's still a slower trip than Willa anticipated. They're about halfway to Bimini when the sun starts to set. They're completely out of sight of land—something neither of them have ever experienced—alone, except for a huge cargo ship in the distance. The sky turns brilliant gold with streaks of rosy pink, sherbet orange, and deep purple. Taylor goes for her cameras, but Willa trains her eye on the place where sky meets sea, watching for the green flash. For centuries, mariners have claimed to see a glimmer of green at the last moment of sunset. It lasts no more than a second or two—a very definite "blink and you'll miss it" moment. Willa waits to look at the sun until it's almost set and then she stares, unblinking.

Then it slips below the horizon and is gone.

"Oh my God," Taylor whispers, almost reverently. "I just saw the green flash. I can't believe it. Did you see it?"

"I must have blinked."

Taylor snaps one more picture of the fading light. "My dad has seen it a bunch of times during overnight regattas. I can't wait to tell him."

Willa blinks rapidly, but she can't keep the tears from trickling down her cheeks.

"Are you okay?" Taylor asks.

"I'm jealous that I didn't see the green flash," she says. "And because I thought—okay, it's ridiculous, but I thought seeing it would be a sign that Finley knows we're going to be okay. And I also feel ridiculous for assigning an emotional value to a scientific phenomenon."

Taylor laughs, but not unkindly. "Yeah, because no one has ever made wishes on shooting stars or when the clock hits 11:11 before."

Willa gives her a grateful smile. "Good point."

"And here's the thing . . . I know we're going to be okay. Don't you?"

"Yeah, I guess I do."

Taylor shrugs. "So you probably didn't need a sign."

As darkness falls, they divide the night into equal shifts and take turns sleeping so they won't be tired when they reach the island. Willa is on the sunrise watch when they cross into shallow water, brilliant green and so crystal clear that she can see starfish the size of dinner plates sitting on the sandy bottom and schools of silver fish flashing in the sunlight. Bimini sits in the near distance, awaiting their arrival.

"We made it," she says as Taylor comes out of the cabin wearing her pajamas.

They stand there for a long moment, taking it all in.

"It doesn't feel real," Willa says finally as she starts the engine. "Like, if someone had told me that someday I'd be sailing to a tropical island, I would have laughed in their face. Kids like me don't usually get to do things like this. I always thought my dreams had to be practical—get a college degree and make enough money to pay the bills—so this is *beyond* beyond."

"You were the one who got us here," Taylor says. "Maybe it was Finley's idea, but you made the whole trip happen. So if anyone is going to land somewhere beyond their wildest dreams, it will be you."

"We've both come so far." Willa laughs to keep her tears at bay, but fails. "I mean, look at you. When we left Sandusky, you didn't even like sailing."

Taylor smiles. "To be honest, it's still not my favorite thing, but I kind of like knowing how to do it."

"It might come in handy if there's ever a zombie apocalypse."

Taylor snorts a laugh as she climbs up on deck to lower the mainsail. "You're such a dork."

According to the rules of entry, they are required to raise a solid yellow quarantine flag to indicate they haven't officially checked into the Bahamas yet. They don't have a Q-flag, so Taylor cuts a rectangle from an old yellow T-shirt. The makeshift flag flutters in the breeze as they motor into the anchorage. Once they've cleared customs and immigration, they return to *Whiskey Tango Foxtrot* long enough only to grab their snorkel gear.

"So what should we do while we're here?" Willa asks as they walk down the King's Highway, the island's main drag. The road is lined with shabby, colorful homes, souvenir shops, corner markets, bars, and local restaurants. They're passed by locals in cars and tourists in rented golf carts.

"Hit the highlights," Taylor says. "Swim, snorkel, eat conch, drink beer that we don't need fake IDs to buy, and sleep out on deck under the stars."

"Yes, yes, yes, and . . . yes."

They cut down a side road leading to the west side of the island, to Radio Beach, where they peel off their clothes, don their flippers and masks, and swim out into the crystalline water. The bottom is white sand with large scattered rocks, where tiny fish dart into the shadows as Willa passes over. She finds a red starfish bigger than her hand, and as she and Taylor move into deeper water, a small green sea turtle swims right up to Willa's face mask. Clearly unafraid of humans, the turtle paddles around the girls, getting close enough for Taylor to make a video with her phone and for Willa to stroke its soft underbelly. The world feels at once huge and tiny, and she feels so overwhelmed with wonder that she surfaces to catch her breath.

After a couple of hours in the water, they walk up the

beach to a waterfront shack, where they share plates of spicy conch salad and battered "crack" conch, washing it down with bottles of cold Sands beer. When they finish, Willa and Taylor each snag an empty conch shell from the mound behind the shack. With holes in them from where the conch were removed, the shells aren't gift-shop quality, but they're perfect anyway.

On their way back across the island, they come across a place called the Dolphin House, a patchwork house made from stones, shells, driftwood, colored tiles, and recycled bottles. The arched entryway is framed by leaping dolphin sculptures, and a sign on the door explains that Dolphin House was built by Ashley Saunders and has been a work-in-progress since 1993.

A brown-skinned man with graying dreadlocks approaches as they read the sign. "Welcome to Dolphin House," he says. "If you would like to take a tour, you can pay just inside the gift shop and come upstairs."

They each pay five dollars, then climb a set of outside stairs decorated with bits of brightly colored tile. The man is waiting in the main room of the house, where mosaic dolphins adorn every wall. He introduces himself as Ashley Saunders and explains that he started working on the house after an encounter with wild dolphins.

"The dolphins touched my heart and awakened the artist

331

in me," he says as they move slowly around the main floor. Ashley points out whole starfish, bits of coral, US license plates gifted to him by visitors, and coins from around the world plastered into the walls. Overhead, multicolored buoys dangle from the ceiling. Taylor snaps what seems like a million pictures. "I built this place by myself as a monument to honor the wild dolphins of Bimini."

Before either of them can reply, Ashley excuses himself to greet an older couple who have wandered in off the street. Leaving the girls in a mermaid-themed bedroom. A Finley room. When he returns, he explains that visitors sometimes donate trinkets to add to the house. He shows them a few pairs of earrings, beer bottles from other countries, and even someone's favorite lipstick. "People want to be a part of the house."

"It's like a group effort," Willa says.

Ashley nods. "Exactly."

He takes them up another flight of stairs to an unfinished third floor where they can see out over the island. As Taylor takes photo after photo of Ashley's work, Willa tries to memorize everything she sees. Maybe she'll return to Bimini one day. Maybe she won't. Either way she wants to remember it all.

Finally, Ashley leads them back down to street level to sign the guest book. Taylor signs—*Whiskey and Tango were here!*—and they slip out when he's greeting another new group of tourists.

"I wasn't sure what to expect," Taylor says as they head back toward the boat. "I thought it might be just a bunch of random crap, but it's not random at all. It's pretty clear he has a vision, and it's so impressive that he did it all by himself."

"It's magical," Willa says. "I mean, no one really needs a house devoted to dolphins, but I feel like its existence makes the world a more hopeful place."

"So . . . I have an idea."

Willa cocks her head and waits for Taylor to go on.

"I've thought a lot about which of us is going to keep the Finley mermaid—"

"I already told you to take it," Willa interrupts.

"I know," Taylor says. "But what if we give her to Ashley? He could incorporate it into the Dolphin House, and people from all over the world would see it."

"Do you think he'd go for that?"

"I mean, you've just seen his house. I'm pretty sure he'll love it."

They motor out to the sailboat and remove the mosaic mermaid from the bulkhead over the sink. On the back, Taylor writes Finley's full name, birthdate, and the day she died. Willa isn't completely sold on the idea—especially since she wants to keep the mermaid for herself—but when she sees the way

Ashley's face lights up, she changes her mind. He is a story-teller and they're offering him a tale.

Back on the boat, they make good chicken tacos and gather their bedding into the cockpit to watch the sunset. Willa doesn't look for the green flash. She lives in the moment and later falls asleep to the sound of gentle waves lapping against the hull.

Taylor

A FEW DAYS AND A GULF STREAM CROSSING LATER, they reach Marathon—a town that spans several of the Florida Keys—where they pick up a mooring ball for the night. They sleep a few hours and ghost out of the harbor before sunrise, like they were never there. Taylor keeps track of the lower Keys as they sail past. Big Pine. Ramrod. Summerland. Cudjoe. Sugarloaf. Saddlebunch. Finally, they round the western tip of Key West, and soon the harbor is within shouting distance. Taylor feels tears building behind her eyes as she unties the halyard to lower the mainsail. Making the detour to Bimini only delayed the inevitable. Soon their promise will be fulfilled. Their lives will diverge, maybe forever.

"I don't know if I can do this," she says. "I just—I'm not ready to go back to the real world."

"Okay," Willa says, starting the engine. "But what if we reject the idea of the real world being different from *this* world? What if we don't have to go back because we're already here?"

Taylor's eyebrows pull together. "I'm not following."

"I'm saying that no one except you gets to decide what makes life real," Willa says. "Key West doesn't have to be the end. It can be the beginning."

"Do you really think it's that easy?" Taylor asks.

"No, but—"

The outboard splutters to a halt.

"What the—" Willa yanks on the starter, but the engine only makes a weird wheezing sound. She tries again. Nothing. Once more. Still nothing. "You have got to be kidding me! You wait until the very last second to die? How the hell am I going to sail this boat into that harbor?" Taylor laughs as she opens the cockpit locker and takes out the towrope. "Still sure about that real-world theory?"

"What are you doing?"

"I have a plan."

"What is it?"

"Just watch."

Taylor lowers herself into the dinghy and motors around to the bow of the boat, where she ties one end of the towrope, ties the other end to the dinghy—and guides the boat into the marina.

24.5465° N, 81.7975° W

Start here.

Willa

WHEN FINLEY DONOGHUE DIED, THE FUNERAL procession was incredibly long. So long that the Sandusky police department had to change the traffic light sequence through town so all the cars could stay together. Even though Finley hadn't wanted that kind of funeral, she would have *loved* knowing she backed up traffic for miles.

In Key West, her procession is much smaller. Just two girls pedaling their bikes at six o'clock in the morning toward the place where Whitehead and South Streets converge. The golden light of sunrise turns the sea bright turquoise and the Key West roosters crow in the distance, welcoming the new day.

Willa and Taylor kickstand their bikes and approach the big concrete buoy that marks the southernmost point of the continental United States. The buoy is taller than both of them, and painted red, black, and gold.

They have reached terminus.

Now there is only one more thing to do before their trip is officially complete.

Taylor places the bottle of Finley's ashes at the base of the buoy, under the words "Key West, FL." Willa feels simultaneously happy and sad, and she tries to understand how it is possible for opposite emotions to take up the same space within a heart.

Taylor snaps a photo of the ashes, then looks at Willa with a tear tracking down her cheek. Her voice cracks. "I thought I was ready to say goodbye, but it turns out I'm not."

Willa smiles through the haze of her own unshed tears. "I know."

"I found a website where you can have someone's ashes fired into a bead that you wear on a bracelet or a necklace," Taylor says. "That way you can always carry them with you."

Willa taps her fingers to her own chest. "She's always going to be with us."

"I know." Taylor sniffles, wiping her face with the side of her hand. "I just thought—"

"Hey," Willa says softly. "Keep some of the ashes for a bead if that's what *you* want."

Taylor shakes her head. "I want to do this."

"You can do both."

Taylor picks up the bottle, and they step up onto the

breakwall. The water laps gently against the rocks below as Taylor pulls open the stopper. She pours some of the ashes into the bowl of Willa's palm and some into her own, leaving a little bit in the bottle.

"Do you think we should say a few words or something?" Taylor asks.

"I feel like we said enough at her funeral. Maybe we should just do 'WTF.'"

"Scatter on 'Foxtrot?'"

Willa reaches for Taylor's free hand as she nods. She smiles. "Whiskey."

Taylor smiles back. "Tango."

"Foxtrot," they say in unison, and they toss their handfuls of ash.

At that moment, a gust of wind kicks up and Finley's ashes scatter backward, catching in their hair, dusting their faces, and blowing into their open mouths. Willa coughs as she inhales a bit of ash into her lungs.

"Oh my God!" Taylor cries out, choking with laughter as tears stream down her face. "This is the most Finley thing ever."

Willa cracks up laughing, the ash like sand on her lips. "When I said we'd always have her with us, this is *not* what I meant."

"We need to record this for posterity." Taylor holds her instant camera at arm's length and they lean into each other.

In the shadow of the buoy, they wait for the photo to develop.

"So, what are you going to do now?" Taylor asks. "Will you stay in Key West for a few more days or . . . ?"

Willa shrugs, but her cheeks dimple as she gestures at the southernmost marker. "I mean, Cuba's only ninety miles away."

"You can't go to Cuba without me!"

She nudges Taylor with her elbow. "We'll save that trip for another time."

"Will we?"

Willa isn't sure how to answer. Taylor is the last person she expected to have as a best friend. But maybe *best* doesn't mean *forever*. Maybe best is the person you get at a time when you need her most and she stays only that long. Tomorrow might be the last time Willa and Taylor ever see each other. Or they might meet up at their tenth class reunion. Or maybe, fifty years from now—when their faces are etched with laughter lines—they'll still be friends. No matter how their lives play out, if anyone ever asks Willa if Taylor Nicholson was her best friend, the answer will always be yes.

Now, though, she smiles. "Let's play it by ear."

Slowly, the picture reveals itself. Taylor, with ash mixed into the dampness on her cheeks. Willa, with gray dust trapped in the spiral of a curl. Finley all over them. Both their faces show smiles and tears. Opposite emotions sharing the same space.

And Willa understands.

1. ~~Start here.~~
2. ~~Music is good for the soul,~~ but sometimes you have to make the playlist as you go.
3. Make time for wonder. (Just don't charge it to your mom's credit card.)
4. ~~Time travel whenever possible.~~ Don't leave your friends behind (even for a cute boy).
5. ~~Don't lose your head.~~ Be flexible with the plans.
6. Take a bite out of life, especially if it means kissing a pretty girl.
7. ~~Make your own luck.~~ Don't gamble with your future, even if it seems like a sure thing.
8. ~~Give a "ship."~~ Leave room for the unexpected.
9. Get a little wild. _and_ believe in fate.
10. ~~Believe the unbelievable.~~ Believe in yourself.
11. ~~Stay young.~~ Stay strong.
12. ~~Reach for the stars.~~ Trust your instincts (but always keep a towrope handy).
13. ~~It's not the destination . . . (You know the rest.)~~ Don't scatter your dead best friend's ashes into the wind. (Seriously. Don't.)
14. Start _here_.

Acknowledgments

Frank Turner wrote a song called "Long Live the Queen" that made me cry. If neither of those things had happened, this book would probably not exist. Thank you, Frank, for all the songs, but especially that one.

Katie Smith and Jessie Zevalkink spent two years aboard a twenty-seven-foot sailboat, traveling America's Great Loop. Their adventures and most especially their friendship were a huge inspiration.

It might be strange to thank a city for existing, but Sandusky was my childhood. It was where I was married and where we raised our children. Some of the stories and memories in this book are *my* stories and *my* memories—and no matter where I live, Sandusky will always be the place I call home.

While I was working on this book, Mary Singler rolled up her sleeves and punched cancer in the face, proving (once again) that my mom is the strongest, bravest, and most resilient woman I know. *I love you, do you love me?*

Life tested my family a lot—too much, really—in 2018, and I owe a debt of gratitude to my agent, Kate Testerman, and my editor, Jennifer Ung, for their patience and kindness when I needed it most.

Suzanne Young always rates her own line in my acknowledgments because she deserves it. Not a day goes by that she's not there for me. Thanks for countless "Does this make sense?" reads, talking me down from ledges, and just being my friend. You're the best, Suz.

Endless thanks to Cristin Bishara, Kathy Boyd, Huntley Fitzpatrick, Annie Gaughen, Miranda Kenneally, Wendy Mills, and Veronica Rossi for reading, listening, brainstorming, and being outstanding human beings. I'm so lucky to have you in my life.

Ginger, Jess, and Jenn . . . you have outstanding taste in music. Thank you for helping me create the soundtrack for this book.

Caroline, Scott, Raquella, and Jack, you are the Very Best People and I am fortunate that you also happen to be my family. (And you, Cobi Jones, are the Very Best Dog.)

Speaking of very bests . . . Phil, I love you the very best. Always.